TALON AND THE SONGBIRD

What Reviewers Say About Julia Underwood's Work

The Mogul Meets Her Match

"*The Mogul Meets Her Match* skillfully blends delectable foods, business negotiations, and sharp-witted dialogue, creating a captivating and engaging story. …The story offers sweet, angsty moments as Claire and Abby navigate their personal and professional lives. Grab your copy immediately!"
—*Lesbian Review*

"Intriguing romance! I had a lot of fun reading this story. …Lots of great moments and really cute sentiments throughout."
—*LESBIreviewed*

Protection in Paradise

"It is an interesting read—you delve into their respective emotional baggage and how that is affecting the decisions they are making while trying to solve the case, move on in life and keep safe. …I enjoyed this and certainly recommend it."—*ThisLesbianIsReading*

By the Author

Dancing to Eternity Romances:

Dancing Toward Stardust

Dancing With Dahlia

The Mogul Meets Her Match

Protection in Paradise

Talon and the Songbird

TALON AND THE SONGBIRD

by

Julia Underwood

2025

TALON AND THE SONGBIRD

ISBN 13: 978-1-63679-970-4

THIS TRADE PAPERBACK ORIGINAL IS PUBLISHED BY
BOLD STROKES BOOKS, INC.
P.O. BOX 249
VALLEY FALLS, NY 12185

FIRST EDITION: DECEMBER 2025

CREDITS
EDITOR: CINDY CRESAP
PRODUCTION DESIGN: SUSAN RAMUNDO
COVER DESIGN BY TAMMY SEIDICK

Acknowledgments

An author is only as good as the people who guide the initial manuscript to the final product. The team at Bold Strokes Books is phenomenal—knowledgeable, supportive, efficient, and inclusive. Rad has opened the door to so many authors, taking a chance on each of us. I need to also thank her for letting me branch out from contemporary romance into this speculative fiction romance because I felt compelled to tell a story that offers hope for the future—the world might change, but there will always be love.

As I mentioned, Bold Strokes Books is a team of talented individuals. Sandy Lowe is always available to offer support and advice whenever needed, as well as keeping everything on track for crossing the publication finish line. Cindy Cresap was my editor for this book. Both she and Ruth Sternglantz have taught me so much. I think their lessons are sinking in. In past draft manuscripts I sprinkled in present participles "like weeds," and in this manuscript I think I managed to blow it with only one very awkward present particle. They've been dedicated to making my current and future manuscripts the best possible. There are also additional people behind the scenes who have helped bring this book to completion with clear and timely publication guidance, cover choices, production design, and eBook design: Tammy, Susan, Toni. This team of dedicated people make Bold Strokes Books the outstanding publisher that it is.

I need to also thank my family and friends for their support of my writing. The younger family members offer me laughs and inspiration for the juvenile minor characters in many of my books. I pursued veterinary medicine because I love animals, and I can't write a novel without animal sidekicks. I hope that including them as minor characters enriches my stories the way that animals enrich our lives. As I work on my manuscripts, and even as I type this acknowledgement, my canine companion is always there by my side. Fin keeps me tethered to the real world with his side-eye looks, delete button presses, and the ultimate laptop lid closures when it's way past dinnertime.

And foremost, there's you, the reader. Without you, there would be no reason to write. I can't thank you enough for your investment of time and resources. And for everyone taking the journey of two hearts…happy endings, always.

Dedication

This romance is set in 2073 in a world changed
by so many of the factors that we're dealing with today,
but still a world filled with humanity and hope and love.
I'd like to dedicate this novel to those three things, and to all
the individuals who are currently striving in whatever ways
they're able to keep humanity and hope and love alive.

Chapter One

Many nights Makayla Odin was so exhausted she didn't dream at all. There were other nights when she dreamed of returning to the enclave she hadn't seen in two years. And on this night, she dreamed of a nameless woman with flawless skin and an alluring shape. Seductive curves that melded into her own gentle contours. Hungry lips that captured her mouth—held it hostage. And ultimately, expert touches that skillfully sculpted exquisite ecstasy from heartache. Heartache she was ready to leave behind as she headed home to Aurora.

Makayla had finally drifted into those dreams as the barely breaking dawn penetrated three dust-coated windows situated fifteen feet up the wall in the aged warehouse where she slipped in and out of fitful slumber.

Now midmorning, full illumination reached the spot where Makayla lay sprawled on a pad unrolled over the hard concrete floor. Her head, chest, and arms were free of the insulation offered by the worn blanket she'd spread to create a barrier to the drafty warehouse chill.

Her most recent buzzcut had been achieved with an end-of-life straight razor Makayla had found a few weeks ago at a stopover that had followed her escape, and her hair had grown out a little more than a quarter of an inch since that shaving.

Two soft swells beneath the shirt that covered her unbound chest were the only visual clues that promised she was a lithe young woman and not a slender boy-man. Thoracic emancipation was a rare liberty that Makayla only took in isolated environments, and last night she'd felt safe removing the constrictive leather vest she wore as protection against both physical injury and being recognized for the female she was.

At the periphery of Makayla's reach sat an inverted wooden crate that served as an improvised bedside table. On the top surface of thinly sawn slats, the corner of a box of matches touched the base of the squat candle that she'd used for light the previous night—rare finds from a different overnight stay. The oval sticker adhered to the bottom of her wax light source read *Made in China*, a place Makayla knew no longer existed as a recognized country with a centralized government that exported products to the West. Not in 2073, after the perfect storm of catastrophic events coalesced into an insurmountable prescription for world change.

A white lace-edged doily left by a prior visitor was also present on the night table. On top of that doily rested a perfect little pendant with negligible utility. Makayla had discovered it in her late-night rummaging through a box of trinkets. It was gold in composition and heart-shaped in configuration. She'd saved the heart because it had reminded her of the love she'd once known in the world. Love she hoped to know again.

When Makayla was finally fully awake, the clear definition of the warehouse interior verified that the day was rapidly progressing. She searched for another hour and discovered several additional discards that had been overlooked in a trash heap in a far back corner—a rain poncho, some freeze-dried meal kits in an air-tight container, a ball of cotton string, a few tea bags, and a handful of rags that might prove useful.

"Lipton." Makayla read a faded tea label. Then she examined the freeze-dried food packets. "Gourmet kale and grains. Savory beef and potatoes." *Gourmet. Savory.* She couldn't suppress a snort as she loaded the items into the large backpack that she'd escaped with in the chaos of her flight from the battlegrounds. Then her mood saddened.

This was food she wouldn't share with her grandfather. She'd lost him three days ago on the thousand-mile trek home when his moist, rumbling cough had escalated to fatal pneumonia. After she'd said her final goodbyes, a passing regional patrol of friendly rebels had agreed to perform his burial—but not before Makayla had collected his slip-on moccasins. She'd worried one of the patrol members would scavenge them.

"I don't want some stranger walking in your shoes, Gramps," she'd told her grandfather's memory. No one could fill those shoes— or that place in her heart that missed him.

Her grandfather had lost so much weight before he'd passed that Makayla was hopeful that the patrol wouldn't identify him. There was no advantage to the world's premature awareness that Shep Odin, commander of the enclave Aurora, was gone along with her father and brother. Homecoming would be bittersweet.

At twenty-five, Makayla would now be in contention to step into the commander role at Aurora—if that was the will of the consultation council, whose members should be the first informed of recent events. If her enclave even still existed.

She gathered her belongings into her pack and then also dropped in the tiny gold heart that stood for love. After a moment's consideration, she added the doily. That doily—of little use, but a touch of beauty that she couldn't leave behind.

Makayla took one last look around last night's accommodations, then she donned her protective vest, her light brown jacket, and a sheathed machete. She hefted the loaded backpack onto her shoulders, then slipped out into the early autumn afternoon to the last leg of this two-year ordeal—an ordeal where she'd toured hell. But now, she was going home to where her heart was.

Not more than a dozen feet from the warehouse door, a young raven swooped down from above in a descent aimed directly for Makayla. She didn't flinch. Instead, she laughed and offered a low whistle. She extended her arm and the bird landed.

"Good afternoon, Al. Did you have a good night?" Al cast her an affable obsidian gaze and returned a welcoming croak as a similar raven glided to the ground and hopped along in front of her. She couldn't help but smile at them.

"Hi, Ed. I'm so glad to see you. Where is that third member of your not-so-unkindness?" Makayla knew several terms to describe a group of ravens: a rave, a treachery, a conspiracy, an unkindness. Such negative labels, but these birds had only been kind to her—they were her avian family. Family like Gramps.

She'd loved them from the time she'd discovered them in the woods near the edge of one of the southern battlegrounds where she'd been taken. The young chicks, prematurely independent, had flourished under her care over the past year and become her not-so-unkindness.

Makayla proceeded along a worn dirt path, comfortable in her own well-being because her escorts would have warned her if she wasn't safe. As she walked, the other member of the triplet of ravens welcomed her out into the daylight with the drop of an acorn and a friendly clicking sound.

"Well, it's about time, Poe." She felt a flood of relief at the confirmation that all three of them were accounted for.

With their accompaniment, Makayla picked up speed. She was closing the distance on Aurora. Her enclave was on the Pacific Coast of WestLand in the area once known as northern Oregon. The former contiguous United States now had three informally recognized regions: WestLand, MidLand, and EastLand.

The failed invasion of the former San Diego area's deep harbor by the MidLanders had been an attempt to gain a well-positioned stronghold for better nautical access to coastal trade. In need of reinforcements, they had ventured north two years ago to capture and transport males down to their front lines in stolen sailboats, as well as females for labor—or worse. That had included Makayla.

As she walked, Makayla thought about her father's fear for her welfare when they'd been taken. "You need to go by Mak, but spell it M-a-c if anyone asks," he'd said. "And I want to cut off your hair with my pocketknife." She'd agreed. Then disguised and accepted as a male, she'd ended up in the conflict but avoided the mistreatment often endured by captured females.

The MidLand army had eventually given up when they couldn't sustain the large numbers of casualties suffered at the hands of local fighters, casualties that had included Makayla's father and brother. She didn't want to dwell on the magnitude of her losses, but the passing of her grandfather was still too recent not to cause her moments of severe grief.

With the MidLand soldiers' defeat, Makayla had set a pace home that her grandfather could maintain in their weeks of travel back north, and she'd slowed as his condition deteriorated. The birds had advised them of danger as they'd journeyed together.

Now, while the three ravens traveled ahead and circled back, Makayla continued northward at a rapid pace along the dusty, rutted path. After they'd passed a disintegrating storefront, they arrived at a hand water pump. From a nearby post, a Steller's jay tried to scare off her threesome with the mimicked call of a hawk.

"I've got to admire your brazen efforts," she told the jay as she offered the well handle a few seesaw swings of her arm. To her surprise and delight, water flowed from the spigot. Like a heart pumping lifeblood, the conduit of this pump reached deep into a groundwater aquifer and bled clear, cool liquid out onto the ground at Makayla's feet.

"Maybe it's our lucky day." Her traveling companions agreed as she leaned into the stream and hummed to herself. Makayla washed her face before she submerged her entire head and rinsed the short cap of hair that protruded from her scalp. And finally, refreshed, Makayla filled the four metal bottles she had in her possession before she moved on.

It was three miles beyond the remains of the defunct town when Poe flew back in a highly agitated state. Al and Ed followed him with repeated shrill calls that warned of trouble ahead. Makayla touched her sheathed machete in an action that assured she had easy access. She advanced covertly through the trees as she cautiously approached a ravine where her ravens sounded the alarm.

She saw that a dead oak tree located on the slope of the ravine had lost its tenuous hold on the damp earth. Mid-incline and now above the ground, the tangled root system was suspended like a tentacled Medusa. The textured trunk traversed downhill until it met the floor of the gulch where it burst into an extended mass of leafless limbs.

Oh, sweet Sappho. After coming closer, Makayla realized there was a body trapped beneath a large branch at the bottom of the gorge and scattered out across several feet were a backpack, a crossbow, and arrows.

Makayla carefully descended and moved toward the form, pinned in place across the mid-torso by a large branch of the felled tree. Her winged not-so-unkindness circled and settled on higher limbs in the downed oak, and then all three offered her their excited opinions.

She cautiously surveyed the scene.

Through the dead limbs and twigs, she could make out an unconscious man positioned flat on his stomach with the branch extended across his back. He appeared toned and slim in tight sepia-colored pants tucked into brown leather mid-calf boots.

A hint of a sepia-colored shirt rimmed his umber jacket collar and peeked through a thick mane of layered hair—the clothing likely colored with walnut-stain dyes. Makayla could discern the up-and-down movement of his upper torso with each respiration. However, it was only the back of his head, covered in that dense mass of dark locks, that remained completely visible without obstruction by vegetation.

Once Makayla verified that he was breathing, she removed her pack, extracted the machete from its sheath at her waist, and began to hack the large limb that held the captive to the ground. It took almost twenty minutes to remove the offending bough. He didn't move the entire time. When the task of freeing the man was complete, she carefully rolled him over. Her eyes grew wide and she gasped.

"Holy fuck, just slay me now." The ravens laughed at Makayla's profane exclamation. They'd obviously sensed the truth when they'd discovered the tree-trapped hostage.

This was a fit woman who lay prostrate on the ground, that sepia shirtfront unbuttoned far enough to reveal an ample cleavage with a slightly paler skin tone than the light bronze of her face. Makayla judged her to be about forty. She was a compelling figure, resplendent and regal.

She had high cheekbones under her sun-kissed skin, a narrow nose, lush full lips, long lashes that curled out from her closed lids, and a faint scar to the side of her right eyebrow. But the most striking feature, by far, was the swathe of hair at the front of her dark, trimmed tresses—a distinctive golden forelock. That startling stroke of light—painted onto the canvas of coffee-hued hair glazed with touches of burnt umber and burnt sienna—created a unique female image that rivaled those that Makayla had once seen in a salvaged tome.

It was also that distinctive slash of gold at the front of her short dark mane that triggered the truth of this woman's identity. The light forelock was almost as legendary as the woman. Makayla had only seen her from a distance about five years ago when her grandfather and father had met with her just outside the entry to Aurora's compound. She and her entourage of fellow riders had returned the body of a fleeing thief who had suffered an unfortunate demise on her land, and Makayla hadn't forgotten.

This was the feared leader of Raptare, Aurora's southern neighboring WestLand enclave whose name was derived from the Latin word for seizure or ravage and also associated with raptors. She was infamous for her fierce devotion to her rebel holdings, to her people, and to her own power.

"Warrior woman." Makayla swallowed hard before she uttered another word. *"Drakaina."*

Some called her a drakaina, or dragon woman, while others related her to a bird of prey. Stories were rampant of past ruthless acts of aggression, bloodshed, and even murders that the commander of Raptare had committed in the acquisition and defense of what she held dear—for the preservation of her enclave, or in accord with her reputation, her den or nest. This woman was Talon. Makayla thought the name was fitting: a sharp-hooked claw. Not just Talon—she was

Talon the Heartless, Talon the Brutal. But she was most notorious as *Talon the Terrible.*

"Talon of the earth…Talon de LaTerre." The woman's official name escaped from Makayla's mouth in a whisper. Heartless, brutal, terrible—those were all warnings Makayla had heard for as long as she could remember. Words assigned to this stunning woman's renown.

The inborn response of fight-or-flight seized Makayla. She inhaled deeply and then let out the air slowly as she seriously contemplated the flight option and an escape from any further engagement with the infamous leader. She'd not been seen. She'd freed the Raptare commander. What more did she owe this woman?

However, Makayla's grandfather had ingrained the simple notion that doing the honorable thing was important. And now here she was, caught in the consideration of an offer of assistance to the injured female. Makayla shook her head in disgust at her hesitation to leave, then took in the scene on the ground before her. The drakaina, Talon de LaTerre, lay recumbent and injured, clothed in her sepias and umbers, merely another patch of fertile terrain blending into the landscape.

As Makayla studied the commander more closely, the image of a beautiful red-tailed hawk, momentarily stunned and supine on the ground, came to mind. She pushed the memory away. This was just a woman. Flesh and blood. Bone and sinew. But there was something more—a physical presentation that wasn't just the gossip and legends that surrounded her public image. She was a striking woman who, even in her current incognizant state, conveyed an imposing aura. Makayla lectured herself—as fascinating as she found the recumbent leader, she should really move on and reach Aurora. But she didn't change course.

After she noted that the sheathed long blade attached at Talon's waist extended at an angle across her lower body and pressed into her inner thigh, Makayla reached to adjust it and make the woman more comfortable.

Suddenly, a slender, but powerful hand shot up and captured Makayla tightly by the wrist. She felt the chill of glacial blue eyes lock with her own. Azure ice. A burst of shock streaked up Makayla's arm and detonated in her chest—captured like prey. She could have sworn her heart arrested for a moment. Makayla fought not to look away. Not to reveal her panic. Not to show a shred of weakness.

CHAPTER TWO

D on't fucking touch it." Talon de LaTerre growled the low-pitched warning as Makayla reached for the leather-encased blade. A flash of confusion momentarily shadowed Talon's expression before she quickly reconfigured it to present one of threat instead of threatened.

Makayla swallowed down her consternation and held that penetrating stare through her mounting state of alarm.

"I just intended to move the blade. It appears to be digging into your leg. If I wanted your weapons, I could have taken them and left you where you are."

Talon pursed her sensual pink lips. "And just where am I? What happened? Who are you?" She spoke with a commanding attitude, even when she was obviously uncertain.

Talon de LaTerre might be frightening, but it was her rich alto voice that connected with something that had lain dormant in Makayla until recently. Makayla scolded herself for her physical reaction to that voice. She needed to focus on the fact that Talon had only reinforced the negatives that defined her reputation—Makayla added *demanding* to that list. Her objective should be to convince Talon that she'd just saved her. That she, Makayla, deserved gratitude. Or at least mercy.

"We're at the bottom of a ravine. This dead tree was uprooted due to the rains. It fell and trapped you here." Makayla worked to keep her voice steady. Reasonable. "I chopped through the offending branch and freed you."

Talon nodded. "I was out on patrol and hunting. Where is my backpack? My crossbow?"

Makayla glanced over toward Talon's belongings, strewn on the ground where they'd landed. Talon followed her gaze. Then she noticed the nearby birds.

"Bloody hell, why are those ravens here?" Talon did not hesitate in her interrogation as she studied them before she scrutinized Makayla.

"They're my not-so-unkindness. They found you—Ed, Al, Poe—and saved your irritating hide." Makayla heard the indignation creep into the appearance of calm she'd been striving so hard to present to Talon.

From her location on the ground, Talon moved her gaze from the birds back to Makayla. Talon spoke quietly—a gauged, steel-toned rebuke. "I could skin you alive and leave *your* irritating hide for the buzzards." The delivery was far more menacing than if she'd made the threat at full volume. Then Talon simply watched Makayla as she assessed Makayla's reaction to her words. It appeared she was taking Makayla's measure.

Makayla didn't dare blink. Her heart rate elevated, but she fought to suppress any outward hint of her thoughts. There might have been an inkling of truth to her initial assessment that Talon was fascinating when she was unconscious, but Makayla now decided she was formidable as hell. And exasperating as hell. Makayla refused to let Talon know how much she unsettled her.

In a change of course, the corners of Talon's mouth twitched up. "Your *not-so-unkindness*?" She seemed to be considering this. "Like an unkindness of ravens that has renounced their malevolent reputation?"

"Exactly," Makayla replied.

Talon inspected her. "*Nevermore*," she whispered. "So, you think I owe you? What could a poor injured party such as myself do to repay you?" Talon's demeanor indicated she was now toying with Makayla. Makayla recalled the time she'd witnessed a raptor toying with its catch before consuming it. She hoped she hadn't gone through two years of hell just to end up as the main entrée on Talon's metaphorical dinner menu. Hell, she'd just rescued her.

Then Talon delivered another demand. "What's your name, boy?"

Boy. Makayla made the choice not to address the error that her extremely short hair and lean form elicited until she saw how things played out. The belief that she was a male had certainly served to her advantage in several dangerous situations these past two years. If circumstances warranted, she could always correct Talon's assumption later.

After some thought, Makayla concluded that Talon did not suffer weakness in others. The best course of action was to assert herself. To not be intimidated. So she threw back, "Your name first." Then she took a deep breath to fortify herself—she hoped she wasn't going to get herself killed.

Talon arched an eyebrow at Makayla's boldness while she obviously considered her options. "*Tal* will work," she finally said. That she lay flat on the ground did not seem to faze her.

"I'm Mak."

"So, Mac, help me sit up." Talon's words might have revealed that she knew she needed assistance, but the command that infiltrated her delivery left no doubt that she had every intention of maintaining her struggle for dominance in her incapacitated condition.

"Ever hear of *please*?" Makayla just couldn't help herself as she set a foot on either side of Talon and leaned down, close enough to breathe in the scent of the woods mixed with Talon's personal scent, a fragrance imbued with floral and citrus hints. She closed her eyes and inhaled. She'd only smelled testosterone-laden sweat mixed with the odors of battle and carnage for so long.

When Makayla opened her eyes, she was looking directly into challenging blue ones. Into the depths of a fathomless sapphire ocean...lost at sea. Makayla turned her head away. There was no way she could deny the resurgence of her hibernating cravings, an inner need that had been sedated and caged because Makayla had just spent two years living among males. But she could not be attracted to Talon—she did not even like her.

Makayla placed a hand on each of Talon's solid shoulders before she pulled her forward to an upright position. To cover her visceral response to this disagreeable woman, Makayla added, "And now, you owe me a *thank you*." Makayla did not hesitate to emphasize those last two words.

The initial shocked reaction of disgust on Talon's face because Makayla had dared to chide her generated a grin she couldn't suppress. She shouldn't find it funny, but Talon's unrelenting delivery of demands, while she simultaneously rejected a simple request for a little appreciation, struck Makayla as absurd in her present weary state. However, Talon didn't seem to be receptive to the grin.

Talon's response did not stop at disgust. The passage of emotions that traversed her face was mesmerizing. Makayla saw disbelief wash over her at Makayla's audacity. Talon's eyes widened and her jaw dropped. Then her eyes lit with indignation so intense Makayla could have sworn they sparked. Talon frowned. She scowled. She impaled Makayla with a threatening stare before she finally threw back her head and laughed. A full, beautiful, melodious laugh, as if she hadn't been this entertained in a long time. It rolled out deep and rich and sultry, like her voice.

Eventually, Talon took control of her delight and grew serious. "Impudent with a touch of imprudence. I could put you on the ground and finish you off without a trace of remorse, you cheeky little bastard," she said with a truly daunting delivery.

Makayla had already made her decision. She refused to be frightened into submission by Talon—she'd fought too long and too hard for survival and being bullied wasn't something she'd relent to if she could help it.

But she'd noticed something interesting during that remarkable facial display of emotions. Those tiny lines of living, the ones at the edges of Talon's eyes and mouth, appeared not so much when she was angry, but when she was amused—they chronicled a history with some measure of levity. Unless she laughed at others' suffering, Talon de LaTerre was more complicated than her reputation.

"You could finish me off. But that would be rude payback for all that this *cheeky little bastard* has done for you." Makayla waved her hand back at herself. "Are you really such an ass?" She struggled to keep her voice restrained and steady in her gambit to establish a level of acceptance from Talon. For some reason, she wanted to make Talon respect her, if only just a little.

Makayla stopped to consider her. Talon supposedly had no qualms regarding the disposal of those she had no use for. That was the image Talon fought to project—the merciless commander. But Makayla had just witnessed a jocular hint that there was a crack in Talon's armor. A crack that had never reached the lore of Talon.

Talon's shapely eyebrows rose, and the subtle scar to the side of the right one danced with the action as she considered Makayla. Then she seemed to make a decision.

"It's your lucky day, Mac. Any other day would have been your last. Do not cross me. Do not test me. You don't know what I'm capable of." Talon scrutinized her. She gave Makayla the impression that she was making sure that her words were received for the intimidation they were intended to be, even in her compromised condition.

Makayla's chest pounded, but she maintained eye contact, even as the inherent threat of Talon sank in. It didn't matter that she was incapacitated, Talon was obviously used to being in charge and unchallenged. This was how the Raptare leader had built her reputation, even if that reputation was part illusion. But Makayla wasn't sure what was facade and what wasn't. They engaged in a visual battle until Talon seemed to be satisfied that her words had landed, that they had reached some sort of a truce that left Talon in control.

"Don't poke the dragon, huh?" Makayla muttered to herself.

"If you've got an ounce of common sense," Talon replied. "Now, help me stand so I can assess the damage."

In order to keep a safe distance from the action that was playing out below, the ravens had taken positions up in a nearby tree—action that had their full attention. They watched as Makayla went behind Talon and put her hands under Talon's armpits to help boost her to her feet. She carefully avoided placing them too far forward and touching her breasts. Talon's back muscles were defined and solid. While she struggled to help her to a standing position, Makayla tried to focus on something besides her body. She took note of Talon's taller height—that seemed like a safe distraction.

"Son-of-a-goat, wretched, pain-in-the-ass torment!" Talon grimaced as she put weight on her right leg. In an obvious decision to continue to carry on their assessment of the situation from a healthy distance, the birds did not budge from their tree.

"I guess that didn't go as well as you'd hoped," Makayla dryly noted as she maintained support of much of Talon's injured weight.

Talon sighed in disgust. "Don't just stand there. Go fetch me a straight stick for support while I work off this boot and check the damage. I think it's just a bad sprain." Talon limped over and lowered herself onto a rock. So that they could observe while she freed her foot from its covering, the ravens landed on the ground close to her. They were a bit cautious but didn't act overly alarmed by her vocal outburst of profanity. Makayla decided that maybe they were braver than she was.

The ravens called to each other and followed Makayla as she hiked out of the ravine into the trees and searched for the perfect branch that could serve as a crutch. After she'd scoured the area, she found a long straight branch close to the requisite height with a few smaller right-angle side limbs. Makayla, accompanied by her three advisors, dragged it back to where Talon sat and cursed.

Makayla held out her hand to assist Talon. "Stand up." Talon glowered at her. Makayla fought the urge to grin again. Talon certainly hated being told what to do. "*Please,*" Makayla drawled the request, then offered Talon the sweetest smile she could muster. She fought not to roll her eyes.

Talon hesitated, then finally complied and took Makayla's hand for assistance. Makayla ignored the stirring that coursed through her at the connection. She held the branch up to Talon, performed measurements and made calculations. Talon sat back down, but she never looked away from Makayla.

Makayla laid the branch in the dirt and unsheathed her machete before proceeding. She hummed as she worked because she needed to distract herself from the unrelenting supervision. She used her blade to cut the long branch to crutch length and then removed all right-angle limbs except for the one Makayla cut into a handhold, and another at the very top of the branch that she shaped into a short support piece that Talon could place under her arm and lean on. Talon remained seated and continued to watch, and Makayla continued to hum.

She considered Talon's scrutiny as she gazed at her out of the corner of her eye and wondered if Talon thought she was halfway competent. She shouldn't care what Talon thought. Makayla took a large scavenged rag and the ball of warehouse cotton string from her pack and attached the cloth as a cushion for the armpit support. When she was done, Makayla set the crutch on the ground and cleaned up her supplies.

As she maintained her close scrutiny of Makayla, Talon finally admitted, "Handy fellow to have around." Then, as if she'd never been anything but pleasant, she offered an appreciative, "Thanks." With that concession, they both looked down and studied the swollen and bruised ankle.

"Can you get your boot back on?" Makayla employed a tone that indicated she had her doubts.

"This is total horse crap. I don't think so." Talon ground out her response as she gave the replacement of her footwear some effort, clearly disgusted with a situation she couldn't control.

Makayla considered for a minute. Someone else walking in her grandfather's shoes—it was just related to a silly idiom. She fished around in her backpack and pulled out Gramps's right moccasin. Makayla went over and dropped it next to the seated Talon, who looked at her in surprise before she gingerly put it on and indicated that the larger size and looser fit was much more amendable than the boot.

"Are you trying to make yourself indispensable so I'm not tempted to dispose of you?" Talon's taunt was delivered with an upward quirk of her mouth as she pushed herself to a standing position and took a few steps with the new slip-on and crutch.

"Yeah, and I think it's working." Makayla dared to give her a wink. Could she get any cheekier?

"Watch it, fledgling." Talon winked right back.

Fledgling. A young bird. A term of affection? Maybe the-cheeky-little-bastard approach was effective. Makayla laughed.

"Don't get too full of yourself. I'm not known for my gratitude," Talon said, but her sparkling eyes couldn't hide the fact she was enjoying the exchange. She looked at all the equipment they had between them. "I can at least carry my pack."

Makayla knew that would be a big help and so held the pack up while Talon shrugged into the shoulder straps. Then Makayla picked up Talon's right boot and placed it into her own backpack before she lifted it to her shoulders, secured her sheathed machete to her waist, and collected and carried Talon's crossbow and arrows. Talon used the crutch and limped along, her jaw set and her teeth clenched with obvious pain.

They progressed down the ravine at a sluggish pace until the birds alerted them to a spot where they could climb out into the woods with a great deal of pushing and pulling and additional cursing. They slowly continued north through the trees until the slant of light that filtered down through the foliage indicated the sun would soon set, and Makayla decided they'd gone far enough for one day. Her ravens needed to find a place to shelter for the night too.

Makayla's pack had a bedroll and blanket attached, but because Talon had only been out for a long day trip, she had no bedding. It certainly wasn't clear to Makayla how sleeping arrangements would work.

"You can hobble along all night if you want, but I'm done for the day. It's not going to rain tonight, so finding a dry shelter isn't a big concern. I haven't eaten a substantial meal in twenty-four hours and I've hit my limit," Makayla said. The not-so-unkindness backed her up with a chorus of gurgling croaks followed by a series of clicking sounds. Poe flew down to strut on the ground beside where she stood.

Talon gave them all a look of displeasure. "And if I say I want to keep going." The tone of her delivery made it clear it wasn't a question.

"Help yourself," Makayla replied. Then she repeated herself in this battle of wills. "I'm done."

Talon's glare was one she'd undoubtedly mastered in order to impose her will on the people she was in charge of, but Makayla had just come from two years of holding her own in a world filled with macho males who made foolish choices to prove their superiority, and she was in no mood to be intimidated by anyone.

She recognized Talon's need to be in charge, that it was necessary for her leadership role, but Makayla's energy was depleted and if they didn't come to some understanding, she couldn't help her. And only female deities knew why she felt compelled to do so—Talon could be so infuriating. Or maybe, Makayla admitted to herself, it was the ancient poet Sappho who inspired her because she'd given up on higher powers.

"I've cut men to ribbons for less insubordination." Talon's tone conveyed she didn't want to be challenged.

"Leaving me here in a pile of ribbons isn't going to get you anywhere. I'm not someone you get to order around, whoever you think you are."

Talon skewered her with a frosty stare, and Makayla gulped as she fought to maintain her nerve.

"Wherever you're headed," Makayla continued as if she didn't know they were on a course to Talon's compound, "it will still be there when we get there, and from what's come out of your mouth, you've also hit your limit for the day." Makayla blamed her own daring on her exhaustion.

"If you think that stopping now will make me any sweeter, you don't know me." Talon huffed her loathing at being compelled to allow Makayla to call the shots, but she finally sat down on a log as Makayla took the warehouse food from her pack and detached the bedding. The ravens called their good nights before they flew off to find dinner and accommodations of their own.

To Makayla's surprise, Talon's mood shifted. "I also have food and water in my pack, Mac." Makayla noted that Talon had to be even more fatigued than she was with the pain and inconvenience of her ankle injury, even if she wouldn't admit it. Makayla was relieved that their current standoff seemed to have been resolved as she gathered fuel for a small fire, heated enough water to hydrate their dinner, and split it into two metal cups. Then they settled into a temporary silence that felt almost comfortable.

❖

After the meal, it was time for Makayla to seriously contemplate their sleeping arrangements. She only had the one bed pad with an accompanying blanket strapped to her backpack. She considered walking a substantial distance from her domineering traveling companion and making her own bed, but she knew that just wasn't her nature. She couldn't just leave Talon out in the cold to freeze. Makayla reasoned that after all the loss she'd experienced, she needed to help preserve life where she could, even if Talon didn't value that.

Makayla tried to ignore the apprehension she felt and turned toward Talon. "We've only got one bedroll and blanket."

"Are you offering them to me?" A hint of a teasing smile played across Talon's attractive face.

"Not a chance. I might share with you...if you promise not to cut me to ribbons while we sleep." Makayla infused as much admonition as she could manage into her delivery. She reprimanded herself for even considering sharing a bed space with Talon, but she didn't see any choice. Not if she wanted to consider herself a decent person.

"And if I did promise, you'd believe me?" Talon cocked an eyebrow at Makayla.

"I think I would." Makayla tried to sound decisive. She wanted to believe Talon was a commander of her word.

Talon studied her. Finally, she gave Makayla a nod. "Okay. No ribbons tonight." There was no missing that twitch at the corners of her mouth, although she quickly suppressed it.

Makayla spread the bedding on the ground in a layout that was perpendicular to how she would have placed it if she'd been alone.

"We can each have half the pad under our upper bodies and share the blanket." Makayla could hear the touch of trepidation evident in her own voice as she turned to look over at Talon.

"Don't worry, Mac. I don't lust after men. You have anything against lesbians?" Talon gave her a sideways glance.

"*Fuck.*" Makayla murmured the profanity before she realized she'd said it out loud.

"And certainly not boys either, fledgling." Talon's voice was almost kind.

Makayla tried to repress her strangled groan. What had she gotten herself into? She stretched out on her side with her half of the pad under her shoulder and ribcage. Her back faced the spot where Talon would sleep next to her, and she rested her cheek on her arm. Fully dressed except for her shoes, Makayla pulled half the blanket over her upper torso and tried to ignore the fact that she hadn't removed the constraining vest for fear of what Talon might discover.

Makayla registered the warmth of Talon's body as she crawled into their bed, the movement of the other half of the blanket as it was tugged and tucked. Makayla closed her eyes and breathed deeply as she lectured herself. She needed to just carry on and maintain the pretense that had served her for two years—that she was a young male. She finally fell asleep after a long day and was consumed by her dreams. Dreams of doing more than simply sleeping next to Talon de LaTerre. Dreams she couldn't control.

CHAPTER THREE

The golden glow of the rising sun was cresting the horizon when Makayla first stirred. She was still on her side with her back to Talon. No blanket covered her, but she wasn't cold. That was because a strong, well-toned arm draped her shoulder, a solid leg crossed her lower thigh, and a firm body with breasts pushed tightly against her back and ass.

"Sorry, I must have gotten cold in my sleep," Talon's warm, throaty voice fanned the back of her neck just behind her ear. Not only was Makayla suddenly fully awake, but now her treacherous libido was too. Then Talon added, "It's a good thing you're not my type."

"Yeah. My lucky day." Makayla rolled out from under the tormenting Talon and stood.

Makayla traipsed far back into the woods out of Talon's view in an effort to create some distance from her. She lingered in the trees while she took care of morning business—she needed to give herself time to subdue her hazardous hormones.

The not-so-unkindness flew in and joined them as Makayla came back to where they'd made camp. The three ravens settled in the trees and carried on a morning discussion as Makayla and Talon shared one of those salvaged Lipton teabags between two tin cups of hot water and a jerky stick apiece from Talon's pack. When it appeared that Talon thought Makayla wasn't watching, she offered each raven a small piece of the dried meat—they each came right up to her and accepted the overture out of her hand, one at a time.

While the three birds were all highly intelligent, they each had different personalities. Al was more cautious and the one who tended to remain closest to Makayla as they traveled. Ed and Poe were willing to roam a wider radius, and although they were all vocal, Ed had mastered a distinct, hoarse *hi* that he used only when he greeted her. Poe was the gifter with a hint of prankster in him; he often dropped presents of rocks and snails and acorns, or pulled Makayla's shoes a few feet from her bedside where she couldn't reach them, and then laughed.

This morning the birds were demonstrating that they liked Talon, and Makayla considered them good judges of character—at least until now. She noted the interaction but said nothing. She didn't want to give Talon any reason to alter her kindly behavior toward them.

Makayla decided to start up a conversation. "How'd you get that scar?" She indicated that small, faint mark on the right side of Talon's face at eyebrow level.

Talon chewed her lower lip. "I could tell you a story about vanquishing enemies. Cutting people to ribbons."

Makayla noted her phrasing. "You could, but is that the truth?"

Talon frowned. "Bad time. Alcohol therapy. A sharp rock ran into me."

"Someone threw a rock at you while you were drunk?" Makayla was incredulous. She couldn't imagine that anyone would dare to throw a rock at her. Or the always-in-charge Talon drunk. She was the queen of control, and too much alcohol meant she'd relinquished that. Makayla could have given her a bad time, but she saw that Talon's mood suggested there was more pain involved than just a small cut. She remained silent.

Talon chewed her lip some more. "Rock was on the ground." Then she pressed her lips tightly together as if she'd said too much.

In an effort to give Talon some time to move past her memories, Makayla decided to say nothing as they packed and headed out. She'd concluded that Talon didn't want to appear weak in any way, but now she knew that Talon was human.

After they'd traveled in silence for a few minutes, Makayla asked, "How far to get you home?"

"Ready to get rid of me, Mac?" There was a touch of humor back in Talon's voice. "With this sprain and slow pace, I think it will take another few days to get there. Where are you headed?"

Makayla ignored her inquiry and decided to redirect the discussion to find out what Talon would admit. "What enclave are you from?" Of course, she knew the answer, but she wasn't ready to let on that she was aware of Talon's identity or her destination. She wanted to hear what Talon would say.

"I live here in the Raptare enclave. We're way south of the compound."

Okay, she'd been honest about that. "I live just north of you, in Aurora." Then Makayla lowered her voice. "If it's still there."

Talon looked at her. "Yeah, it's still there. A bit worse for the wear from what I hear. They're waiting for the leadership to return. I've been told that MidLanders took Shep Odin and his heirs off to their battlegrounds in the south, as well as several other able-bodied males they were able to capture. Maybe a few females too—for no good outcome." The look on Talon's face was murderous. It made Makayla believe that Talon would kill someone if she felt they deserved it. Makayla couldn't fault her if it was someone abusing women.

"I know," Makayla admitted as she continued to conceal her gender and tried to keep the sadness out of her voice for the loss of the family she'd loved. She knew that Aurora wouldn't be the same with her family gone. "They took us in the sailboats we use for fishing and sailing the coast to regions where we trade. They sailed us south."

"Ahhh. You were one of those males. That makes sense," Talon said. "The MidLanders took many of our men too. We didn't lose any women; we put up a ferocious fight and several escaped. We killed some MidLanders before it was over, but they surprised us and then outgunned us." Talon shook her head as she recounted the events. "After they finally lost down south and returned to MidLand, our men began returning—the ones who survived. I'm waiting for

Shep Odin to return to Aurora so we can broker a way to unite our forces and defend ourselves better next time. I want to meet and discuss some sort of cooperative agreement between our enclaves—strength in numbers."

Makayla didn't tell the leader of Raptare that Shep Odin would never return to his enclave, Aurora. She needed to tell Aurora's consultation council first. And she needed to come to her own terms with the loss.

❖

Talon's compound at Raptare was about twelve miles south of Aurora's compound, and Raptare's total enclave territory was similar in size and composition to Aurora's. But Makayla knew that unlike herself, Talon had been the leader of Raptare for several years. The infamous leader.

Makayla considered their enclaves. Enclave communities were the outcome of huge, failed, centralized governance that had succumbed to the coalescence of disastrous circumstances that had significantly altered the world's population and social structure. To be successful, with less energy wasted on inner turmoil, most enclaves had evolved a governance structure based on an elected advisory council that acted in a consulting role and chose their commander. They often kept these leaders for years, barring scandal or incompetence. That had been the case at Aurora with her grandfather, Shep Odin, and at Raptare with Talon. While generational leadership wasn't the norm in most enclaves, her family had a proclivity for leadership roles. Makayla's father had held positions that had readied him to become Aurora's next leader, and she and her brother had been exposed to leadership roles since their childhoods in an effort to also prepare either of them to eventually step into the commander position if it became the will of the elected consultation council.

Makayla knew that survivors in enclave communities had no interest in returning to a large centralized government and the outsized influence of the wealthy, the power seeking, and a vocal minority who forced their beliefs on others as they often represented a governance shift toward totalitarianism. Adjacent and neighboring enclave communities had come to tenuous unwritten understandings of cooperation, or at a minimum, an informal "live-and-let-live" tenet because the expenditure of constant energy on regional feuds wasn't productive. Raptare and Aurora had informal arrangements. Talon was proposing a more formal agreement sanctioned by the leadership of the two enclaves.

"We already exchange furniture from Raptare's woodshop for items from Aurora's reclamation center," Talon said. "It's a rather informal commerce exchange, which works fairly well. But with what happened to both our enclaves, the number of people hurt and lost, I think some sort of talks that result in a more official defense agreement would help both Raptare and Aurora."

Makayla nodded. She wanted additional information about what Talon was suggesting without giving anything away. "So, what specifically are you thinking?" she asked as nonchalantly as she could manage.

"Probably a meeting of the members of the leadership teams of each enclave," Talon told her. "Commanders, seconds-in-command, or other members of each enclave's consultation council. It's nothing you need to be concerned with. I'm sure our enclaves can work it out when Shep Odin gets back."

As it became obvious to Makayla that a formal agreement between the enclaves could likely bring both Talon and Makayla to the negotiation table, Makayla looked away—the death of her grandfather was too raw. Luckily, Talon mistook Makayla's contemplation about her own role in a likely leadership position at Aurora as something very different—as just a simple reflection on future negotiations with Raptare. She certainly didn't intend to enlighten Talon that she would undoubtedly be at a deliberation table, or that she'd recognized Talon. She would escort Talon to her compound and then complete her own journey home.

"Don't worry, Mac. I'm sure our leadership can work out an agreement beneficial to both our enclaves." Talon didn't let on that she would be at the table either.

❖

By the second day, Makayla appreciated that they had arrived at a fragile working dynamic based on this alpha woman interacting with her as an apparent boy-man who did not want to be intimidated. Progress was slow as Makayla helped Talon travel. Makayla couldn't help but admire Talon's tenacity as she gritted her teeth and limped forward until she almost dropped, the crutch always in use.

Makayla couldn't deny that Talon fed that newly awakened physical longing she'd suppressed for two years. As inconvenient as this physical attraction was, Makayla wasn't surprised that her body was responding to the resolution of her battlefield stress. And while she suspected the worst of Talon's recent threats had been bravado and bluffs in her compromised condition, Makayla didn't doubt that she could be an ass. That conclusion helped Makayla put a bridle of common sense on her reemerging desire as she worked to rein it in. She had no business being physically attracted to a complex woman whose only focus in life was her role as Raptare's commander. In fact, Makayla needed to do the same for her own enclave.

With her focus on a return to Aurora affirmed, Makayla began to whistle. She was helping Talon, she was on her way home, and she knew what her future likely held.

As the morning passed, Makayla decided it was time to take a break and give Talon a rest, but she couldn't make that declaration without completely offending Talon. She didn't want to incite her wrath. Makayla just wanted to succeed at the challenge of getting her safely home to her enclave. Talon would only push herself harder to prove she wasn't slowing them down if she suspected she was the reason for the stop.

"Could we stop for a break?" Makayla called up the path to get Talon's attention.

Talon called back over her shoulder. "Don't tell me you're having trouble keeping up with me."

"And if I am?"

"I'd say you're wearing yourself out whistling." Talon slowed down.

"I'm just trying to keep my mind on getting home. But I think it's time to give the birds a break." Makayla didn't think the ravens would mind if she used them as an excuse to stop for a bit.

"The birds, huh? When all else fails, blame the birds." Talon seemed to suspect Makayla might have another motive.

"Hey. It's their lunchtime."

Well, if it's for the birds, we'd better do it." Talon limped over to a log and leaned her crutch against it, then lifted off her backpack and set it on the ground before she sat down.

Talon reached into her pack to pull out some dried meat, and Makayla sat on the log a few feet from her. All three ravens swooped in and landed at Talon's feet. She broke off small pieces of the food and gently extended her hand, and they came to retrieve it.

"It looks as if they like you." Makayla couldn't help but insert a bit of teasing incredulity into her voice.

"Don't act so surprised. What's not to like?" Talon pressed her lips together, and Makayla inferred that she was deadly serious as the birds persisted in crowding her for the treats. Then she reached over and handed Makayla a large piece of dried meat too.

"I could mention demanding." Makayla enjoyed giving Talon a playful verbal poke, but then decided she needed to acknowledge Talon's interactions with her birds. "But I think the not-so-unkindness would agree with you—what's not to like?"

Talon resumed feeding the ravens, and Makayla recognized the hint of something softer working its way to the surface from where it was hidden beneath all those protective layers. And much to her chagrin, there in her chest, Makayla felt the flutterings of an emotional attraction to Talon.

❖

At the end of that second day, they repeated the same dinner and sleeping routine they'd navigated the day before. Again, Makayla didn't relinquish a stitch of clothing for fear of being discovered for the female she was and changing their entire dynamic. It was on the third day that her carefully constructed strategy went straight to hell.

Clouds had gathered by midmorning on that third day. The not-so-unkindness urged them along and stayed close as they cautioned that a major storm was fast approaching. Talon watched the ravens and the darkening sky with the attention of someone who had spent years interacting with nature, and she pushed herself even harder as she took their warnings seriously.

Those threatening clouds continued to gather throughout the late afternoon until the temperature plunged and a torrent of heavy drops began to fall in the early evening. Makayla took out the poncho she'd scavenged from the warehouse and put it over her pack and the attached bedding in an effort to protect her supplies and their sleeping materials for the night. Then she began to look for shelter from the storm as the rains and the wind roared through the woods with such force that there was no relief for any of them.

Ed and Al led the way to a sheltered overhang in a rock outcropping as Poe urged them from behind. Once Makayla reached the space, the birds departed to find a refuge of their own. Makayla dove into the dry sanctuary, dropped her pack, and headed back into the squall to guide the struggling Talon to the shelter.

"Are you okay?" Makayla managed through chattering teeth when they were both safe.

"Yes, but we have to get out of these wet clothes before we catch pneumonia." Talon had already discarded her soggy jacket.

Makayla didn't move.

"*Now*, Mac." Talon's tone was commanding as she shed her footwear, stripped off her drenched shirt, detached her sheathed knife, and started on her pants. As she undressed, she turned enough so that Makayla caught a glimpse of Talon's back, angled in her direction. A dragon tattoo defined the pale landscape, and Makayla would have commented except she was too cold and miserable.

When Makayla made no effort to strip, Talon took on an even more authoritative air. "I'm used to my orders being followed," she said in a forceful voice. The cold consumed Makayla, and Talon shifted to a more comforting tone. "As I said before, you're safe with me. I don't like boys—at least not in that way—although I have to admit I've grown fond of you."

Talon peeled off the last of her own clothing, then reached for Makayla and held her steady as she removed Makayla's drenched jacket. When Talon began on her vest, Makayla pulled away, turned her back to Talon, and began taking off the vest herself. Talon seized the collar and helped her shake out of the soaked garment.

"The shirt and pants," Talon said as she stood there in all her stripped glory. "We have to get dry and warm if we don't want severe hypothermia."

Makayla lifted the shirt over her head, tossed her shoes, and lowered her pants as she tried to figure out how she could keep her secret. As she stood there in contemplation, Talon grabbed her shoulder and turned her around. Makayla let out a deep sigh.

"Well, fuck me." Talon conducted an appreciative assessment.

As she shook from the numbing temperature, Makayla looked down at her bare feet.

"Those hips and that ass were the giveaway, Mac. Or whatever your name is." There was amusement interlaced with the increased huskiness of Talon's tone that revealed she was entertained by her discovery.

"It's Mak with a *k*. Everyone who counts calls me Mak." She didn't want to give her full name and she didn't want to lie, so *Mak* was all she was willing to reveal. She was afraid that Talon might have heard who *Makayla* was, and she wasn't ready to deal with that.

Talon nodded before she addressed her again. "Let me help you get out of those wet underclothes." Then she softly added, "Please," before she stepped up to Makayla and efficiently peeled her out of her remaining attire. Makayla would have appreciated the "please," but she was just too miserable to acknowledge it.

As Makayla's shivering escalated, Talon turned to spread out the bedding. Then she pushed Makayla down onto it, stretched out next to her, and covered them both with the blanket. She wrapped her body around Makayla and held her.

"I wouldn't hesitate to hurt someone if I thought it was warranted, including you, Mak with a *k*," she said into Mak's ear, "but I would never coerce you, as gorgeous as you are. I have plenty of willing bed partners."

The events of the last several days slammed into Makayla and added sobs to her shaking. It was difficult to tell if it was the cold, or the sorrow for all she'd suffered and lost that had finally broken her. "I'm sorry." Makayla wept into Talon's embrace. Somehow, the embrace strengthened and softened at the same time.

"Shhhh," Talon said. "You're not weak. Too much has been asked of you for too long." Then Talon just held her and rocked her for almost an hour as she maintained a tranquility that offered no hint of her own feelings. When Makayla finally calmed down a bit, Talon leaned back and put on a stern face. "If you think there's an ounce of tenderness in me, you're mistaken. I don't do sympathy. I don't do kindness. And I certainly don't do romance." She hesitated before she added, "I just need you healthy so you can help me get home." Then Talon continued to gently hold her while breathing warm air into her ear.

As the chill gradually abandoned Makayla, it was replaced by a growing heat that settled at her core. They lay naked on their sides and faced each other, breasts and hips and thighs pressed into a confluence of curves, Makayla's face buried against Talon's neck—into a throat that still carried a hint of the oh-so-intoxicating fragrance that was pure Talon.

They didn't move as time ticked away. Not until Makayla's sobbing completely stopped. Not until Makayla's trembling halted. Not until Makayla was warm and comfortable again. And not until Makayla celebrated that smooth, inviting throat with several sensual, caressing kisses.

Talon responded to the play of Makayla's warm mouth on her neck by rolling Makayla onto her back. She held Makayla's hands above her head before she probed Makayla's beseeching eyes with her darkened, dilated indigo ones. Makayla had no doubt that Talon wanted to feed the same desire that hungered in her. Talon conveyed the same need that she felt: lust, ardor, desire. Makayla assured herself that was all it was.

"How old are you?" Talon shook her head as if to clear the erotic thoughts that consumed her.

"Twenty-five. And you?" Makayla didn't care how old Talon was. Circumstances had finally quashed all her good intentions. What persisted was her overwhelming need for this naked woman who had tormented her since the moment of their encounter.

"Forty." Talon continued to scrutinize Makayla. "Is this really what you want? Because as pleased as I am to understand why I've been wanting to do more than sleep next to you these last few days, I'm not going to fuck you unless that's what you want too."

"You're not only a romantic, but chivalrous as well," Makayla wryly noted. "And yes, I'm sure."

"Romantic and chivalrous?" Talon raised her eyebrows. "I have a reputation to uphold. I'm offended." Talon huffed her indignation before her armor crumbled and she chuckled. Then she shook her head. "You're dangerous, fledgling."

Makayla raised her head and shut Talon up by kissing her on the lips. Makayla knew this wasn't a good idea, but it had been so long—and even then, it had only been limited kissing and inexperienced touching with another girl in the compound, Nellie Smith. Those had been encounters of exploration—for both of them. Appropriate partners at Aurora had been scarce, and then she'd been taken by the MidLanders—but she wasn't going to tell that to Talon.

Makayla had endured so much in the past two years. She knew that she was a different person than she'd been before; she was more certain of herself and what she wanted now—who she wanted. Drawn to Talon in a way she'd never been drawn to another woman, she was ready to give herself up to the pleasure of sex with Talon tonight. To unleash her desire. To let it run free. To feel the scorch of Talon's seductive blaze. This one night.

Talon moved to cradle Makayla beneath her. She tenderly held Makayla's jaw as she wreaked havoc on her mouth and tasted her with palpable passion. First it was just soft moist lips, then it became a tangle of tongues as Makayla kissed her back. This was followed by a trail of sensation down Makayla's neck and across the valley of her cleavage. Talon slowly scaled each breast until she reached the peak. She ruthlessly owned each nipple, one and then the other. Makayla arched up into Talon until she was on the verge of release.

"We're not nearly done," Talon said. First, she moved to the side and in one swift motion, rotated Makayla so that she was now stretched out face down. Talon shifted to her knees. With her legs between Makayla's thighs, she was situated to reveal the space that led to the heat of Makayla's longing. "I'm in charge." Talon's tone left no doubt that she was in full control.

"Of course you are," Makayla mumbled into the pad beneath her. She would have laughed if she hadn't been so distracted. Talon didn't seem to break character in bed either. Although Makayla had to admit that she had no inclination to complain.

Talon knelt behind Makayla and guided her. She masterfully pulled and lifted Makayla backward. As the world narrowed to simply the sensation of flesh igniting flesh, Makayla completely forgot they were in the woods, in the cold, without a proper mattress. The downpour dissipated, and slivers of moonlight bathed their human storm. Makayla offered herself to Talon, who now blessed her with the nip of teeth and the relentless stroke of fingertips across the curve of skin that Makayla presented to her. Makayla's prayers for release escaped in a stream of primal pleas that echoed through the trees. Talon embraced Makayla with one hand to further steady her hips before she walked her other hand to the saturated area of Makayla's greatest need. Makayla writhed in pleasure until Talon suddenly halted her ministrations.

"Have you done this before?" Talon's tone was gentle. When Makayla didn't answer, she spoke again. "The truth." Her tone had shifted to one that insisted on a response.

"Not exactly, but I'm not naive. I want you." Makayla couldn't speak above a whisper, her natural volume overwhelmed by just how much she wanted Talon, even with her reputation as a drakaina who she'd been taught to fear. But this wasn't fear lodged in her throat, only desire.

Talon shook her head in obvious confusion, then surprise, as she acknowledged what Makayla had just offered her. "You're still okay with this, Mak?"

Makayla nodded her affirmation, embarrassed that Talon had suspected her level of inexperience.

"Say that it's okay. I need to be sure."

"I want you." Makayla repeated her whisper. "It's okay."

Talon sucked in a bracing breath, hesitated in apparent consideration, and then allowed the fingers of one hand to find refuge in the intimate passage to Makayla's unexplored depths. She used her other hand to reach around and masterfully massage the primed place at the front of Makayla's waiting delicate folds. Talon repeatedly took Makayla to the edge of fulfillment before she slowed down each time and held Makayla at the tipping point to completion without allowing her to fall over.

"*Tal*" was the only discernable word that floated breathlessly through the night. And the fervent manner in which Makayla emitted the name—it defined the wild in the wilderness.

"Patience, fledgling," Talon purred as she kissed and massaged and skillfully stroked Makayla. She pushed her toward the precipice and then finally released her to that place where the need at Makayla's center exploded and diffused in rolling spasms of pleasure. And when Makayla was sated and collapsed, Talon warmed and gently caressed her in their makeshift bed.

When enough time had passed, Talon rolled Makayla to her back and gave her a soft kiss. "You should have told me before we started." Her low, husky reprimand suggested maybe she preferred that Makayla hadn't.

"And you would still have made love to me?" With her forefinger, Makayla delicately mapped the reminder of past pain that marked the side of Talon's right eyebrow.

Talon brushed Makayla's cheek with her thumb. "Don't make me out to be more honorable than I am. I probably would have taken advantage of you and then regretted it." Talon shook her head. "I can't be who you want me to be. I never spend the night after sex." Then she sighed. "But I don't have much choice tonight."

She gave Makayla another gentle kiss. "Fuck. I'm breaking my own rules."

"In that case"—Makayla moved on top of Talon—"there's something else that you don't get much say in. Consider it adding to my education." And before she could object, Makayla took charge and explored Talon with her hands, her lips, her tongue, her teeth. With Talon's guidance, she took Talon to the same place she'd just been.

When they were both finally, fully, undone by their own storm of surrender, Makayla offered her a tender kiss before rolling away, and she was surprised when Talon pulled her close and held her as they soundly slept through the rest of the night.

Chapter Four

The sun was barely teasing the emergence of dawn when Makayla woke and realized that even though it wasn't raining, their clothing was still wet. While Talon slept, Makayla donned the poncho to cover her nudity and looked around until she found some dry wood under a second smaller overhang. She built a fire several feet from their shelter and hung the soggy clothing from branches close enough so that the heat would dry the soaked items. After placing her matching pair of shoes and Talon's mismatched footwear near the fire, she watched for her birds.

The ravens had done well on the trek, but humans created Makayla's biggest worry for them. They gave a wide berth to unfamiliar people, and she'd worried less about them being hunted for food as they'd moved north when she realized that they wouldn't get close enough to strangers for an arrow's strike, and there were not enough available bullets for a hunter to waste one on a puny bird when a shot aimed at a deer or feral hog would produce much more nutrition. Ammunition was reserved for defense and major food acquisition.

Makayla smiled as her not-so-unkindness began to arrive. "Good morning, Poe," she said as he flew in and delivered a rock. "Have a good night?" she asked Ed and Al, not far behind Poe. Then Makayla sat and rotated the attire to speed up the drying process.

The small feathered creatures in the woods were singing this morning, and she decided to join the serenade. Makayla remembered the song sparrows from the sunrises she'd spent with her grandfather. As she accompanied the birds, she realized it was the first time she'd sung in over two years. It wasn't long before she felt Talon watching her from the comfort of the bed.

She continued to sing and tend the fire. When she knew the clothing was no longer damp, she removed it from the makeshift branch hangers and handed Talon her garments and footwear. Then she removed the poncho and slowly dressed her own bare body under Talon's watchful gaze.

"I saw the dragon tattoo on your back last night. Is it why some people started to refer to you as a drakaina?" Makayla hoped she hadn't insulted Talon by acknowledging the label.

"I earned that designation before I got the body art. Protecting Raptare. I had the tattoo done in Gull Town as a reminder of my priorities." Talon seemed to have embraced the designation.

"Well, it suits you. It's gorgeous." Makayla would have liked to have added "like you," but Talon might not appreciate that. She'd made it clear that the symbol was about keeping her enclave safe— her commander role—not beauty. It could be about both, Makayla thought, like Talon herself.

"Your not-so-unkindness proved their worth last night. And it looks like they made it through the night in good shape. I'm glad." Talon nodded toward the birds.

"I wouldn't want to travel without them. Did you sleep all right?" Makayla wasn't going to bring up what they'd done, besides sleep. Not unless Talon indicated she was willing to go there. She didn't know how Talon would feel about it this morning, but the night had been exquisite. Talon had been exquisite. Makayla couldn't help but consider how much she would enjoy more than one night savoring their intimacy. But last night was a single indulgence, she reminded herself.

"Never better," Talon answered Makayla in a purring morning-after voice. "But the best part wasn't the sleeping. You completely surprised me, Mak. And that's rare," she went on to softly allow. "Can't be having that."

Makayla blushed. "Can I get you some tea?"

Talon ignored Makayla's question. "Regrets?"

"No regrets." Makayla only wanted more.

"But we each have our own goals, our own mission—getting home is at the top of the agenda." Talon clarified what Makayla should be thinking—getting home needed to be the priority. "And what we did probably isn't in the strategic plan," Talon added with a soft chuckle.

Makayla still wanted her—goals and mission be damned. "I think it's included in the first paragraph." Makayla side-eyed her as she offered a smile. Talon might be better at sex, but she wasn't going to give her the upper hand in repartee.

Talon responded with another of her captivating, resonant laughs. "Nice to know. But now that paragraph number one is crossed off, it's time to get on with things. Territories to defend. Enemies to vanquish. Wrongs to right."

"Spoken like *a leader*," Makayla said, trying to get an admission.

Talon ignored the intimation. "There are innocents to protect. And you are an innocent." She frowned at Makayla. "You have no business becoming attached to the likes of me. You practically chirp with your cheeky attitude. And you're humming and whistling— and now singing. You're a songbird, fledgling."

Makayla was surprised that Talon sounded almost wistful, and then her tone changed.

"I'm someone who takes what I want, and then I move on." Her expression darkened as she murmured, "Dangerous." Makayla wasn't sure which one of them she was referring to.

Makayla felt the fluttering of emotional attraction, and she thought that Talon was cautioning her. Getting hurt was inevitable when you cared for someone, and Talon threatened to be a deep, penetrating wound. She didn't want to care for Talon.

There was also the physical desire Makayla felt. A primal desire that she had no control over and that played out as a deep throb between her legs, as if her pulse now resided there. Castigating herself, Makayla turned her back to afford Talon some privacy, as much as she wanted to watch Talon dress the way she'd been watched. As much as she wanted to revisit paragraph number one of that strategic plan.

❖

They broke camp after eating, and then they headed out to finish the last leg of the trek back to Talon's home, after which Makayla could complete the last twelve miles of her journey to Aurora. The location of the Raptare compound at the northern end of Talon's enclave territory was stipulated by the same factor that placed the Aurora compound toward the southern end of Makayla's enclave territory—essential water. While the combined territories of the two enclaves covered over a thousand square miles, the respective compounds were only a dozen miles apart because functional aquifers and access to surface water determined their locations.

Makayla thought about the stories she'd heard since she was a child: the world changing drastically over the last several decades, fewer people remaining in a struggling society with most survivors fleeing, then banding together to form communities that established and defended their own individual smaller territories—enclaves.

As the social structure collapsed, additional enclaves formed until the landscape was composed almost solely of these enclaves—each often founded as an aggregate of family or friends, or people with shared political, cultural, religious, or other leanings that they had in common.

Makayla brought her mental meandering back to the woods they traversed as her not-so-unkindness flew ahead, circled, and returned, shadowing their progress. When they were finally within three miles of the Raptare compound, the ravens sounded an alert. Makayla saw an approaching group, comprised of an older man who looked to be in his mid-fifties, a younger man in his late twenties with a strong resemblance to the older man, and a paler, blond-haired woman, likely in her late forties, leading a dapple gray horse. Two large dogs remained close to the woman and she ordered them to sit.

"Where have you been? We've been looking everywhere for you." The older man with shaggy dark hair salted with gray stepped forward, a note of relief in his voice. Then he nodded at the crutch. "Are you okay? What happened?"

"Mak here is a trespasser," Talon replied.

Makayla was surprised and a bit perturbed. Where was Talon going with this? She watched the three-person Raptare search party, observing their reaction, but they didn't seem the least bit concerned. In fact, the older man glanced over at Makayla, smiled at her, and rolled his eyes.

"An oak tree uprooted in a ravine toward the southern edge of our territory and pinned me under a large branch. My ankle—I'm sure it's just a sprain," Talon said. "Mak redeemed herself by rescuing me—so we won't have to hang her." An undercurrent of levity crept into her delivery at that last part of her statement.

Humor or not, Makayla still registered the words. *Trespasser? Hang her?* Talon certainly knew how to be the one defining the situation. *Sappho give me strength.*

Then Talon did a little redeeming of her own. "She and her three ravens—nobody harms any of them. Not a hair. Not a feather. That's an order." She issued the command with the authority of an enclave leader.

"Got it. And I'm glad you're safe, Talon." The man shifted his attention away from Talon and addressed Makayla. "I'm Brock. Talon's second-in-command. This is my son and assistant, Ash, and holding the horse is Willow, our head of defense—also into agriculture. Glad to meet you, trespasser." His eyes twinkled as he said that last word.

Ash and Willow nodded at Makayla, and she nodded back. Maybe they weren't taking the trespasser comment seriously, but hopefully, they would take the instructions to protect her ravens seriously.

"Glad we don't have to hang you," Brock added with a chuckle.

Makayla looked at Talon and feigned an expression of surprise as she decided it was her turn to speak. "*Talon,* huh?" She drew out the name. "Leader of the enclave Raptare." Makayla was interested in how Talon would respond to having been found out.

As if she was reminding herself, Talon quietly answered, "That's me, trespasser." Then she approached the dappled mare and stroked her muzzle. "How are you, Babe? Ready to take me home?" Brock and Ash boosted her onto the mare's back.

Trespasser—Makayla wondered if maybe she'd encroached on Talon's heart, at least a little bit.

❖

They moved to cover the last three miles through wild lands, fields of pastureland, acres of planted orchards, and past a full running stream. Makayla knew that most enclaves had a compound where the humans and domesticated animals were aggregated, and she assumed that was their destination. A windmill came into view before an outcropping of distant structures appeared that let Makayla know they'd finally reached Raptare's compound. Talon's home.

They proceeded through a guarded gate, part of a mix of stone, wood, and wire fencing that surrounded the compound acreage.

"How's it going?" Brock asked the young woman who stood guard with a dog as they passed. "We found Talon, and we've got a guest."

Inside the fence, there were over two dozen various sized wooden buildings, some with salvaged solar panels. Makayla noted that this was a very similar layout to her own enclave's compound area. There appeared to be a mixture of housing, both individual and multi-unit dwellings, a leadership building, two large storage structures, a barn with stables, a large building that Makayla assumed was the woodshop Talon had mentioned, as well as a huge garden and greenhouse, multiple small courtyards and walkways, several corrals with goats, sheep, six more horses, and several bird enclosures with chickens, ducks, and geese.

It seemed that the Raptare compound construction was also similar to Aurora's in that the materials were either salvaged or refurbished components from previous times, or new materials from the natural setting, mostly wood and stone. While direct enclave-to-enclave trading occurred, Makayla knew that the rarer exception was a product that was traded for with other products or credits in an evolving system of barter that was more far-reaching than just between neighboring enclaves.

As they drew closer, Makayla couldn't help but contemplate the situation and how she'd come to be walking into Talon de LaTerre's enclave on her journey home, now 2073 with two years' absence from Aurora—such a confluence of multiple factors and failures that had brought her to this moment.

Centralized governments in country after country had crumbled after the prolonged perfect storm of ingredients. Ingredients that would have been less catastrophic individually, but added and mixed, had created a recipe for worldwide chaos and societal upheaval. The slow creep of incompetent authoritarian and oligarchy governance, social discord that had culminated in widespread urban warfare combined with relentless military conflicts and terrorist activity that destroyed city after city, climate change, poorly regulated artificial intelligence, overpopulation, pollution, pandemics, unparalleled solar storm activity, wildlands encroachment, manufacturing stoppages, a gradual and nearly complete economic collapse…It had been a merging of determinants that had all played a role in the elimination of centralized governments and led to the establishment of enclaves like Raptare and Aurora.

Makayla knew that this had once been both a digital and energy-driven world. But with the loss of the ability to maintain the essential components of digital technology there had been cataclysmic impacts on telecommunications, data processing, transportation, medicine, industrial processes, community water access, global trade, energy production…The list was long and life-changing. Many of these things had been in decline or gone before she was born.

Gramps had often talked to Makayla about his younger years, so she understood how much the world had transformed. As with digital technology, the changes to energy production were no less devastating. Fossil fuels had been mostly phased out, and safe, affordable thermonuclear-fusion energy production had stalled in its implementation. The ability to easily repair or replace the damaged and destroyed equipment essential to electrical power grids and large-scale renewable energy sources no longer existed.

Only small-scale opportunities remained. The energy production that was now familiar to Makayla was often primitive. Some was generated from salvaged components from the past, but that was limited and localized. Makayla's own enclave, Aurora, had a reclamation shop. Raptare had traded furniture from its woodshop, as well as agricultural goods, for Aurora's salvaged products. Those scattered rooftop solar panels she'd just noticed were probably examples of their inter-enclave trading.

Makayla concluded that all these changes had a role in bringing her to this moment. New territory boundaries and governing structures were now established at a local level by those who had survived, Raptare and Aurora being examples. It was a world where people were both struggling and thriving under the circumstances. Those circumstances had led to her capture two years ago, and now to this enclave in the WestLand region of the former United States of America on her trek back north to her own enclave—where there undoubtedly would be expectations for her role in that enclave's governing structure.

"You seem lost in thought. We're here. You ready for a real bed, trespasser?" Brock asked Makayla.

Before she had a chance to tell Brock "Hell, yes," Talon addressed him. "Will you see that her birds are safely settled and she gets a room in the residence hall? Then you can give me a quick rundown on what I've missed."

Yup, it was obvious that Talon was home.

It was evening and Makayla had been separated from Talon since their arrival. Willow had taken Makayla to a bedroom in a wooden building that was set up as one of the compound's multiple residence halls to provide sleeping quarters for most of the single residents. Before she left Makayla in the bedroom where she would sleep, Willow asked if she wanted a warm bath.

Makayla didn't hesitate at the invitation to what sounded like heaven. After her agreement, a young woman in her early twenties wearing a berry-dyed shirt tucked into brown slacks arrived and led her to a room with what appeared to be a large horse trough half-full of clear water. She poured in two full buckets of steaming water that had already been brought to the room before saying anything.

"Hi, Mak. I'm Willow's daughter, Ivy. Plant names run in the family for us women—my grandmother was Daisy."

Makayla nodded as she noted that Ivy had a darker complexion than her paler, blond-haired mother, but similar delicate features.

Ivy carried on with the sharing of her family history. "My mom and dad haven't been together for years. He runs the woodshop. I'm a mix of the two of them."

"I appreciate you helping me out."

"No problem. I'm happy to help—you're undoubtedly exhausted. It's ready for you." Ivy tilted her head toward the trough, which made a perfect place to soak. It had a pipe that could drain the water, probably to an outside garden area. Ivy turned her back while Makayla undressed and climbed in. Then she turned back to face the tub, paying no attention to Makayla's nakedness. "How many days were you traveling with Talon?"

When Makayla told her that this had been the fourth day, Ivy's mouth dropped open. After she'd had a minute to process the information, she chuckled. "Holy crap, Mak. Talon is fearsome—her own force. She doesn't tolerate much, and if she was injured, she was probably even *more Talon* than usual." Ivy used two fingers to put "more Talon" in quotes as she drew out the words with widened eyes.

Makayla smiled at Ivy's theatrics. "We did okay. I think she knew she needed my help. I saw her fierce side, but I saw a soft side too." It was the first time Makayla had hinted out loud that she had an attraction to Talon, that maybe there was an emotional appeal and not just a physical one. That this wasn't just lust. It didn't matter—she needed to return to Aurora. That had been her only goal for ages and had gotten her through hell. "But don't tell Talon that I said she has a soft side."

"An actual soft side, huh?" Ivy's tone was dubious. "Our secret, because nobody would believe me." Ivy made the sideways motion of sealing her lips with her index finger and thumb. "She has a lot of support as our leader, for being completely dedicated to Raptare. And good working relationships as long as she's in charge, but nothing like any long-term romance."

Makayla just listened, interested in what Ivy would reveal about Talon.

"Emotional bonding, that's a nope, except maybe with some of the others serving the enclave too. And then there's a tomcat, and maybe a few other animals like Babe, the horse. And the compound dogs like her." Ivy handed her a small washcloth before she added, "Romance—she's notorious for love 'em and leave 'em. Nothing of duration with any human when it comes to her heart. She's pretty upfront about that. Shuts it down if someone tries to get close, and a few women have tried. Her reputation is for one-night liaisons only. You do know she likes women, don't you?" Ivy chattered away.

Makayla didn't answer. She wasn't going to mention the intimate night they'd shared. That was between Talon and her. She was digesting all that Ivy had told her while Ivy left and then returned with a folded white flour-sack towel and some clothing.

"Here's something to dry off with when you get out, and a nightshirt you can wear. I'll take your clothes to be washed and dried by the fire in the laundry area—return them to you in the morning." Ivy collected Makayla's clothes off the floor and turned toward the door. "Now, I'm going to leave you to take your bath. I've been studying under our enclave's healer, May Lin, and I want to observe while she examines Talon's leg. I'll come back with dinner later, after you've had a long soak and relaxed."

She thanked Ivy before she left, then Makayla submerged her entire body in the luxury of the warm water and scrubbed her short hair as she held her breath. After she'd resurfaced, Makayla reclined back, fully submerged except for her head and upper shoulders. She hadn't been in warm water in two years and it truly was heaven. She'd started to nod off when there was a sudden sharp knock.

"It's Talon." The unmistakable voice came through the closed door. "May I come in? I want to talk to you for a moment."

Makayla wasn't used to carrying on conversations in the nude. First it was Ivy who had paid no attention to her state of undress. Now it was Talon, who she felt disconcertingly and absurdly attracted to in an unrequited way.

"Sure, come on in," she muttered quietly to herself; she would just relax here without a stitch of clothes on and have a friendly chat with Commander Talon de LaTerre. Then she decided that what she and Talon had shared was well beyond simple nudity, so she conceded more loudly that Talon could enter.

The door swung open and Talon came in using her crutch. She shut the door to maintain some level of privacy for Makayla. The crutch didn't diminish her aura of now owning the encounter. Once in the room, Talon just stood there and slowly took in Makayla's full exposure in the bath. Talon's eyes darkened, and she pushed her tongue into her cheek.

After a long appraisal, Talon swallowed before she spoke. "Ivy will bring some dinner to your room, then you can get a good night's sleep. Your birds have found accommodations in the barn. Tomorrow, Ash and another young man will escort you home. If there's anything else you need, just ask."

"Thanks." Makayla would have liked another night with Talon, but that did not seem to be in the plans.

"Don't thank me. You're the one who found me and got me home."

"I'm going to miss you," Makayla replied. "I won't forget our time together."

Talon raised her eyebrows and turned to leave. "No attachments." She took a deep breath. "I've got to catch up with things around here tonight, and I could use a proper bath too, before a good night's sleep. I'll see you at breakfast before you leave." She gave Makayla a long look before shaking her head, and then she was gone.

❖

Ivy brought Makayla her clean clothes the next morning, waited while she dressed, and then led her to a mess hall to collect a plate of breakfast. She mentioned that the omelet came from the compound's chickens and the applesauce from the orchards. As she filled her own mug, Ivy directed Makayla to collect some lavender tea. Makayla knew that coffee was scarce because it was a credit-based trade item from Gull Town, only brewed on rare occasions. The mess hall was full of people of all ages. People turned to look at Makayla as she collected her food, and she smiled at them while Ivy filled a second plate.

"Bring your food and follow me. I'll take you to Talon's office to eat. She wants to see you before you leave. I heard that Ash, and probably another rider or two, will be the ones to see you home. Ash is my boyfriend." Ivy led her across a courtyard and into another building, clearly the leadership building. Makayla followed her to Talon's office door where Ivy knocked with her foot because her hands were full.

"Come in." Talon stood up from a desk piled with papers. With her hair washed and the golden forelock prominent in her thick dark tresses, she presented her usual arresting figure as she stood in her sepia clothing behind the mammoth wooden desk with maps and notes tacked to the wall at her back. The crutch leaned against a bookshelf where Talon could reach it. There was a case of knives and guns over to one side of the desk, and on top of the case was a brass, monocular scope. A small cabinet sat against the wall on the other side of Talon's work surface.

Makayla noted that the room complemented the image of Talon as the indisputable leader of Raptare—all except the plush mauve chair in the corner of the room where a chubby cat concentrated on achieving a morning nap. On the floor to the side of the chair were food and water bowls. Makayla remembered that Ivy had mentioned a tomcat that Talon had an attachment to. That tomcat now opened one amber eye for a moment to take in the intruders, then went back to his slumber. He was very well-fleshed, but the edges of both ears were heavily tattered. And of course, Talon would have a dark brown cat with a golden M marking his forehead.

"I brought you a plate of food too," Ivy said before she handed it to Talon. Talon nodded at Ivy before she left, and then Talon tilted her head toward an empty office chair that faced the other side of the desk. Makayla set her plate on the edge of the oak workspace and sat down when Talon did.

"How did your leg check out?" Makayla remembered Ivy had said that the enclave healer was going to examine it yesterday.

"May Lin thinks it's just a bad sprain. I'm tougher than a downed tree."

"You look good. Rested. I guess a full-size bed agrees with you," Makayla commented after she'd looked Talon over more closely.

"A full-size bed was nice. But I sort of missed sharing it with a fledgling," Talon said with a touch of drawl in her voice before she pressed her mouth closed, the only hint she was flustered for having made an admission of actually missing Makayla. And Makayla knew it was probably just her body she missed.

Makayla looked at the delicate scar to the side of that right brow, studied the forelock that helped physically distinguish Talon, and realized the role their encounter would have on her emotions. On her memories. "My bed was a bit lonely too. No domineering woman to warm me up." Makayla offered her a smile.

Talon shook her head as if disgusted with the label, but she couldn't hide the twinkle of amusement in her eyes. "Domineering? I haven't met my quota of cutting cheeky little bastards to ribbons yet today, but it's early."

"Well, I guess it's a good thing you discovered I'm not a cheeky little bastard then." Makayla did her best to add a touch of sass to her delivery before she wiggled her eyebrows at Talon. "If memory serves me right, for a reason besides avoiding your wrath."

At the reference to their intimate night together, an unguarded, resplendent laugh floated from Talon's throat and filled the room. "So much better than ribbon cutting."

Just then, Brock stuck his head in. He looked surprised. "I don't know what you did, trespasser, but keep it up. I don't believe I've ever heard her laugh like that." Makayla liked the kindly face and easy demeanor of Talon's second-in-command.

Talon pulled herself back under control and gave him a stern glance. "I was just laughing about shredding people who piss me off."

"In that case, I'm on my way out of here." Brock offered Makayla a conspiratorial wink. "Just let me know when you're ready to go." He started to leave and then turned back. "I checked and your birds are fine." He headed on down the hallway, leaving Talon and Makayla alone again.

They settled in to eat their food in silence. After a few minutes, Makayla's plate was empty and Talon's only had a few spoonfuls of scrambled eggs left, but she didn't touch the remains.

Makayla nodded at the food. "Aren't you going to finish?"

"It's for Betty." Talon looked over at the sleeping tomcat.

"Betty? You have a tomcat named Betty?" Makayla couldn't help but break into peels of hilarity.

"Don't blame me. That cat came to me with the name Betty. He likes it. Who was I to tell him that he's a Tom, or a Bandit, or a Lucifer?"

"Hey, Tom," Makayla called, and the cat ignored her as he slept. "Come over here and steal some breakfast, Bandit." Makayla tried again, but the cat never stirred. "Okay, Lucifer, how about a bit of tabby evil eye?" Makayla asked with no response from the cat. "I guess Betty really is your name." Betty barely opened one eye and cast her a look that communicated his feline indifference.

Talon clucked and placed her dish on the floor. "Breakfast, Betty. Come and get it." She actually cooed, and the cat quickly leapt from his chair to consume the leftovers. Talon reached down and caressed him while Makayla's heart did a little flutter.

"Yeah. Who are you, except the dragon woman who loves a tomcat named Betty?" Makayla muttered as she stopped to reflect on the fact that she wished she weren't so drawn to Talon, this woman with hidden facets.

Talon frowned at Makayla's accusation of love and straightened her shoulders before she changed the subject.

"You'll be glad to get home, Mak. It's been a long time. Brock's son, Ash, will get you there safe and sound." Talon cleared her throat before she stood up to grab the crutch. She led them to the door. "So, this is it." Talon gave a deep sigh and pulled Makayla into a hug before kissing her lightly on the forehead. "I'm going to miss the cheekiness," she softly said into Makayla's ear.

Makayla held on to her and sniffed. "I'm going to miss the bossiness." She was going to miss a whole lot more, but she didn't think Talon wanted to hear how much Makayla would miss her. That initial low belly physical desire had turned into something more—nesting deep in her chest. She'd probably experienced all the sentimentality from Talon that she was going to receive.

Talon chewed on her lower lip before she moved both lips to Makayla's mouth, and they exchanged a slow, long kiss. "Cheeky little charmer," Talon murmured. "Cinnamon-colored locks, huh? When it grows out." She ran her hand over Makayla's short cap of hair.

Makayla dried her eyes as best she could. She didn't want Talon to see her cry.

"Stay a songbird, fledgling," Talon whispered before she let Makayla go. She led the way down to Brock's office where she left Makayla with her second-in-command after she gave Makayla a last long stare—it felt as if she was committing Makayla to memory. Makayla hoped so. Then Talon turned and headed back toward her own office.

❖

Makayla stood there for a moment with Brock. She debated, then decided to ask him the question that was on her mind. "Can I ask you about Betty? I'm just curious how Talon came to have a tomcat with that name."

Brock chuckled. "Betty's a lucky cat. Got his name as a kitten when the jerk who had him named him, and it stuck—thought he was a female kitten. Betty was neglected and mistreated. Then abandoned in bad shape when that same jerk left the enclave. Talon took the cat in. Nursed him back to health. Saved his life, although she'd never confess that to anyone. Talon was happy to let him keep his name—he liked it." Brock looked directly at her to make sure he had Makayla's full attention. "Don't believe everything you hear about our commander."

Makayla nodded. She'd already surmised that the common lore about Talon didn't align with the depths that were surfacing. She wanted more—more than just satisfying her lust. Makayla was becoming even more aware of her strong emotional draw to Talon. Too strong. Caring. That fluttering she'd felt...a moth to the flame.

Brock had Ivy take Makayla back to her room so that she could collect her backpack and machete. While Ivy gazed out the window, Makayla reached into her pack and pulled out the right boot that she'd carried for Talon. She quickly stuffed the lace-edged doily from the warehouse inside it. She set the footwear containing the doily next to the pillow on the bed. Then she shouldered the pack, strapped on her blade, and headed out the door with Ivy in order to join Brock at the barn.

Ed, Al, and Poe were perched near the barn when Brock escorted Makayla to where Brock's son, Ash, and another young man introduced as Derrick waited with saddled horses to accompany her on her last dozen miles home. It was about half a day's ride to the Aurora compound. With a midmorning start, they should deliver Makayla by midafternoon. Then they planned to head back south and ride until dark, when they'd stop to camp for the night. The birds accompanied them in their usual manner of flying ahead, backtracking, and stopping to comment when they halted for a break. Derrick chattered away to Makayla as they rode, but her mind was on Aurora. And Talon.

As they entered the southern border of the enclave of Aurora, Makayla's heart rate accelerated. It had been two years. She wasn't the same person that she'd been when she was taken by the MidLand soldiers to fight in the south. She'd lost so much. Changed so much. Coming home wasn't simply the happy return she'd dreamed about at the beginning of her abduction, but it was the bittersweet return she'd come to anticipate with all that had passed.

Her not-so-unkindness accompanied her, and for that she was grateful as they drew closer to Aurora's compound. Makayla noted that the agricultural land looked good, the trees appeared healthy, and the open fields sported thick, lush grass and wildflowers—there had been adequate rain.

A few miles from the home base, a patrol from Aurora met up with them. They acted thrilled to see her. They recognized her, even with her leanness and short hair. Her hair had been shoulder-length the day she'd been taken, before her father had helped her cut it all off after their capture, and she'd had a much softer physique.

Years ago, among the leaders and patrols in Makayla's enclave, they'd established a hand-on-chest signal to warn each other of the need to only make idle chatter and to use caution regarding the disclosure of other information. Makayla now employed the gesture as the two groups approached each other. She did not want to disclose that her full name was Makayla Odin and take a chance that Ash or Derrick might take back information to Talon that revealed she was likely to become part of the leadership of Aurora. While she suspected that word of the deaths of her father and brother six months ago had reached the compound, she didn't think anyone knew of her grandfather's death. She needed to tell the current consultation council before anyone else. And she just wanted to remain *Mak* to Talon for now.

"It's me. Mak," she greeted the leader of the patrol, Ned, as they approached. "You know me. Mak," she repeated. "I'll bring you up to speed once we get back to the compound." Makayla kept her hand on her chest as she spoke.

Ned nodded his understanding of her signal and took her lead. "We're so glad to see you home, Mak. Everyone will be overjoyed. We can talk later." He turned to Ash and Derrick and thanked them for escorting her, and then the two groups parted ways. Makayla introduced the Aurora patrol to her ravens and made sure that as they accompanied her to her final destination, the rest of the compound would be informed that they were to come to no harm.

The compound looked the same to Makayla as she entered the gate, but she knew it would be different. She was different. And her family was no longer here. She fought not to dwell on that. After she'd accepted brief greetings from a few members of Aurora's current leadership team, Makayla excused herself, pleading exhaustion. She had her not-so-unkindness to take care of.

First, Makayla made sure the birds had a safe place to roost in the barn. When she was satisfied that they were settled, she informed the interim enclave commander, Quinn, of the deaths of her three family members, and they'd agreed to meet the following day so she could be brought up to speed on all that had occurred, and all that was currently happening—so that decisions could be made. Then she headed straight to her old room. She was so tired, more emotionally than even physically, after almost two tumultuous years of astounding losses. And she was already missing Talon.

Finally, Makayla slipped between her own sheets again, so long since the last time she'd slept between them. So much had changed. She dreamed of the battlefields, of her deceased family members, and of the notorious Talon de LaTerre. Talon now held a piece of her heart. And she was someone who Makayla needed to forget.

CHAPTER FIVE

When Makayla had finally arrived at Aurora, after two years of turmoil and loss she never could have imagined, after she'd experienced an encounter she never could have anticipated, she'd given the consultation council a quick update before completely isolating herself for several days—except for checking on her ravens. She tried to let the past drain from her mind. She marinated in the present. And when she finally felt that she was ready, she filled her days with the familiar, feasted on old comfortable connections and the safety of Aurora. She thought about being home.

Makayla knew the history of her enclave and family. Aurora—named for the Latin term meaning dawn or daybreak, because her grandfather had wanted it to represent a new day. Thirty years ago, Makayla's grandfather and her parents had driven until their vehicle could go no farther, then they walked on in their search for a sustainable future. Her grandfather, Shep Odin, had been middle-aged when the initial commune was formed with family and friends. Her brother had been born three years later. Then two years after his birth, her mother had died giving birth to her. Over the years, additional like-minded nomads had joined the commune, and it had evolved into one of the numerous independent enclave communities that now populated the country.

Aurora was in the WestLand region of the former United States, the former northern Oregon area. It was on the Pacific coastline, where elements of the geography had been redefined by climate change. But Aurora was no longer the same place it had been when she'd had family here. The people who had held Makayla's heart were no longer present. It wasn't the home it had once been.

As she recovered from her ordeal, from all she'd lost, Makayla could not completely move past what she'd also gained while she was gone. She was grateful for the three ravens she'd raised and now loved, and she spent hours wandering the orchards out beyond the compound fences with them. Makayla could not stop thinking about Talon. Her physical attraction to Talon was understandable, but her emotions confused her.

"I shouldn't even like her," Makayla told the birds. "Masquerading as a fire breather."

Poe swooped down from the orchard tree he'd been perched in and delivered an apple core to Makayla. "But I've seen something else. Hints of a breath-taking hawk, or falcon, or eagle. A raptor—fierce, powerful, intelligent. She's willing to do battle for what's hers. And she hides a heart."

Makayla had been held against that heart—gently held. She'd glimpsed the buried, sensitive heart that Talon fought to keep concealed.

❖

There were many mornings when Makayla woke early. She loved to sit and watch the sun crest the horizon, taking in the morning symphony of feathered vocalists. The coo of doves, the honk of geese, the cheery tune of robins. And her grandfather's favorite, and hers, those little russet-colored, white-chested singers that were prevalent throughout the region. Song sparrows.

Makayla Melospiza melodia, her grandfather had called her—his sweet little song sparrow. And that memory brought her back to when Talon had called her a songbird. Shep Odin had taught her the scientific name for the bird, *Melospiza melodia* and had reveled in her joy at the alliteration with her own name and the melodious way he would say it.

"How could you not love a song sparrow?" Gramps would ask as they'd shared the sunrise and beauty of the crisp, clear notes followed by a trill—sung for the ear of a mate. *Love is a song sparrow trilling at dawn.*

As she walked the solitary pathways at night when she couldn't sleep, dirt byways without light except for the lunar illumination, Makayla reminded herself that she was home. This was the place where she'd grown up. Where the buildings held familiarity. Where so much was just memories. She'd sat and scrutinized the dark sky, the moon, the constellations, and a few passing clouds that put the winter celestial landscape in motion.

This was the same sky she'd lived under while she was gone. The same sky she'd shared with Talon—the moon, the stars, the clouds. The clouds that brought a severe storm and the special night they had spent together because of that storm.

Emotions ambushed Makayla. Not the joy of being home, but the pain of what she'd left behind at Raptare. How the hell had that happened? She needed to resolve that her feelings were just physical. Or at least belonged in the past—history. She couldn't have an emotional attachment to someone like Talon.

There was such a mix of jumbled feelings. The monstrous, magnificent role that their encounter had come to play in her life. But this wasn't play—this was reality—her reality, and she needed to figure it out. There were bewildering things she carried in her heart that made no sense. If Makayla was going to settle back into life at the Aurora compound, she concluded that she needed to fill her days—the best solution to her distress was to have a purpose.

Makayla focused on the legacy she'd inherited—on thoughts that she could likely step into her grandfather's role, a role that from all indications would have been her father's. A role that could have eventually become her brother's, and now a role possibly destined to be her own if that turned out to be the decision of the elected consultation council. But before that could happen, she needed far more personal leadership experience. Those considerations returned Makayla's thoughts to Talon. To her leadership role that held Raptare together, moved them forward.

To her swagger, her infuriating dominance, to the buried charm that Talon embodied.

Makayla resolved that if she was to hold a leadership role in her own enclave, she needed to consider those features that would make her a good leader too. Her people deserved that. So, Makayla pledged to take lessons from Talon. Not the overbearing, because that wasn't in her makeup and it wasn't how she wanted to lead, but at least the strength, the confidence, the commitment, and the emphasis on a successful survival.

She'd taken the winter three months to recover and reflect, to work at settling into a different life without her family. During that period, Makayla had met informally with Rosa, the chair of the consultation council. Now she was ready to meet with Quinn, the interim commander, and after that, the entire consultation council as the season shifted and spring arrived. To put purpose into her life.

Quinn was over a decade older than Makayla, in their late thirties, and nonbinary. Makayla had known them for several years. Quinn informed Makayla that the consultation council members, elected as advisors and responsible for the selection of the enclave's commander, had been waiting for her to indicate when she was ready to sit down for a meeting to discuss her future.

"I have no interest in creating discord by advocating for a permanent role as commander," Quinn told her.

Quinn told her that they'd escaped the MidLander capture and deployment two years ago by climbing a tree out in the orchards when the compound had been raided. They'd realized that they couldn't stop the invading soldiers after fighting them as best they could. Quinn had been injured during the invasion but had recovered.

"I've heard that you love agriculture, the plants and the animals," Makayla said.

Quinn smiled. "A full-time leadership role wouldn't allow me to pursue the things I'm good at and want to do. I'm already stretched in my duties at the compound, and I've added the duty of oversight of the enclave's reclamation shop, although there are several workers who do most of the labor. I'm happy to help with the commander role, but I don't want the entire job to fall to me."

"Well, let's see what the consultation council has in mind. I'm more than willing to listen to what they suggest. I'd be happy to have help. In fact, I'd definitely need help, if the council even wants to consider me."

Quinn then informed Makayla that one of the patrol scouts, a rebel named Bull Puckett, who'd also avoided the battlegrounds, was someone who wanted power. Bull had vied for top leadership in the absence of the Odin family, but he wasn't well-liked by many in the compound. He was rash, egotistical, and autocratic—traits they'd all experienced as destructive. The consultation council, with more women advanced to its ranks when the enclave was in crisis after the MidLanders' assault, had shunned Bull in favor of Quinn as the interim leader.

Makayla had spent her formative years with her grandfather and her father. She'd been exposed to years of their enclave oversight. Her grandfather had begun to slowly transition the leadership role to her father with the enclave's approval, and both of them had started to share leadership skills with Makayla and her brother. So, despite her insecurities, she knew that she had the foundation and the intellect to take on a position of authority. But she also knew that she didn't want to be the sole leader—at least not yet.

The morning that Makayla walked into Aurora's leadership building to attend an arranged meeting with the consultation council, she was finally ready to put some purpose back into her life. The three months since her return had allowed her to begin to reconcile the deaths of her family and the role she was ready to consider, whatever that might be in terms of what the council advised and the enclave needed.

As she entered the room, she took in the long wooden conference table with seven members of her enclave seated around it, all older, and all but Quinn elected as head of one of the various enclave interests that currently constituted the consultation council. They selected and advised the commander of Aurora. At the head of the table was Rosa, who Makayla had met with about a month ago. Rosa was a gray-haired, fiftyish-year-old woman with a comfortable air of self-assurance—someone Makayla recognized as smart and who worked well with her grandfather and father. Three women sat on one side of the table, and two men on the other, with the addition of Quinn in the third chair on that side. The idle chatting halted and Makayla took the seat at the opposite end of the table from Rosa.

"Thanks for meeting with us. It appears you're doing well." Rosa smiled at her. "I see you've added a little more weight and your hair is growing back out and looking great."

After over three months of additional growth since her return, Makayla's hair was almost two inches long. Fran, a grandmotherly woman who years ago had brought her cosmetology skills with her to the enclave, had styled it. Fran had described it as "a thick and curly nest of arresting auburn ringlets with darker brown striations." She'd proposed leaving the top longer, but with a much shorter undercut that still maintained the lighter cinnamon tint, and Makayla had accepted her advice. Fran had shown Makayla the final result in a mirror when she'd finished. In contrast to the starkness of her former fully-shaved head, Makayla thought that the new presentation complemented her almost-too-wholesome face with a touch of orchestrated edginess—exactly the image Makayla had asked Fran to create. She was ready for a major shift from both her feminine shoulder-length hair of a few years ago and the shaved head that represented her capture. Fran had assured her that with her fitted, off-white shirt tucked into her tight, light-brown pants, she left no doubt that she was a young woman. Fran's exact words had been "a very attractive young woman."

"It's nice to have regular meals again." Makayla returned Rosa's smile.

"On behalf of the council, I want to extend our sympathies for the loss of your family. Your grandfather, your father, and your brother were all integral to the success of Aurora. We're all so sorry for what happened."

"Thank you."

A loud banging interrupted their discussion, then the door flew open. A tall, stocky man burst in. His dark hair was in disarray and he swayed a bit, as if he'd been drinking.

"I heard you're discussing the commander role. You need a real man...not that Quinn person, and not her, another Odin." He pointed at Makayla and scowled.

Makayla studied him and realized that she knew who he was. He was Bull Puckett. Quinn had recently mentioned Bull's push to be named to the commander position.

"Bull, you're interrupting our meeting with Makayla. We interviewed you when the interim position was first open after the MidLand invasion, and we made our selection—Quinn. It was all done according to protocol. You never indicated interest in these most recent discussions when we put out the word, but if you'd like to be reinterviewed, you need to tell us now. We're at the end of the process of deciding how to fill the position going forward. We can even arrange to meet with you later today, before we make any final decisions," Rosa said.

"I'm not sitting through that again. This group wouldn't recognize great leadership if it bit 'em in the ass."

"Just so there's no misunderstanding," Rosa replied, "you're not willing to meet with us?"

"You deaf? I said hell no." Bull shook his head in apparent disgust.

"Okay, then. Anything else we need to hear from you before we continue with our meeting?"

Makayla had to admire how Rosa was making every effort to be as fair to Bull as possible, even if he didn't appreciate it.

"Maybe I need to be sitting on the council making these decisions." Bull gave them a challenging stare.

"As you know, Bull, we're elected by the residents of the enclave. You're free to run for a position in the next election if you'd like to see if the enclave supports having you on the consulting council," Rosa said.

"I don't have time for this." Bull shook his head, then turned and headed back out of the room with a slam of the door as he left.

Rosa gazed around the table. "Everyone good to continue?" The council members glanced at each other and nodded, so Rosa went on. "Well, as a reminder then, the council has been through several meetings and discussions which have brought us to this point in the process and this discussion with you, Makayla. We need to move forward after the repercussions of the MidLand invasion."

Even though she'd seen plenty of difficult men during these past few years, Makayla needed a moment to refocus after Bull's interruption. She made a note to remember how Rosa had not let him ruffle her.

"The council has been willing to meet with and consider anyone who's interested. We've discussed our options in the finalization of the commander role. You met with me informally about a month ago. You were still recovering—but an interview per se. I've shared that information and my thoughts with the rest of the group. I need to say that members of the council have always been impressed with your maturity." Rosa smiled at Makayla.

"Thanks." Makayla appreciated Rosa's kind words and was anxious to hear the rest of what Rosa and the council had in mind.

"Let me repeat. It's time to move forward. Quinn agreed to be our full-time interim commander during the turmoil, but they have additional interests they'd like to put more focus on. The council's met and deliberated. What we've concluded is that you seem the best fit to make a transition. We'd like to name you as co-commander, with Quinn continuing to hold the position in conjunction with you. In that role, we can expand your knowledge and experience." Makayla listened carefully, and Rosa allowed her time to digest and respond to what had just been proposed.

"I'm just starting to contemplate my future. At this point in my life, I'm pleased to support the enclave in whatever way I can. I'm happy to have a purpose," Makayla replied.

Rosa nodded. "We'd be pleased to have you share the role with Quinn. Over the next year or more, you can discover your strengths and we can revisit our leadership structure over time. You'll both have the entire consultation council as backup." Rosa looked at each individual around the table. "Several of us on the consultation council hold key leadership positions in specific areas, as you know, while other enclave members serve under each of us. I'd like to clarify each of our positions if that's all right."

Makayla nodded in agreement with what had been said so far.

"I'm second-in-command and the head of defense, as well as chair of the consultation council." Then Rosa proceeded to move around the table. She indicated the woman who was head of training and education for both adults and children, and the man who was chief engineer, critical to maintaining solar, wind, and hydro programs, and also overseeing carpentry and facilities.

As each person was introduced, Makayla locked gazes and smiled.

"You already know our acting interim commander," Rosa said. "Quinn also oversees our reclamation shop, and our agriculture—plants, animals, and our bee colony. You probably also know that we trade a lot of our reclamation shop products for additional woodshop and agriculture products produced at Raptare, as well as for exchange credits in Gull Town where we acquire other needed items."

Makayla felt her heart skip a beat at the mention of Raptare.

Rosa proceeded to introduce the head of inventory, acquisitions, and finance, a stocky woman in her sixties who offered Makayla a broad smile. Rosa completed the introductions with a woman who oversaw onsite law enforcement, and then a woman who was the head strategist, as well as filling in where needed.

"We'll expect you to work closely with Quinn in the co-commander position, and it's the norm for whomever is in the position to confer with the council regarding big decisions so that we're all working together," Rosa concluded. "We welcome you back to Aurora." The entire table cheered and Makayla relaxed at the warm reception.

Her grandfather had insisted that LGBTQIA+ individuals be accepted and respected at Aurora, and anyone who had an issue wasn't welcome. There were other enclaves, especially the Christian evangelical-based ones, that were more antagonistic to anyone who didn't adopt their religious beliefs, but Aurora and Raptare were interested in what an individual could contribute to survival, including the trait of being able to get along with others.

"I know that while I've grown a lot in the past two years, I'm certainly not ready to fly solo as a commander." Makayla agreed with Rosa's assessment. "It was never my grandfather's or my father's plan for either my brother or me to even be considered for that role for years. But if I have Quinn as an equal, and the rest of you working with me, I think we can present the leadership image you want. Organized and cohesive. I know that's critical."

"Exactly, Makayla. You've got a great head on your shoulders—what you just said backs that up. However, you're lacking experience. This co-commander position should better prepare you for the future and is in the best interest of everyone." Rosa seemed pleased with the discussion so far. "An added bonus is that with your grandfather's and father's stellar reputations, it can only help us in the eyes of an often tumultuous world to have an Odin in leadership, while our plan allows you to rotate through different disciplines and fully grow into the position. You may find an area you want to concentrate on and we can discuss things as they evolve. How does that sound?" Rosa had a strong, but kind voice and Makayla appreciated that.

"This sounds like a wise plan for both Aurora and for me. And I think I'm ready to begin learning from all of you as soon as you're ready," Makayla replied. "I appreciate the time you've allowed me to miss my family and begin to recover."

"That's settled then." Rosa glanced around the table and everyone agreed. "I'll make sure that the rest of the enclave is informed of the decision and that it's made clear that it has the full support of the consultation council. Now is there anything else for today?"

Makayla cleared her throat. "I just want to add that I traveled back from the southern boundary of Raptare with Talon de LaTerre."

The entire table turned their focus from Rosa's end of the table to hers. She had everyone's full attention now. "And the night I stayed at Raptare, I met her second-in-command, Brock, and their head of defense, Willow. They seemed reasonable."

The group at the table nodded, so Makayla went on. "Talon was injured in the southern area of her territory and I helped her get home to her compound. That's why Ash, the son of their second-in-command, Brock, escorted me back here. Talon only knows me as Mak and has no inkling that I'm an Odin, or of my potential leadership role. I didn't mention the death of my family either because that information belonged with this council first." Makayla waited for questions or comments as she followed the protocol she'd witnessed her grandfather and father implement in the past. "If we announce that Makayla Odin is now leading Aurora with Quinn, I don't know that Talon will make the connection between Mak and Makayla, which was my thinking until things are more settled here."

"An element of surprise might not be a bad thing in our next dealings with Raptare." The woman who was head of training and education spoke up. "Never hurts to keep Talon de LaTerre a bit off-balance. She's just so good at getting what she wants from what I hear, although I've never dealt with her personally."

"Speaking of dealing with her personally, I should add that Talon mentioned to me that she hoped we could get a delegation from each of our enclaves to meet so that we could discuss and maybe negotiate some plan of combined defense for the future." Makayla looked at the group to judge their response. "To prevent the kind of horror that happened with the MidLanders."

"After the MidLanders' attack on both our compounds, that sounds like a very good idea," Rosa replied. "We're still missing eight people, and several others are deceased. These were our family and friends." Rosa gave Makayla a sympathetic look. "And I agree that the element of surprise that our new leader turns out to be Makayla, the one who saved her, might just be to our advantage at the table with *Talon the Terrible*." Rosa chuckled as she emphasized Talon's moniker. "If nothing else, just to see her face. Maybe you can head our consortium as your first primary task, Makayla, since you know the woman. Our team would also include Quinn as co-commander, and myself as second-in-command and head of defense."

Makayla gulped, then nodded. "We traveled together over four days, and I'd say that we eventually worked out an understanding. We managed." Makayla fought a smile but lost. She wasn't going to mention how well they'd managed. "Although I don't know how she'll react when she realizes who I am with regard to Aurora."

"Anyone who can spend four days with that woman and smile about it deserves our respect," the woman in charge of onsite law enforcement quipped, and they all laughed.

Rosa looked at Makayla to see if she had anything else to say, and when she didn't, Rosa moved the meeting toward a wrap-up. The council concluded that a cooperative defense pact with Raptare would be to everyone's benefit. It was decided that the invitation would come from Rosa, in her position as chief strategist, defense head, and chair of the consultation council, and she would send a horseman to invite and arrange for the Raptare consortium to come to Aurora to negotiate.

"Having them on our home territory seems to be to our advantage," Rosa said. "We'll try to set a meeting in the next few months. That should allow this group to meet and discuss our position regarding a pact before we meet with a Raptare group."

When no one else had anything to add, Rosa adjourned the meeting. Makayla tried to settle her pounding heart as it rejoiced that she was going to see Talon again.

Chapter Six

The Raptare leadership readily consented to a meeting at the Aurora compound to negotiate an agreement that would offer better defense for both enclaves against outside attack. The planned event was set for spring, two months after Makayla had brought the topic up to the consultation council.

Raptare's representatives were due to arrive late on a Sunday afternoon, to meet and eat dinner with the Aurora group before they settled into the rooms provided at Aurora, and then they'd all begin negotiations on Monday. Makayla was torn between anticipation and nervousness. Not so much because of her role in heading the discussions, but because she would be spending time with Talon, who had occupied her thoughts for the past five months.

She wondered if Talon had thought about her at all. She tried to control her emotions because it wasn't likely that Talon had given her a second thought once she'd departed. As Talon had told Makayla, she wasn't short of willing female companions, she didn't do romance, and she certainly didn't do attachments. Makayla kept reminding herself that there was so much not to like about her. Or at least so many reasons not to let herself care.

When that Sunday afternoon finally arrived, the three black ravens were the first to fly to Makayla to inform her that Talon and her group were approaching. The birds hadn't forgotten her. Makayla went to the leadership building where the consultation council usually met and watched through a window because she wanted to take in Talon before Talon saw her. She reminded herself again that it wasn't Talon she'd be meeting with, but Raptare's commander.

As the party on horseback entered through the Aurora compound gate, there was no mistaking Talon, perched atop her equine. Not Babe, but a spirited black stallion. Her distinctive dark hair and golden forelock, and her well-proportioned figure clad in that signature sepia clothing and umber jacket only served to remind Makayla just how stunning she was. Makayla couldn't take her eyes off Commander de LaTerre.

Talon led the group, tall and dignified astride the ebony horse. To everyone's surprise, the ravens circled above her until she stopped and stretched out her arm. Ed swooped in and landed on her extended forearm. Talon smiled and exchanged greetings with him before he took off. The crowd seemed to realize there was more to Talon the Terrible than the stories they'd heard. She was everything that Makayla remembered—and more.

Makayla sucked in her breath as she realized her desire for Talon hadn't diminished, even though she'd hoped it would over the past months—five long months when she'd thought of her every day. She'd repeatedly told herself that her physical desire for Talon was understandable and controllable. And there was no place for an emotional attachment to someone who didn't want one, to someone who worked so hard to create the image of being as tyrannical as Talon was reputed to be. But damn, this was going to be a challenge. The physical desire and emotional attraction Makayla had managed to hold at an even keel for so long seemed to be catching an upward draft.

Talon scanned the crowd of onlookers as she, Brock, and Willow completed the ride into the Aurora enclosure. Again, Makayla compared Talon's visual search to that of a raptor. A gorgeous predator on the hunt. As she continued to scrutinize the bystanders, Talon's firm mouth turned downward as she surveyed the crowd. After the riders had dismounted and their horses were taken to the stables, Rosa introduced herself. She led the three Raptare leaders into the leadership building for introductions before the planned drinks and an early dinner with the Aurora team. Makayla nervously waited in the seat at the head of the long wooden conference table, with Quinn and an empty chair for Rosa to either side at her end. The remainder of the chairs were waiting for the visitors.

As Talon was escorted into the room, Makayla's heart flailed frantically, a wild bird trapped in her chest. She fought to tame it back to a normal rhythm. Talon's crystal-blue eyes widened when they locked on Makayla's, but only for a moment. Makayla suspected Talon had found her prey. Then Talon returned her demeanor to one of complete composure as she took the seat at the opposite end of the table. Only Makayla had noted her initial transitory shock before her rapid recovery.

Once everyone was seated, Rosa spoke. "I think you've met our newest co-commander, Makayla Odin, who will head our contingent in these negotiations."

Makayla fought to keep her face neutral and get her turbulent heart under control. Talon cocked her head and studied Makayla while she inhaled deeply through her nose. Her nostrils flared a fraction—the only hint that the usually regal Talon was buying a moment to collect herself before she spoke.

"Makayla." The name rolled off Talon's tongue as she arched an eyebrow. Then she cleared her throat. "Yes, we know each other well. Hello, Mak," she drawled.

Makayla swallowed down the emotions that constricted her throat. "It's good to see you again, Talon. You too, Brock and Willow...uh, could you acquaint everyone with your contingent, please?"

Brock leaned in and introduced their group to everyone— Talon as their commander, himself as second-in-command, and Willow as the head of defense and also involved in their agriculture. Raptare had a division of duties among their leadership that was a bit different from Aurora, but they were not dealing with two co-commanders either. Makayla followed by introducing Quinn as her co-commander, and Rosa in her roles as chair of the consultation council and second-in-command, as well as the head of defense.

She avoided eye contact with Talon as she told the group that the plan was for them to dish themselves dinner from a side table buffet in the room next door. This was a carefully selected menu chosen to showcase an array of enticing dishes—from chicken-laced pasta with a tomato sauce, to garden vegetables and orchard fruit, to a huge leafy salad with components from the compound greenhouse built with salvaged glass panels.

This spread purposefully demonstrated the agricultural capabilities and culinary expertise of the Aurora compound. After inviting everyone to partake, Makayla added that they could come sit around the table while they ate, so they could get to know each other better before negotiations commenced the next morning. Only after Makayla had turned everyone loose to follow up on her directive to dish up next door did she take a deep breath and reflect on how alluring Talon had sounded when she'd drawled Makayla's name. She might as well just shoot herself right now and get past this friggin' one-sided yearning.

When everyone had exited the conference room to go collect dinner, Talon silently reentered and moved in behind Makayla. Talon casually trapped her against the far end of the table where Makayla had been trying to distract herself with a quick sort of her notes. Talon's solid form fenced her in place and reminded her that she had a traitorous body. That she was willing prey, and Talon knew it.

Whispered breath heated Makayla's ear. "Commander, huh? It seems you're full of surprises, Makayla Odin."

Makayla took in Talon's familiar scent. She loved the floral-citrus imbued with a fragrance unique to Talon. "And I remember when I found out that Tal was short for Talon, the commander of Raptare," Makayla replied quietly over her shoulder. "Talon the Terrible if the stories I've heard since childhood are to be believed."

"Oh, they're true, fledgling," Talon replied with Makayla still trapped from behind in a gentle block that heightened the thunderous pounding in Makayla's chest and resurrected the suppressed desire that ached at her core. Talon's soft, smooth voice continued to tease her ear. "So, we both neglected to disclose our leadership roles."

"I was no leader when we met." Makayla tried to keep the squeak out of her voice, but Talon's closeness was disconcerting.

"But Mak was short for Makayla. Makayla Odin. As if I wouldn't have recognized your name." Talon's words might be intended as reproval, but the delivery was low and sultry.

"Exactly. And I owed it to the people here, if not to the legacy of my grandfather, to tell Aurora of his passing first. I didn't want you to recognize me," Makayla admitted. "He died three days before I found you."

"I knew you'd been through a lot. I'm sorry." Talon squeezed her shoulder as Makayla nodded, remembering her breakdown. "And don't forget that you neglected to tell me that you weren't the cheeky little bastard I thought you were." Her effort at an admonishing tone didn't hide the hint of humor that Makayla had learned to detect. "Definitely not a boy. By the way, I love that hair." Talon's lips lightly brushed the back of Makayla's neck. Then she pushed in even closer, her firm warm body enveloping the length of Makayla's, her breasts pressed solidly against Makayla's shoulder blades. "Almost four days together. Three nights together. I remember our nights together, Mak. One in particular."

Talon exhaled a heavy sigh that blew down Makayla's shirt and warmed her upper back. Then she shifted away. Makayla felt the loss of intimacy and missed it. Talon turned Makayla around to face her, straightened, then took another deep breath and looked directly into Makayla's eyes. Makayla knew they were reluctant eyes because she was afraid of what Talon would say next.

"It's history—time to get on with our lives and the work we each need to do." Talon shook her head as if trying to clear other tempting thoughts and focus solely on the task at hand. "History," she firmly repeated as she gave Makayla the impression she needed to convince herself as much as convince Makayla.

Makayla had been working to persuade herself for months that she wanted it to be history, and yet all it took was a short time with Talon and that conviction evaporated. Makayla quietly replied, "That one night. You keep reminding me it was just one night in your history of countless physical conquests. That I'm just an insignificant part of that history. But I can't forget it, or you. Even if you can forget me."

Talon's jaw clenched before she murmured, "Don't underestimate yourself, charmer." Then she turned and walked away to go dish her dinner, leaving Makayla to wonder what in the hell that meant.

As Makayla entered the room next door to collect some food, she heard Brock ask Talon, "Are you okay?"

"Of course I'm okay. Why wouldn't I be?"

After a fitful night, Makayla went to breakfast in the compound mess hall. She saw the other Aurora consortium members sitting with Brock and Willow from Raptare, but there was no sign of Talon. Makayla joined the group for a quick bite and an exchange of dutiful pleasantries with the contingent from Raptare. Then she headed over alone to the leadership building where they were all meeting today.

As she entered the conference room with her notebook, she saw Talon studying some paperwork in her designated seat at the other end of the table from where Makayla would sit. Rather than sit close to Talon for the moment, Makayla took her assigned place.

"Afraid I might bite?" Talon's mouth twitched as she looked down the length of the table.

"Well, I know you nip." Makayla looked down at her notebook, aware of the flush rising to her cheeks.

Talon's eyes danced and laughter rumbled in her chest before she made an effort to subdue it. "Oh, fledgling, I've missed you." Then catching herself, Talon sobered.

Makayla brought her gaze up. "History," she reminded Talon, who was as enthralling as ever.

"It's for the best. I take what I want, and then I move on."

Even if Talon was only trying to persuade herself, if she was by chance conflicted, Makayla suspected there would be no budging her from her stance. Not that Makayla should want to—she'd just spent five months working hard to assure herself that it had been a single night of lust, at least on Talon's part. Makayla couldn't want anything more from her because Raptare was all Talon cared about. She'd told Makayla she didn't do relationships. So, why was Makayla feeling so torn about walking away? She decided it must be because she loved a challenge. A challenge that would undoubtedly hurt.

As if reading Makayla's thoughts, Talon softly said, "You'll only get burned. I'm no good for you, Mak. Raptare is my first priority, and I'm a self-gratifying, egotistical, self-absorbed—"

"Ass," Makayla finished for her.

Talon scowled at her.

She couldn't have hurt the feelings of someone who claimed not to care, could she? "Drakaina," Makayla amended. She wanted to tell Talon she was a beautiful hawk with a heart of hidden secrets that the world did not know, but Talon wouldn't want to hear that.

Talon nodded her affirmation. Drakaina—she didn't seem to mind a label that referred to her powerful side, even if it was linked to the lore of her brutality.

"What if I'm a dragon tamer?" Makayla challenged her as she pushed a little tease into her voice.

"Dragon tamer? Dangerous for sure." Talon's tone had softened again.

"Dangerous, huh?" Makayla looked down at herself. "Well, you must mean that in the best sort of way."

"The best." Talon chewed on the words. She didn't break her scrutiny of Makayla. "I don't want to hurt you, fledgling. And coming from a reliable source, I'm an ass."

"Then don't," Makayla replied as the others started to stream into the room and Talon gave her a last long, unsettled look.

The negotiations went well. Makayla's leadership confidence grew as the talks progressed and the members of both contingents openly discussed their interests, as well as how they could cooperate in the event of a future attack. A defense plan was the impetus for the negotiations, but they also entertained suggestions related to how they might cooperate in other ways that included trading supplies and sharing expertise beyond the dealings they were currently undertaking.

They discussed Raptare's specialized workshop that produced wooden furniture and Aurora's large reclamation shop. Makayla knew that her enclave refurbished and repaired salvaged items for use and trade that included a wide range of items not limited to windows, cloth, paper, metal items, useful structural and energy components, and oddities. The shop included a small charcoal furnace.

Because the volume of materials available for scavenging wasn't insignificant after so much infrastructure had been destroyed or abandoned when established communities had collapsed, scavenged or recycled items were a major feature of Aurora and Raptare, as was handmade wooden furniture. The two enclaves had informally traded their commodities for years, as well as surplus food supplies, but the current talks focused on more regular and larger scale exchanges of goods and knowledge.

It was on the third day of discussions, Wednesday, and after the agreement between Aurora and Raptare had been finalized by everyone, that Brock broached another topic.

"If you all remember your history, before we reached our current state, there used to be NATO, the North Atlantic Treaty Organization, an intergovernmental military alliance of former European and North American countries founded well over a hundred years ago, in 1949."

Makayla wondered where Brock was going with his history lesson.

"It was created to prevent Russian advancement across Europe after the Second World War," Brock continued. "If one country came under armed attack, the others joined in the defense. It worked well for many decades—until so many factors started to destabilize and then topple global governments and alliances."

Everyone nodded and Rosa spoke up. "What are you proposing, Brock?"

"I'm suggesting that an alliance with other enclaves in WestLand's northern region, more than the agreement between just our two, might be preventative, or at least a winning defense in a future attack on any of us, either from within WestLand, or by MidLand or EastLand fighters."

As Brock's idea sank in, the leaders around the table looked at each other and nodded.

"Maybe a northern enclave treaty among an additional four of WestLand's enclaves near us," Rosa said. "At least initially. Six collaborative enclaves in this region of northern WestLand would be a good start. We can always consider inviting more later."

"Six...to see how it goes and make it manageable to implement." Willow spoke up in her role as the head of defense for Raptare.

"That makes sense," Brock said.

"How do you propose we move forward with this idea?" Rosa asked.

Makayla gazed down the table at Talon, who was obviously surprised by the suggestion and paying close attention.

Brock avoided looking at Talon. "I'm thinking that since you have two co-commanders at Aurora, and since she's the one leading these negotiations, that you send Makayla Odin down to stay at Raptare. She can work closely with Talon. They can flesh out an agreement and present it to the leaders of the other four regional WestLand enclaves they decide would be a good fit. We need to start with a strong core group. Those enclaves can be invited and conferred with, one by one, or in groups of two. Once that's been accomplished, Talon and Makayla can meet with all interested parties together, to finalize an alliance among these six northern region WestLand enclaves."

Talon's mouth dropped open before she quickly closed it. She glowered at Makayla, and Makayla had to bite her cheeks to keep from laughing at the undercurrent of shock she saw on her face. Then Brock snuck Makayla a subtle wink.

What the hell? Makayla had no doubt that Brock knew what he had just suggested with regard to Talon and her. Maybe Talon would be shredding her after all, because days in close proximity to

Talon without being allowed to touch her would only lead Makayla to goad her—she didn't know if she could do this. But she didn't believe that she could simply walk away from Talon either. And she had a job to do for her enclave.

After some discussion, Rosa and Quinn agreed it was a good idea. So did Brock and Willow from Raptare's contingent. Talon remained silent as she obviously struggled to remain stoic.

"What do you think, Makayla? Can we count on you?" Willow asked.

Makayla considered her grandfather's legacy and her own new leadership role. This would offer her some additional experience. The proposal would also allow her to be close to Talon, allow her to chase the inferno that Talon ignited in her. She took a deep breath and decided to go all in—poke Talon a bit now, just because she couldn't help herself.

"I can see eventually inviting all the other enclaves in the north region of WestLand once we have a strong core six on board. We could even name it NATO, for *North Area Tactical Optimization.*" Then she looked directly at Talon. "In deference to the original historical alliance. *History.* Because sometimes it's good not to relegate everything to history. There are some very good things that shouldn't be considered just history."

Everyone nodded in agreement. Everyone except Talon, who understood just what Makayla was actually referring to when she mentioned history.

"Well, it looks like it's settled," Quinn said. "Thank you, Brock."

"To Talon and Makayla then," Brock said. "And to the future."

Talon skewered him with a displeased look, and Makayla only hoped he wouldn't be the next pile of ribbons. Brock just smiled. Obviously, he had dealt with Talon before.

CHAPTER SEVEN

The Raptare group planned to head back to their compound the day after the new NATO plan had been proposed. Early that morning before Makayla was even out of bed, there was a sharp rap on her door. She crawled from her sheets in her shorts and shirt, still half asleep. She knew that her wild, curly top-mop was thoroughly tousled, and she had no idea who was outside. She cracked the door. There stood Talon, fully dressed in her distinctive brown attire. Makayla gulped before she moved back and motioned her in.

Talon stepped into the bedroom and closed the door. She took in Makayla's unmade bed, then Talon surveyed Makayla, who knew that while she was now wide-awake, she was disheveled. Talon didn't try to hide her predatory expression.

She stepped past Makayla, turned her around, and firmly backed her up against the door so that she had Makayla corralled there with her body. Talon rolled her lips between her teeth as if she was making an effort to control her mouth. Penning Makayla in seemed to be Talon's signature move—not that Makayla was complaining. Makayla scrutinized those beautiful blue eyes and that layered brown hair with the streak of gold, then she took a deep breath and closed her own eyes tight. The urge to kiss Talon was so overwhelming that Makayla couldn't even look at her.

"So, Brock told me that you knew nothing about his proposal," Talon growled. Makayla swallowed hard—she shouldn't find that growl so arousing.

"That's true, Tal." Makayla kept her eyes tightly shut in an effort to deprive Talon of the opportunity to reprove Makayla with her visual wrath.

"I'm still furious." Talon's tone was laced with displeasure, even though she seemed to be calming down as she kept Makayla in such close proximity that her enticing fragrance wafted into Makayla's nostrils. Makayla opened one eye to a slit.

"It can't be the implementation of a multi-enclave defense alliance because you were the one who first brought up the concept of an agreement between our two enclaves. This is just expanding on your brilliant idea." It couldn't hurt to give Talon the credit she deserved. Makayla opened both eyes and looked directly at Talon. She contemplated the name NATO. If Talon was going to pin her, half naked, up against her bedroom door, Makayla was going to engage her.

"Maybe you don't like what the acronym now stands for with regard to our defense—North Area Tactical Optimization. Maybe we should change it." Makayla couldn't completely suppress the mirth in her voice. "N-A-T-O: *Never Anger Talon Or...*" Makayla drew her index finger across her neck in a throat-slitting gesture and played up the delivery by rolling her eyes upward and sticking her tongue out the side of her mouth before she offered Talon her most innocent smile.

A chuckle escaped from Talon before she quashed it and shifted to a stance of aggrieved glare in an effort to convey her irritation. But those sapphire eyes couldn't hide the hint of amusement and an abundance of desire. Talon shook her head in an obvious effort to clear it, then spoke. "Huh-uh. You don't get to tease your way out of this, you cheeky little charmer. I'm in a ribbon-cutting mood. Angry with you."

"Because?" Makayla's gaze met Talon's visual scrutiny. Makayla wanted her. And she wanted Talon to spell out her anger.

"Because *we* need to be history," Talon barked at her.

"Because?" Makayla repeated, as the heat of Talon spread downward to settle at her feminine core. There must be something wrong with her because she was way too attracted to this fire-breathing version of Talon.

Talon eased her stance a bit and cocked an eyebrow. "You're lucky I've got you pressed against this door instead of that unmade bed of yours."

Makayla sucked in a deep breath and shut her eyes again so she didn't let Talon know how appealing her threat was. Or maybe Talon was aware and was torturing her on purpose. She let Talon rant on.

"You don't know how much I want to take you right here, right now, and fuck you senseless. I know it would be consensual, and desire has never stopped me before. I'll be damned if I haven't grown a conscience—don't want to cause you emotional pain." Talon ran her hand through her own hair, then let her fingers gently caress Makayla's ringlets. "Pisses me off."

Makayla opened her eyes and looked into those electric blue ones. "Maybe because you like me." Then she leaned forward and planted her lips on Talon's moist ones. Talon lowered her lids and deepened the kiss before she pulled back.

"The dragon's not looking to be tamed, Mak. I don't know how to not just take what I want and move on anymore. I'm trying not to do that to you."

Makayla seemed stuck on the same word. "Because?"

"It's got to be because you undoubtedly saved my life," Talon replied, but Makayla didn't hear conviction in her voice.

"I don't want this to be about me saving your life. Or you probably saving mine when I was drenched and cold." Makayla decided to go along with the life-saving theme. While she wanted to relegate it to just lust, Makayla remembered Talon's tenderness that night. Makayla knew it was time to be honest, if only with herself. "I want this to be about the fact that there's a part of me that really likes you. And I want you to be interested in me for the same reason." Makayla gestured between herself and Talon. "Even though you can be such an ass sometimes, I want to see if this grows." Then she admitted, "And I don't have a fucking clue why. There are so many people who are so much nicer who I could like."

Talon shook her head, as though she was hearing things she didn't want to hear, but she didn't say anything. She just stood and studied Makayla in her skimpy attire.

"This isn't about life-saving debt, Talon. And it's not about me being enamored by your power. I've spent my life around powerful people in this enclave. It's about feelings. Not just physical. Emotional." Well, she'd certainly laid it all out there now.

"And I can't have those, Mak. I don't have feelings for any woman beyond that initial lust." And with that, Talon tenderly kissed Makayla before she pulled her away from the door. "I'll see you at Raptare in a few days." She started to move past Makayla, but not before she released a final growl. "To do some work." And with that, Talon left.

Makayla had to smile—it could have gone worse. Talon had kissed her. And she hoped there was more to it than simple lust.

Makayla stayed at Aurora to talk with Quinn and Rosa about their goals for a future regional alliance, and Makayla took notes. One of the additional things they discussed was the fact that while all the enclaves lived within the scope of the mostly primitive technology currently available to them, there had been the know-how in the past for much more advanced technology. Advances would undoubtedly come about again, minimally in the form of communication, transportation, weapons, and eventually additional areas that could prove threatening in the hands of aggressors. Makayla's consultation council asked that they include that topic in their future defense discussions—how a multi-enclave coalition might share and utilize that information to their advantage, for both quality of life and protection.

Makayla received a haircut from Fran, who left her top curls at the three-inch length they'd finally reached, but maintained her undercut. Talon had well-kept, layered hair, so Raptare undoubtedly had a decent haircutter that she could probably use. She packed enough clothing to last her for an extended period of time. She would head to Raptare at the beginning of the next week—four days after her last encounter with Talon.

Before she left, Quinn pulled Makayla aside to assure her that they would handle the onsite command role while she was gone. Not only was Rosa a great second-in-command, there were others who could step up. Makayla was happy to leave it to them. Then Quinn mentioned something that had come up.

"You know the rebel scout Bull Puckett—he burst in on that council meeting. He caused trouble when I was first named by the consultation council as interim leader because he wanted the power of the position. I just want you to know that he has been mouthing off again about the fact that a formal agreement has been reached between the leaders of the two enclaves, but he was unsuccessful in spinning it into anything that upset the rest of the Aurora residents. People think our agreement with Raptare makes sense and would like to see it expand. Onsite law enforcement will help keep tabs on him."

Preparations for her departure were in place by the beginning of the next week, and Makayla bid goodbye to the consultation council members, all people she found very supportive. Makayla rode a horse ahead of the one that bore her backpack and a large bag of extra travel belongings. She was followed by Ned, the leader of the patrol that had met her when she'd first arrived back at Aurora, and two of his men. Her not-so-unkindness flew along with the caravan as they traveled south to Raptare. She noted the touch of excitement she felt as she left the compound this time, so different from the last time when she'd been taken by the MidLanders. This time she was departing to face the challenge of her new leadership role, and to face the challenge of Talon de LaTerre. But it didn't feel like she was leaving home. Home was where the heart was, and it wasn't feeling so much like Aurora anymore.

Brock met the group when they arrived about noon, after their early departure from Aurora. Ash made sure that the horses and the ravens were settled in the barn. Then Brock offered everyone a quick lunch in the mess hall before Ned and his men left for the return to Aurora. There was no sign of Talon.

After lunch, Brock took Makayla and her belongings to the same residence hall bedroom she'd slept in during her last visit. She took a moment to glance around the quarters where she'd spent a single night. She'd never suspected that she'd be back in this same room for an extended stay. Brock leaned back against the doorframe and waited.

"Are you ready for this?" he asked with a touch of amusement in his eyes. Makayla had judged him to be in his mid-fifties with the requisite wrinkles. Many of those around his eyes and mouth seemed to be associated with his good nature.

"Am I ready for what? Do you mean the negotiations…or your commander?" She considered that both would likely stretch her interpersonal skills.

Brock laughed. "I like you. No beating around the bush."

"If only your boss liked me." Makayla shrugged and let out a sigh.

"Oh, she does. Too much for her liking. You get away with things I never would have thought anyone could get away with."

"You could have fooled me." Makayla was surprised by his admission. And interested.

"I've known her for a long time. She's fierce because she's had to be. But complicated." Brock offered a shrug of his own.

"That's one way of putting it." Makayla smiled at his description—complicated. "Can you tell me something?"

"Maybe. What is it?"

"Why is she known as Talon the Terrible?"

Brock contemplated her. He furrowed his brow in thought, and then made a decision.

"She fought like the devil for this place. Others were trying to tear it apart for their own personal gain when our commander, Lucas, died. He'd taken her under his wing." Brock stopped and cleared his throat. "This was years ago. She became the new chosen leader and showed no mercy to those who would destroy us. She's killed people, and so have I. It was kill or be killed during some terrible times. Circumstances have changed, but this compound is still her heart and soul. She tolerates no threat to it. Talon had been

adrift when she arrived here—for personal reasons. After she..."
Brock's voice trailed off and he refused to continue. He probably
thought he'd said too much, but Makayla wished he'd continue.

After an extended moment of silence, Makayla finally spoke.
"Thanks, Brock."

"Hang in there, trespasser. She just might be worth it." Brock
patted her on the shoulder.

"I'm too foolish or too stubborn to walk away." Makayla
wished she could.

"You're good for her. Just don't give up too easily. She's worth
some perseverance, even if she can be stubborn." Brock didn't seem
to be afraid of Talon. Probably because of their personal history. It
seemed like they had an extended history.

"Ohhh, now you're asking for her wrath." Makayla couldn't
help but tease him. "And the wrath of Talon the Terrible—word has
it that she'll..."

"Cut me to ribbons." Brock finished the sentence for her.

Makayla nodded. He knew of Talon's misdeeds, and yet it was
obvious he liked and respected her.

"She's mellowed as the enclave has succeeded. No dead bodies
in a while. At least not any that didn't totally deserve it." Brock
chuckled.

"Met her current quota, huh?" Makayla didn't know if he was
kidding or not. She was still trying to figure Talon out. What she'd
heard versus the many sides of Talon that she'd witnessed. What
she felt.

Brock laughed as he started to turn and leave. "Ivy will collect
you later and escort you to dinner. Feel free to wander around a bit.
Your birds are over at the barn."

"Thanks, Brock." Makayla was growing to trust Talon's
second-in-command the more she interacted with him. She hoped
her trust was well-founded. Maybe he could enlighten her more
about what motivated Talon. What else was in her personal history?

"You're welcome, trespasser." Brock tapped the doorframe as
he left her to settle in.

❖

After Brock was gone, Makayla unpacked her clothes and arranged them in the three drawers of the pine chest in her room before she placed the wooden comb her father had carved for her on top of the chest. She suspected the wooden dresser had been made in Raptare's woodshop because it was similar to the ones at Aurora, dressers that had likely been traded for items from the Aurora reclamation shop. She studied the room and noted that Talon's brown boot stuffed with the doily that she'd brought from the warehouse and left next to the bed pillow five months ago was nowhere to be seen. Talon had worn a different pair of dress boots when she'd come to Aurora last week.

There was little for Makayla to do in her new quarters, so she headed out to the barn area to make sure her birds were happy. She offered them a whistle and they greeted her with enthusiasm, but stayed up in the high rafters. Makayla surveyed the large barn interior as she stood at the door. There was a dark-shadowed corner area beyond the common entry space, several stalls off a center corridor, and probably a tack room, a feed room, and a clinical room for examining and treating the livestock further back in the building if it was similar to Aurora's barn.

As she stood there in the entry, Makayla took a closer look at five barn cats that her birds were avoiding. She was surprised to recognize the pudgy brown tomcat with the golden M on his forehead among them. He seemed to remember Makayla and approached her, rubbing against her legs.

Makayla picked him up and rocked him like a baby as she hummed to him and stroked the little fellow's plump belly. He began to purr and rub his head under her chin, his tattered ears soft against her skin. This was the tomcat who had adopted Talon—heaven forbid that anyone would suggest that Talon had adopted a cat, that she might have rescued a distraught kitten, taken him in and nurtured him, provided him with a plush, soft chair in her office, and probably a place to sleep at the foot of her bed. She'd let him keep his name, Betty, because the bloomin' cat liked that name—at least that's what Talon would tell you. Makayla shook her head at all she'd learned about Talon. At all that touched her heart.

"What are you doing out here, Betty?" She kissed his head.

As Makayla stood there holding him, surrounded by the other barn rat catchers, there was movement in the shadowed corner. Someone was sitting on a bale of hay observing her. As Makayla watched, Talon stood up and appeared out of those shadows.

Makayla took in her signature attire. The light forelock, the chestnut-toned tresses. The fact that not just the top button, not just the second button, but three buttons were undone on her sepia shirt. Her smooth tan neck descended to soft cleavage. Her shapely hips were attired in tight sepia pants. She had on the brown boots that she'd worn when she'd been injured—obviously the right boot that Makayla had left on the bed five months ago was back in Talon's possession. Makayla raised her gaze to address Talon's ocean-blue eyes. Deep blue ones, with an undertow.

"Good morning, Commander de LaTerre." Makayla inhaled, then smiled. Those growing feelings for Talon stirred and flapped their wings inside her chest, and that primal need in an area much lower stirred as well.

"Yes, it is, Commander Odin. Trying to steal my cat's affection?" Talon raised an attractive eyebrow. "He's visiting his associates and deciding if he's going to have mouse for dinner." She stepped forward, and Makayla felt the scrutiny of her gaze as it roamed from her head to her feet. "So, what are you doing out here?"

"You caught me. I came out in search of a rodent appetizer too." Makayla grinned as she inspected Talon right back. She found her just as appealing as she'd been four days ago at Aurora, even with all the lectures she'd given herself over the past few days regarding imprudent physical attraction. And even more imprudent emotional attraction. "So, why's a busy leader like you hanging out here in the barn with a cat? Don't you have enemies to vanquish?"

Talon looked down at her boots as if she'd been caught doing something she didn't want to admit. Interesting. Then she looked up and nodded at the feline in Makayla's arms. "I'm just conducting an onsite inspection of the barn. Betty's my accomplice."

"You wouldn't be offering a mostly indoor cat a bit of safe outdoor activity, would you?" Makayla surmised Talon's motivation for being out here.

"Well, we need every mouser we have. There are dogs and predators that could harm a cat." Talon defended herself as her hungry scrutiny settled on Makayla's mouth.

"The drakaina is a Betty babysitter," Makayla muttered to herself as she focused on the cat in her arms. *Oh, sublime Sappho, this woman has layers.* She looked back up at Talon. "I thought I'd walk a bit and tour the compound with the ravens—I just ducked in here to collect them. You could join us with Betty if you want."

"You're tempting me, Mak, but I've got a meeting with Brock, as well as with our head of defense, our chief engineer, and our head of training and education in a few minutes." Talon did look rather sorry.

"Well, that's a shame because Betty just told me that he's looking forward to a large prospective mouse meal he'd like to share, and then he wants a bit more fresh air. I can take him on my walk before I return him to you when I'm done."

"You go do that, but I don't want to interrupt my meeting. If you'd take him to your room, I'll send Ivy to collect him later." Talon cocked an eyebrow and waited for an answer.

"Perfect." Makayla turned her attention back to the cat. "It's you and me, Betty. Let's take a stroll. Come on, you corvids." She didn't let on, but she was sorry it would be Ivy and not Talon collecting the cat.

The birds flew outside, and Makayla set Betty down. They both followed Talon toward the door of the barn. Just before they reached the opening, Talon swung around, grabbed her by the shoulders, and captured Makayla's lips with her own in an action so sudden that Makayla didn't have a chance to respond.

"Shit," Talon said as she turned back to the exit. Makayla blinked a few times, touched her lips where she'd just been branded with proof that Talon wasn't indifferent, and then stared at the sway of those provocative hips as Talon headed back to the leadership building. Makayla didn't even try to suppress a grin.

Betty followed Makayla and her not-so-unkindness as they headed in the opposite direction to tour the compound and bask in the warmth of the sun. Makayla headed to the garden area, visited the animals in the corrals, and willed herself not to think about the kiss Talon had just given her. With the feline following her, she headed back to her room in the late afternoon. Makayla wished that Talon would be the one to come fetch Betty, but she suspected that after the barn kiss and Talon's profanity, Talon probably didn't want to be alone in a bedroom with her. That meant there was hope—Talon wanted her.

❖

As dinner time approached, Ivy came and collected the cat, then returned to escort Makayla to the mess hall where they joined Ash and Derrick for a foursome.

They talked about their lives and Makayla learned more about each of them. All were in their twenties. Ash, Brock's son, sat next to Ivy, who was his girlfriend. Derrick was Ash's friend and spent some of his time in the woodshop under the supervision of the enclave's senior craftsman, Vince, who was Ivy's father. Derrick also worked in the greenhouse and in the orchards, so he had a more tanned complexion than Ash.

"Would you like to go to the dance with me next month—in a few weeks?" Derrick asked Makayla. "They move the tables here in the mess hall to create open space, and there's fiddling. And of course, dancing to all that music too. Raptare has a hoedown about twice a year."

She choked on her bite of stew. She decided she just wanted to be the visiting leader from Aurora. She didn't want to explain her reasons for not being interested in a relationship. At least not for now.

"Thank you so much, Derrick, but I've got enough on my plate without dating while I'm here." Makayla wasn't ready to get into the personal reasons for her lack of interest in him after all the upheaval in her life.

"No dating. Just our luck," Derrick grumbled and furrowed his brow.

"But I'll probably be at the dance—just to socialize," Makayla said.

Derrick nodded, and they all talked some more about their favorite desserts and the amount of rain so far this year before they prepared to call it an evening. Just before they abandoned their table, a light-brown-haired young man about the same age as the others in the group approached and Ivy made introductions.

"Makayla, this is Joe. He works here in the mess hall. Helps cook and serve us this delicious food. He also works out in the orchards." Then she turned to Joe. "This is Makayla Odin, co-commander of Aurora. She's working with Talon on a defense proposal."

Joe scrutinized Makayla before he dipped his head. "Nice to meet you. I hope you're liking our food."

"Nice to meet you too, Joe. And yes, the food's terrific."

The others chatted with Joe for a few minutes, then they all said good night. Makayla walked back to the residence hall with Ivy, and they parted company in the hallway. She stretched out on her bed and contemplated her arrival at Raptare before she turned in for an early night of fitful rest. Talon filled her dreams.

CHAPTER EIGHT

W illow and Ivy collected Makayla the following morning and had her fill a plate of food in the mess hall while Willow filled another plate and Ivy filled two mugs. Without coffee, it was another morning of tea, as usual. Omelets, biscuits, and sliced fruit were the breakfast menu.

Ivy and Makayla saw Joe back by the kitchen and waved. Then the three of them headed to the leadership building with food and drinks. Makayla took a deep breath as they approached the closed door that was Talon's office, the same office where she'd shared breakfast with Talon five months ago. Willow knocked with her free hand.

"Enter," a low, resonant command that could only be Talon's came from behind the barrier, so Willow opened the door and headed into the office with Ivy behind her, and Makayla behind them.

Talon sat at her desk and was focused on some papers. She didn't look up, but Betty jumped down from his mauve chair and headed toward Makayla in a show of feline welcome. At least someone was happy to see her. From her pants pocket, Makayla extracted a piece of the cotton string she'd salvaged five months ago in the warehouse. She still carried that roll in her backpack and had cut some off, specifically for Betty to play with. She waved it around now as she waited for Talon. Betty batted and chewed as Makayla dangled and twirled. She noted that Talon covertly watched them while pretending to pay no attention at all.

Willow waited for Talon to indicate she was ready for the plate of food to be set on the desk in front of her. Then Willow took one cup of tea from Ivy and placed it on a cloth coaster to the side of Talon's plate. Ivy set the other cup of tea in the same spot where Makayla had eaten before, an indication that the plan was for Makayla to consume her breakfast on the opposite side of the desk from Talon.

"Thanks," Talon said into her paperwork as Willow and Ivy exited the room. Makayla was left standing next to the empty chair opposite Talon with her plate in her hands.

Betty returned to his chair to watch them. Talon kept her attention on her work. It seemed clear that she was making a show of acknowledging Makayla on her own terms. Finally, she glanced up and nodded in an indication that Makayla should sit down.

Talon leaned back and contemplated her as she took her seat. Makayla stared right back, not willing to yield and not wanting to appear weak because weakness wouldn't work to get her to a closer relationship with Talon—at least not to the kind of personal relationship she wanted.

Talon cleared her throat and broke Makayla's train of thought. "Good trip, Commander Odin?"

So, this was going to be how Talon interacted with her, as if the barn encounter and kiss had never happened the day before. Talon was now addressing her by her formal name—creating a barrier to any informal banter. That was undoubtedly Talon's intent.

"Commander Odin, huh? So, I should address you as Commander de LaTerre? That's a hell of a mouthful. And maybe too formal, since I've always heard it as Talon the Terrible." Makayla didn't break eye contact with her.

Talon sat a moment before she eventually broke the silence. "Talon will do."

"And just Mak for me. Or even *fledgling*, or *charmer*. I'm kind of fond of those names too." Makayla exaggerated the names.

Talon's expression softened, and then she drew back her shoulders. "Mak," she clarified. "Now that's settled, eat up." Talon took a bite of her omelet. Makayla's gaze followed her hand as she reached for her tea mug. Makayla saw that the cloth coaster it sat on was the lace-edged doily that she'd purposefully left behind five months ago. Left behind for Talon.

Talon noted Makayla's discovery and seemed to be considering how to address it. Finally, she looked at Makayla over her mug. "Someone left this in the room you used. Somehow, it ended up inside my boot. I might as well make use of it."

"Dragon lady's a bit sentimental," Makayla muttered.

"Don't get cheeky."

"Your quota and all." Makayla cocked an eyebrow as she teased Talon.

Talon was obviously fighting to maintain a stern demeanor. She cleared her throat. "Mak." She locked gazes with Makayla. "I normally work with subordinates, giving orders. You are my equal."

"Glad to hear it. Your equal...who you've slept with." Makayla wasn't sure why she needed to bring that up, but Talon's impromptu kiss yesterday had only resurfaced their night together—made her long for more. That kiss had suggested that Talon wanted her, if only physically, but she hoped for other reasons too. It was confusing.

"It can't happen again, Mak. We need to accomplish what our enclaves need—a professional relationship is necessary."

Makayla took a deep breath and chastised herself for letting her feelings take over. She could do this. Besides, she didn't want to be just another notch on Talon's bedpost. For the long haul, for her own sanity, she needed to be either in Talon's life or out—and ending up out of Talon's life was likely a much easier scenario to accomplish than the former, not that she had a clue how to accomplish either scenario. But when had she ever chosen easy?

As they finished their breakfast, she watched Talon set the last of her eggs on the ground for Betty. The cat let out a loud meow of approval and headed to the plate. Makayla watched him dive into the food. "N-A-T-O. *Narcissistic Animals Tout Omelets.*"

"Are you calling my cat narcissistic, Commander Odin?"

Makayla watched Talon bite her cheeks to keep from smiling.

"Just giving you some other options for the acronym, NATO, Commander de La Terre. It could be any whiskered critter, and I happen to like that cat of yours. But now that you bring it up, what cat isn't narcissistic?"

Talon shook her head, but her expression indicated she was enjoying the discussion. Then she grew serious. "We've got important enclave work to do."

"So, what's the plan?" Makayla straightened her shoulders and addressed Talon. "Shall we start with the agreement our two groups reached and work from there?"

Talon nodded. She gently stroked the doily with her forefinger. And then they spent the rest of the morning and the afternoon, after Ivy delivered lunch, beginning a discussion of how they could apply the defense portion of the agreement that their two enclaves had already reached—an exploration of how that agreement or a variation would work to achieve a broader new negotiated NATO alliance that included at least four additional neighboring north area WestLand enclaves.

Talon had other obligations as commander of Raptare, but she made time for the NATO work every day. Makayla was pleased with how well she and Talon worked together in their discussions. Talon treated her as an equal and listened to what she had to say, and she worked to treat Talon the same way.

They shared ideas on which enclaves should be approached, the known personalities of each enclave commander, and the logistics of meeting and communicating with those enclaves. A few times when their hands touched while they were passing papers, there was no denying the current of attraction that passed between them, but Talon ignored it, so Makayla did the same. She dreamed of a whole lot more than talking with Talon, but she tried to keep her focus on the fact that she was accomplishing what she'd been sent to Raptare to do.

There was serious discussion and little banter between them until late one afternoon the following week when they were talking about their approach to the coming meetings. They'd concluded that in their initial talks with the other enclave leaders, the presentation of the mission and goals seemed like a logical initial step to bring additional enclaves on board, and then they could move on to deeper discussions of the implementation specifics that their leadership teams had agreed to. Makayla was both surprised and pleased at what she and Talon accomplished together.

During a break from serious discussion, Makayla tilted her head at Talon. "Mission statement and goals. We're talking about first presenting some of the elements of a strategic plan, and if I'm not mistaken, it was paragraph number one that I liked best."

Talon gave her a confused look that indicated she wasn't sure what Makayla was talking about. Makayla felt the heat of embarrassment flush her face, which then sparked obvious understanding and scrutiny from Talon. Makayla could tell that Talon was a bit bored and ready for a little amusement, especially at her expense.

"Care to elaborate, Mak? I suspect this might be a bit more enjoyable than what we've been talking about."

"Uh, paragraph number one," Makayla repeated, feeling more heat wash her cheeks.

"And paragraph number one contains what?" Talon couldn't suppress the delight that danced in her eyes and tugged at the corners of her mouth. She clearly remembered exactly what Makayla was referencing. "Don't leave me hanging, Mak."

"Uh. Sex," Makayla blurted.

"Damn, you're entertaining." Talon chortled, and Makayla knew her face was now flaming.

Makayla was unhappy that Talon had managed to make her blush after she'd been the one to bring the topic up. "Okay, physical encounters off the table—history," Makayla said. "But I'm only behaving myself if you do too."

Talon's eyes continued to sparkle with mirth, then she sobered. "You're right. We have a job to do. However, I have barely been out of this room in over a week, and it wouldn't hurt to be seen around the compound. Shall we take a break and see if the tomcat wants a little outdoor exercise?" She stood and looked over at the feline. "Your opinion, Betty?"

Betty jumped from his chair and leisurely walked to the door, glancing at them over his shoulder. They followed him outside as he headed toward the barn where Poe swooped down to the ground and caught Betty's long tail in his beak and hopped along behind. Betty turned and hissed at Poe, and he gave the chubby cat a chuckling gurgle before he flew off to join Ed and Al, who had exited the barn.

They approached the gate with the four animals in order to head on out into the orchards. Talon greeted the young male guard, who ordered the canine with him to sit and stay. Outside the fence, they walked the distance necessary to engage in a tour through the trees. Al stayed close to Makayla as the other two birds scouted further out, and Betty remained on Talon's heels. It was spring, and buds preceded blossoms on many of the fruit trees while others were already in bloom. Song sparrows trilled and foraged for food, and they stopped to observe the activity.

"My grandfather loved those little birds. My favorites too," Makayla admitted wistfully. She hadn't told Talon about her grandfather's name for her, and she debated now.

"*Melospiza melodia*," Talon offered to Makayla's amazement.

"The scientific name for song sparrows. How do you know that?"

"I could say I once had a grandfather too, but I didn't." Talon's tone was subdued. "Someone else who loved birds told me. Loved ornithology." Talon let out a sigh. That was all the personal information she seemed willing to offer before she redirected the conversation. "This was Shep Odin who loved birds?"

Makayla smiled at the memory. "Yes. He used to take me out to the orchards at Aurora when I was little. Sometimes at sunrise. He'd named the enclave Aurora, which means dawn or daybreak in Latin," she said. "Gramps loved that time of day. The songbirds were out foraging then."

Talon nodded as she paid close attention.

"He called me *Makayla Melospiza melodia*. His sweet little song sparrow."

"I knew you were a songbird, fledgling," Talon said softly, her blue eyes studying Makayla.

"My grandfather and I, we had a saying. *Love is a song sparrow trilling at dawn.*" Makayla wanted Talon to understand how she came to care about birds.

Talon remained silent. Then she turned and stepped forward so they could continue on their walk. Betty led the way as they headed through the different orchards to the outskirts of the fruit trees. With Talon lost in her thoughts, Makayla also remained silent and simply enjoyed the sunshine until they reached the pear orchard. When they finally came to the far edge of the trees, the three ravens circled back with a display of excitement, sharing a call to alarm. Six full-sized pear trees had been chopped down.

The trunks had been cut through at the base, apparently felled with an ax. They were at the far end of the orchards, so the sound of the ax blows wouldn't have been easily heard. It was spring, and the branches were fully leafed and showing signs of flowering because these trees usually bore fruit between August and October. Makayla knew that it would take four to six years for new trees to mature enough to produce pears, so the enclave wouldn't have a full pear harvest again for an extended time. These pears were part of the food supply at Raptare, and while the vandalism wouldn't have catastrophic results, it was nevertheless a loss.

Makayla and Talon stopped and studied the damage while Betty explored the area nearby, and the ravens continued to sound the alarm and chatter. Talon did not say a word as she inspected the situation. She took a closer look at the ground where there were no clear footprints, and then examined the remaining stumps and the severed ends of the trunks. She showed Makayla where the vandal, or vandals, had made a wedged, hinge cut on the same side of each tree, then proceeded to place several chops through the other side of each trunk. She explained that the six trees had then toppled in the direction of the wedge cut and were now lined up neatly side-by-side where they'd fallen. These carefully planned cuts allowed the vandal to remain clear of the destruction. Someone knew what they were doing.

"I'm going to kill the son-of-a-bastard who did this." Talon's tone was controlled, but lethal. She scooped up Betty and began the march back to the compound gate with Makayla and the birds following. During the entire walk back Talon seethed her anger as she threatened all manner of painful termination for whomever had cut the six trees down. Makayla let her vent, understanding Talon's rage. This was an intentional attack on the enclave she commanded. An attack on the food supply of the compound, and Talon undoubtedly took it personally and felt responsible for catching whomever was responsible.

When they finally reached the gate, Makayla accepted the tomcat from Talon so that she'd be free to take control of the situation. Makayla escorted the birds to the barn and dropped Betty off on his chair in Talon's office while Talon went to find Brock and alert him to what had occurred. Makayla decided to retreat to her room until she was ready for dinner. She didn't need to get in Talon's way.

Makayla waited until dusk before she headed to the mess hall. There was a buzz in the large room, focused on the damaged trees—news like this always traveled fast in an enclave. Ivy waved Makayla over to her table.

Ivy made the introductions. "Hi, Makayla. This is Nina Clark, my good friend. She's one of the teachers at the compound school—at the elementary level."

Makayla greeted her new acquaintance. Before anyone could introduce any other topic, Ivy asked Makayla about the trees. As she started to recount what she knew about the vandalism, others joined them. Joe headed over from the kitchen to listen. The tree cutting was of interest to everyone. Makayla told them what she and Talon had found in the orchards, and Joe discussed the foods he helped create with the fruit. The trees would be missed. Finally, after a great deal of lamenting, much of the crowd left, including Ivy.

"I've worked out in the orchard with those pear trees, and then here in the kitchen to create delicious foods with the literal fruits of that labor…" Joe stopped and shook his head. "Pear turnovers are a favorite enclave dessert."

"I'm sorry," Nina said. "It sounds like you've had a deeper vested interest in those trees than just the loss of turnovers."

Joe nodded and turned to leave. "See you later. I need to get back to work."

Once he was gone, Makayla and Nina sat and chatted some more. Makayla discovered that Nina had a salvaged collection of old books that included one published in the early 2000s, a fanfiction book that she'd always wanted to read about a domineering fictional fashion magazine editor.

It wasn't simply the popularity that the book had attracted in its day—Makayla's interest was piqued with regard to how she might relate the prose to her situation with Talon. Nina offered to loan it to her, and Makayla jumped at the opportunity. Nina promised to track her down and deliver the book in the next few days. Makayla was happy to have made a new friend, especially one who was a bibliophile and owned a library of old books.

After Nina departed, Makayla considered that Talon probably hadn't eaten dinner, so she filled a plate with food for Talon in the chance she would still be in her office this late. She also collected a mug of goat milk and an empty bowl. When she arrived in the leadership building, she found Talon's office door was closed, but light leaked out underneath, so Makayla gently knocked.

"Who the bloody bother is it?" Talon barked before Makayla identified herself. Talon ordered her to come in with a terse *enter* command. Talon had a frown on her face as she ran her fingers back through her dark disheveled hair. Those locks had clearly been the recipient of a lot of finger-combing frustration as she'd sat and fumed from the chair behind her desk. Even her golden forelock was swept back from her forehead rather than falling forward. Brock sat in the chair opposite Talon, the same spot Makayla had been using, and Betty was in his mauve chair watching the show.

Makayla looked at Talon first. Even furious and tousled, Talon was the most striking female she knew. "I'm sorry to bother you, but

I was afraid you wouldn't eat. I brought you some dinner." Makayla wasn't sure how Talon would react to her nurturing, so she took a deep breath and swerved her attention to Brock and apologized. "I didn't know you were here, Brock, or I would have brought you a plate too."

"I think that Talon and I have done all we can for today." Brock stood. "I'm also off right now to get some food. Willow invited me over, so I'd better go before she closes down her chow line." He tilted his head toward Talon as he looked at Makayla. "Keep her calm, trespasser." Then on his way out the door, he called back over his shoulder, "I'll see you in the morning, Talon. Get some sleep."

Talon turned her attention to Makayla, who set the plate of food on the desktop in front of her. Talon indicated that Makayla should take a seat in the now-empty chair.

"I can use the food, but I don't want the milk." Talon stood up and went to a small cabinet and pulled out two metal tankards.

"The plate's for you, Talon. The milk's for Betty." As Makayla set the bowl on the floor and poured the mug of goat milk into it, the feline dove from his chair and beelined to the treat.

Talon watched Betty lap up the liquid. "Trying to steal my cat again, Mak?" She arched a shapely eyebrow. It was the right one, and Makayla had a powerful urge to stroke that faint scar next to it. The one Talon had admitted came from a bad time in her life.

"Nope." Makayla put her jacket over the back of the chair and sat down, her hands clasped in her lap. *I'm not trying to steal your cat—just your heart,* she clarified silently to herself. "What are we drinking?" She nodded at the two tankards Talon had placed on the desktop.

"Presumptive little commander, aren't you?" Talon side-eyed her as she reached for the jug and set it on the desk too. "How do you know I'm not planning to drink two tankards myself? Or offer one to Betty?"

"Because I'm a presumptive little commander." Makayla grinned at her. "And I bet the beverage in that tankard would be enough to embalm poor old Betty. Besides, I brought you dinner. You owe me."

"So, there's no free dinner?" Talon replied. "It's hard apple cider. For limited, discretionary, therapeutic use. How much do you want?"

"Only half. I've rarely had alcohol. No opportunity." Makayla kept her attention locked on the jug.

"A lightweight." Talon gave a slow smile as she filled the two tankards only halfway full with an orange-brown liquid before she pushed one across the desk to Makayla. "I should keep my head clear too, as much as I need to relax." Then Talon sat down and took a long draw from her own drink followed by a bite of the wild boar casserole that Makayla had brought her.

"This attack on the trees is going to take at least my morning tomorrow. I've already increased the patrols for tonight including making sure they have dogs with them, but the consultation council is going to have to discuss what else we want to do. Outside the compound fence means it could be one of our own, or not. And it could be one person, or more." Talon took another slow sip of her cider, swallowed, and closed her eyes.

"I understand," Makayla told her. "Do you want to come and get me at my room tomorrow when you're available to get back to our planning?"

"That sounds fine. But stay here for now and finish your drink with me while I polish off my dinner." Talon ate until she'd consumed her last bite of casserole, and then she leaned back into her chair to savor her drink and a moment of quiet.

As Makayla sipped, a smoldering, alcohol-induced hunger spread through her body. A hunger that had nothing to do with food. However, she was determined not to carry on a one-sided, emotional pursuit, or even a short-term physical affair, no matter how much the spiked cider encouraged it. She could sit here and share a moment with Talon though. An enjoyable, marinated moment.

After they'd both drained the hard cider from their metal tankards, Talon stood up. "I'll escort you back to your residence hall before I take a quick pass around the compound."

"It sounds like you care that I get back safely." Makayla wanted her to care.

"Wouldn't want anything to happen to Aurora's commander under my watch. They might not approve." Then Talon drawled, "I'm not tucking you in, though."

"Not tucking me in?" Makayla acknowledged Talon's declaration and tamped down the arousal the drawled words prompted. "Well, I might have to report that lack of diplomacy to my consultation council." Makayla couldn't deny that the effects of the cider had her feeling hopeful, and a bit cheeky.

"Not taking you to bed tonight either, charmer. Much as a one-night stand might relax me." Talon looked across the oak desk and locked the gleam in her eyes with what Makayla knew was the want in her own. Makayla watched the azure hue of Talon's eyes deepen to indigo as her pupils dilated, and she suspected hers revealed more a sienna emerald coloration than their usual lighter hazel.

Makayla hiccupped. "We already had a one-night stand. Wouldn't another one-night stand make our relationship a two-night stand?"

Talon shared one of her rich deep laughs. "Come on, Betty. Let's get this tipsy trespasser back to her room." Then she grew serious. "A two-night stand sounds like the start of a relationship to me. I don't do romance. Remember."

Talon put on her umber jacket in preparation to head out into the cool spring night. Then she took the lighter brown one off the back of Makayla's chair and helped her into it. She buttoned the front up to Makayla's chin, her face close to Makayla's. Talon stood a moment before she cleared her throat, turned Makayla around, and then placed her hand on Makayla's back. After guiding Makayla out of the office, Talon followed her to the entry of the residence hall building where her room was. She leaned in, and Makayla closed her eyes and took a deep breath of Talon's essence.

"Betty thanks you for your goat-milk thoughtfulness." Talon brushed her lips across Makayla's closed lids. "Drink some water and then sleep well, fledgling. I'll let you know when we can get back to work." Talon opened the door to the residence hall and gently pushed Makayla inside before she turned and headed out into the night with Betty on her heels.

CHAPTER NINE

Makayla slept later than usual the next morning because there was no reason to get up early. It was overcast outside and a good day to stay indoors. She finally decided to head to the barn to check on her birds before she went to the mess hall for a late breakfast and tea. The mess hall was fairly empty, so she didn't stay to chat with anyone. She waved at Joe as he worked in the kitchen and then returned to her room to review the notes she'd taken during her recent meetings with Talon.

It was almost noon when Makayla heard a knock on her door. She opened it, thinking it might be Talon, but it was Ivy's friend Nina instead.

"Hi, Nina. It's good to see you again. What can I do for you?" Makayla welcomed her in and left the door partly open.

"I found my copy of the book that you said you wanted to read. It's a classic. I think you'll enjoy it. I have a small library in my room if you want to borrow more when you're done with this one." Nina smiled. "I'm a real book lover, so I collect them whenever I get the chance—not that there are many of the classics available."

They sat side by side on the edge of Makayla's bed because there was no other place for two people to sit in the small room. They spent time discussing the book, set in a world with a fashion industry that no longer existed. Nina assured Makayla that she would enjoy reading about the relationship between the fictionalized tyrannical boss and the younger employee who found herself working for the older, powerful woman, even though it wasn't about a romance between the two.

Makayla didn't mention it to Nina, but she was interested in the book because she wanted to see how Talon might compare to the story's job-oriented female leader, and while Talon's reputation might measure up, she knew that Talon possessed a softer side.

After discussing the book, they moved on to discuss other topics, including Nina's teaching. Nina talked about her job at the elementary level and the other two teachers who taught the middle and high schoolers, as well as mentioning her boss, Calvin, who was in charge of training and education. Makayla told Nina about how she'd ended up down south on the battlefield, and her new role in leadership at Aurora.

"So, Willow told me that your last name is Odin. I also heard that the three ravens in the barn are yours and that you found and raised them."

"That's true." Makayla shared the history of her not-so-unkindness. How she'd rescued the young birds in the woods down south. How they were now her family.

"Do you know that your last name, Odin, was the name of the chief of the Norse gods, and he's considered the raven god because he had two ravens that he sent out every day to bring him back news of the world?"

"My grandfather told me that after I found them." Makayla remembered how Gramps's story gave new meaning to her last name.

"So, I guess it was destined for you to be the raven girl." Nina chuckled. "What are their names?"

"Ed, Al, and Poe."

The reference to Edgar Allan Poe and the poem, "The Raven," registered with Nina and she couldn't stop laughing as she leaned closer and bumped Makayla on the shoulder. Makayla was laughing along with Nina when there was a quick knock and the door flew the rest of the way open. Talon stepped inside the room and took in the two of them sitting close together on the bed engaged in merriment, then she glared at Makayla.

"Hi, Talon." Makayla greeted her, still chuckling. "Do you know Nina?"

"I do," Talon said with a perceptible undercurrent of anger. Then she gave Nina a perfunctory nod.

Uh-oh. Makayla sobered. Was Talon jealous because she thought Makayla was encroaching on one of her girlfriends? Makayla wasn't even sure what Nina's sexual orientation was.

"Are you ready to finally get to work?" Talon's tone was terse.

"I was just waiting for word from you."

"I can certainly see that." Talon didn't even try to hide the sarcasm as she turned and headed to wait in the hallway.

Makayla's eyes widened as she looked at Nina, then thanked her for the book and the visit as she grabbed her notebook and headed toward the hallway too. Makayla shut her door, and they followed Talon outside. Nina pressed her mouth tightly closed as she looked at Talon, then mumbled wishes for them to have a good afternoon before she turned in the direction of the mess hall for her midday meal.

"Can you wait up?" Makayla asked the back of Talon's head as she rapidly followed her back to the leadership building.

"We'll talk in my office." Talon gruffly threw out her reply and didn't slow down.

❖

Once in Talon's office, Makayla took her normal seat and waited for Talon to take her chair behind the desk. Makayla decided she wasn't going to let Talon lambaste her first, for whatever misdeed she'd supposedly committed.

"Are you mad because you thought I was interested in one of your girlfriends? Not that I even know if Nina likes women, or if you two have had a relationship." Makayla addressed the fuming Talon. "I met Nina in the mess hall through Willow and Ivy yesterday, and we talked about a book she has. She brought it for me to borrow. I'm not interested in her as more than a friend." Because she was only interested in Talon. Makayla fought to remain calm. Talon's outrage was exasperating.

"It looked like more than that." Talon snapped out the response.

"So, are you jealous because you think I was poaching one of your girlfriends?" Makayla repeated her question.

Talon looked down at her desktop and shuffled some papers. Then she looked up at Makayla, the embers of her fury smoldered in her eyes.

"No, Mak. Any time I spent with Nina was a long time ago. I'd be happy for her to find someone appropriate for a long-term relationship. And I *do not* have girlfriends, remember. No attachments." Talon rolled her lower lip between her teeth after she'd made it clear that Makayla's poaching assumption wasn't the source of her anger.

Makayla struggled to keep her focus on figuring out the issue because a fiery, jealous Talon was so mesmerizing that she had a hard time thinking. Then the truth dawned on Makayla.

"You're jealous because you think I was being hit on. It's not about Nina. It's about me." Then Makayla whispered, "You're upset because you like me."

Talon kept her face neutral after that observation. She was so much more practiced than Makayla was at hiding her feelings. Talon had shifted into her stoic demeanor; it seemed she thought that she'd already revealed too much. Makayla fought to convey dispassion too but knew she hadn't fully suppressed the elation from her gaze as the realization dawned. This was indisputable proof of emotional involvement by Talon, even if she wouldn't admit it. Makayla was now certain Talon had at least budding feelings for her, and not only physical either.

Talon didn't deny Makayla's conclusion. She sat in her chair and waited, her only hint of being flustered was a momentary darkening of her eyes. Makayla was starting to understand it was a touch of nature Talon couldn't control, that innate reaction that overrode her efforts to appear dispassionate.

Then Talon dipped her head at Makayla and declared it was time to get back to work. Makayla wanted lunch, but she paid no attention to her rumbling stomach. It had been a great morning, and she could ignore a little hunger. Luckily, Willow brought two full plates of food to the office a half hour later and covertly patted Makayla on the shoulder before she left.

❖

Almost two weeks passed and no clue had been uncovered as to who had damaged the trees. Talon had shifted her attention back to their NATO alliance work. She'd maintained a professional demeanor around Makayla as they finalized the presentation plans for their first meeting with two enclave leaders. Sylvan was the enclave mostly east and slightly south of Aurora and Eden was directly north. Talon was much more familiar than Makayla with the leaders and the politics of each of the enclaves they would be interacting with. She'd had much more experience in regional dealings. The first two enclave leaders were scheduled for talks on Monday of the following week, and the second two on Friday.

After she'd revealed her jealousy, Talon maintained her Commander de LaTerre persona. Her demeanor was all business, and she was unwilling to engage in any banter. She went so far as to look away when Makayla caught Talon studying her. Makayla missed their lighthearted exchanges, but several times, she noticed Talon gently touch the doily under her drink.

The revelation that Talon had been jealous of Nina's possible interest in her, that there was some emotional involvement on Talon's part, encouraged Makayla. That fed her belief that romance could be part of their relationship. She was tired of Talon's cool deportment. Talon had feelings for her, and she was out of patience. It was time to prod Talon again.

Once they'd finished their official discussions for the week late on Friday afternoon, Makayla asked Talon, "So, are you going to the event tomorrow night in the mess hall?"

"And what event might that be?" Talon asked her in what Makayla assumed was mock ignorance because Talon knew almost everything that was happening at Raptare.

"The dance." Makayla gave Talon an eye roll. "Don't tell me that Commander de LaTerre doesn't have it on her calendar."

Talon ignored the jibe. "I heard Derrick invited you a few weeks ago."

"Then you heard I turned him down." Makayla shook her head at their sparring.

"Do I dare ask why you would do that?" Talon relaxed back into her chair, long, slender fingers steepled in front of her that suggested an effort at casualness as she waited for the answer.

"Besides the fact that I'm busy with this leadership role, I like women, as you already know." She held Talon's gaze. "Firsthand." Then Makayla decided to push the topic. "One woman in particular."

"Is that so." Talon focused down on her hands. "Maybe you need to ask that particular woman for a dance." She lifted her attention and Makayla felt piercing blue eyes capture her in a hungry assessment.

"And would she accept?" Makayla's heart rate increased with just the chance Talon might agree to a dance.

"Maybe you should save the last dance for her." Talon's reply was barely audible, but Makayla was elated with her mutter.

Makayla pulled a small piece of paper out of her notebook and held it up. "Dance card," she clarified. Then she picked up her quill, dipped it in the bottle of walnut ink she used for writing, and made a show of jotting a note across the page. "Last dance. Talon the Tempting." She couldn't stop smiling.

"Mak." Talon addressed Makayla in her lecturing voice, but the light that shone from those dancing eyes gave her away. "Cheeky little…" she struggled for the label, "…menace." Talon pronounced the last word at normal volume before she whispered, "Charmer." Talon unconsciously brought her hand to her chest—a likely gesture of protecting her heart. Then she took back control of the situation. "I hope you know how to dance."

"You'll just have to find out." Makayla stood up, walked around behind Talon, and quickly dropped a kiss onto her neck. "Thank you. You won't be sorry." Makayla released Talon, grabbed her notebook, and sauntered to the door. She added all the sway to her hips that she could manage as she looked back over her shoulder and grinned at Talon.

Talon shook her head as she fought to keep a straight face. "Regretting it already."

CHAPTER TEN

Saturday evening, after the dinner crowd had cleared and people had started to gather for the scheduled Saturday night entertainment, Makayla entered the mess hall. She'd been busy in her room fussing with her curly hair and selecting a tighter top than her normal looser shirts, a top that clung to her upper torso and showcased her shape. The fabric in the slacks she'd chosen hugged her hips and ass in a way that she hoped left no doubt that she was out to impress Talon.

Music mixed with the buzz of an energized crowd. Makayla looked around and saw that the interior of the mess hall had been rearranged. The wooden tables and chairs that were usually scattered throughout the room now haloed the perimeter of three sides of a central floor area open for dancing. On the fourth side of the large room, in front of the normal serving area with the kitchen behind it, an elevated platform had been constructed for the event.

Three fiddlers, a banjo player, and a guitarist stroked their stringed instruments and offered vocals to produce the heartbeat of the room, while the chatter and laughter of the attendees created a steady background accompaniment that transformed the normally more subdued mess hall into a symphony of celebration.

Several people were dancing in the open space. Younger kids moved freely to the music as they pursued their own solo performances. Some adults performed choreographed steps and turns in lines, while others danced as couples, rocking in companionable union and then stepping apart in twirling gyrations with only a hand-to-hand connection before they returned to more intimate proximity. As some of the dancing couples strutted and nodded and extended their arms, Makayla thought of the courtship dances of so many bird species. Humans weren't that different, she thought to herself—everyone just looking for love.

Makayla spotted Nina, Derrick, and Joe at a table and headed in their direction. Ash and Ivy were one of the couples out on the dance floor. Joe stood and collected an empty chair for her.

"Can I get you a drink? There's plum wine, apple juice, and water." Joe offered Makayla a nod as he looked her up and down. "And I can probably wrangle you some hard cider if you want."

Nope. Makayla fought to keep her thoughts to herself. She wanted to remain polite, so she forced a smile. She wasn't good at balancing social situations like this, at juggling her attraction to women with the attraction males had for her. A declaration that clarified her sexual identity might be something she'd soon need to do, but it wasn't going to be in this crowded room tonight. She'd just be careful to do some congenial talking and a little dancing, but she'd make no moves that could be misconstrued as more than friendly interaction appropriate to a community dance. At least she hoped she could pull it off.

"Thanks for the seat. I can head over and get myself a little water in a bit. I'm not much of an imbiber and don't want to embarrass myself tonight." Joe's face fell at her words.

Makayla accepted an invitation from Ash when Ivy decided she needed a break from the dance floor, and then Derrick made an attempt to engage her on the dance floor as well. She did a quick number with him and hoped that after that, she could turn him down without hurting his feelings.

She was grateful that none of the music included songs that would require close dancing. Joe just sat and watched, but didn't try to recruit her to the dance floor after she'd turned down his drink offer. She knew, like males across many species, that tonight's event put males in competition with each other. She'd spent two years maneuvering through the intricacies of the male ego, especially the unsettled ones, and she felt no real need to do so anymore.

Derrick and Joe finally joined Nina in the line dancing. After she'd observed for a while, Makayla gravitated to the line dancing too and slipped in between Nina and Joe. There was an unencumbering ease to moving in synchrony with a dozen other people who had made no social commitment to a designated partner. Nina smiled and Joe gave her a reserved nod.

Makayla spent more time at the table as the evening wore on, listening to the conversation of her tablemates and joining on occasion. She enjoyed Ivy's friendly chatter, and Nina knew a lot about several books. She scanned the room for Talon, and when she didn't see her, she kept an eye on the door. Nina's boss, Calvin, head of the enclave's training and education, came over to the table and requested a dance with Nina before he insisted that Makayla dance with him. Makayla didn't want to join him, but Nina gave her an imploring look that made it obvious she wanted Makayla to appease him and free her up.

"Thanks," Nina said when Makayla finally managed to escape Calvin after a dance. "I owe you. He's my boss and I don't want to rock the boat, but I don't want to encourage him either. He's not my type if you get my drift. And even if he was, he's a creep."

Makayla smiled. "Not my type either. If you get my drift." Nina nodded. From what Talon had indicated, Nina liked women too.

"It looks like you're waiting for someone," Nina said.

"Talon." Makayla was worn out from all the navigating she'd done so far that evening and decided to just enlighten Nina.

Makayla worried that maybe even the one word had been too much when Nina's eyebrows rose and her eyes widened as realization seemed to dawn. She'd hoped that if anyone would understand, it would be Nina. Then Nina's eyebrows lowered and she studied Makayla before offering her a ghost of a nod in understanding. "Good luck. She's skittish as hell."

Nina's willingness to respond emboldened Makayla to confirm what she pretty much already knew. "So, you're a lesbian?"

"I am," Nina replied. Then a blush infused her cheeks. "But Talon was a long time ago. And only once." She stuttered the clarification.

"Skittish as hell." Makayla repeated Nina's declaration. "What's that about?" Makayla had thought she might feel some jealousy, but the "long time ago" seemed to save her from those feelings. She knew Talon had a past. And Talon hadn't chosen Nina for anything more than a night.

"I don't know exactly why she's so skittish, but something to do with her past."

"Thanks." Makayla considered this as she left the table to get something to drink. She didn't shift her attention from the door.

Makayla began to wonder if Talon was even going to show up as the evening progressed and she nursed a mug of apple cider. Not hard apple cider. She wanted to be sober, so she could handle her elation or disappointment without the haze of alcohol coursing through her veins and addling her brain. Makayla had no doubt that they'd agreed on the last dance—the only dance Makayla cared about that night.

Finally, it was toward the end of the last band set of the gathering when Makayla saw Talon slip into the room. She watched Talon head toward the musicians, then lean in to speak to one of the fiddle players as the song ended.

That moth-to-the-flame fluttering in Makayla's chest had become a wild, full-feathered creature that caught the climbing currents and floated on air. Makayla closed her eyes and took a deep calming breath. The fiddle player smiled and turned to converse with the rest of the band.

"Last call for a dance this evening." The guitarist made the announcement as he watched Talon cross to Makayla. "And we've had a special request to make it a slow one." He winked at the crowd.

"I believe this dance belongs to me." Talon held out her hand and pulled Makayla from her chair as the slow dance commenced. The eyes of everyone in the room went to Talon, and that included Ash, Joe, and Derrick's. Nina and Ivy were paying attention too. Realization played across their faces as Talon led Makayla out onto the dance floor.

With her arms placed over Makayla's shoulders and her hands locked around the back of Makayla's neck, Talon pulled her close until there was no space between their two bodies. They swayed in unison under Talon's lead as the slow strains of the melody escaped the strings of the instruments and filled the room. Talon was a bit taller, but their bodies fit perfectly together, front to front; the topography of hills and valleys, dips and swells, juxtaposed so that two melded into one.

"I guess I've been outed now." Makayla chuckled, her mouth against Talon's throat.

Talon tilted her head down to offer a warm whisper into Makayla's ear. "I believe this dance is on your dance card, Mak, and you seemed to be looking forward to it based on the sway of your ass as you exited my office yesterday." Talon exhaled against the side of Makayla's head and her heated breath warmed Makayla's ear.

"You were looking at my ass? I'm shocked," Makayla gasped as if she were taken aback. Then she added, "I've never hidden who I am, except when I've had to for survival. I don't think those at Aurora have much doubt, so I see no reason that all of Raptare shouldn't know."

Talon nodded toward the table where Makayla had been sitting. "I get the impression that a few of your admirers might be disappointed."

"I've never led them on. I've known who I want for quite a while now." Makayla mirrored the movement of Talon's form while Talon slowly moved to the music as she held Makayla as closely as possible.

"And what would it be that you wanted?" Talon leaned back and gently lifted Makayla's chin, earnestly locking sapphire eyes directly with Makayla's.

"You."

"We're from two different enclaves. We're two different ages. Two different temperaments. And we have two different histories. As I said before, I'm not good for you."

Makayla wasn't ready to capitulate. "I thought you were Talon the Tenacious. Are you giving up already?"

Talon shook her head and chuckled. "Insulting me, cheeky little charmer?"

"Is it working?"

"The insult, or the charm?" Talon pulled her back in so their bodies were pressed tightly together.

Makayla returned her face to Talon's neck and inhaled that signature scent—so intoxicating. "Whichever one gets me what I want."

The song had ended and Talon continued to hold Makayla close, hesitant with her response.

"I can't make you any promises." Talon finally spoke into Makayla's hair. Then she lowered her voice to a level that sounded more like she was talking to herself than to Makayla. "I'm damaged goods."

What had hurt her so deeply? "Then don't make me any promises. One day at a time."

"Crap," Talon swore. "Easy to say. But what happens when there isn't another day? When you're left holding a shattered heart?" Talon leaned back and studied her. "Smashed into a million pieces." Makayla surmised that Talon was talking about herself. A rare unguarded disclosure. Who had shattered Talon's heart?

What would happen if there wasn't another day? There was no easy answer as to how Makayla would be able to go on. The deaths of her father, her brother, and her grandfather had broken her heart—cracked, but still beating. Even with a profound ache in her chest, Makayla had kept going.

But she already couldn't imagine a life without Talon. Even one limited to the business-only relationship that Talon had imposed these past weeks had been bearable. She'd been existing on hope. So how would she go on if Talon turned that hope into heaven, and then walked away? She didn't know that she'd be able to survive the resulting despair—shattered beyond repair.

"Will you talk to me, Talon?" They were still on the dance floor, but people had begun to move the furniture back for breakfast in the morning. The dance was over. Makayla took Talon's hand and led her out through the mess hall door into the night.

"Talking won't help. I don't want to hurt you. It would be so easy to take you home for the night." Desire emanated from

Talon's husky response. "I haven't slept with anyone since our night together," Talon softly murmured.

Makayla tried not to grin at the admission, but she couldn't suppress her elation. She hoped Talon couldn't see her jubilation in the low light. Talon hadn't been busy having one-night stands since their dark and stormy night several months ago.

Talon growled. A low sexy growl. "I didn't intend to say that. Wipe that shit-eating grin off your face."

"No wonder you're so grouchy." Makayla laughed.

"Ribbons, fledgling. Ribbons." Talon pulled Makayla around the corner of the building and out of sight of any onlookers before pushing her up against the exterior mess hall wall, her own body holding Makayla in place—signature move. Makayla felt the clench of arousal between her legs, the flood of need.

Talon stepped back enough to be able to reach between their two bodies and grasp Makayla's shirt, to tug and free it from her pants. Makayla leaned forward and skimmed Talon's lips with her own. Her now familiar essence caused Makayla to savor her fragrance and escalate the kiss—to explore Talon's mouth with her tongue as she grabbed the waistband of Talon's slacks.

"What are you doing to me?" Talon shook her head as she rolled her hips forward and pressed into Makayla while she moved her hands to Makayla's ass. Makayla was certain that she was aware of the physical effect she had on her—Talon knew so much more about carnal pleasure. She was the queen of sexual encounters, or at least that had been the rumor. A master of seduction and one-night stands.

But "What are you doing to me?" was an admission that Talon's heart was involved—that Talon felt the awakening of caring, maybe even the need to get off her perch and catch those rising currents of an emotional connection too. And that made Makayla even more determined not to give up on her. Talon the Tormented.

They were on a course that neither one seemed able to wield any control over. No matter how much Makayla wanted it to continue, or how ill-advised Talon professed it to be, this was pure explosive chemistry that coursed through both of them. Makayla considered that only an interruption could interfere and calculated that if she suggested that they head to a bedroom, the disruption might be enough to cause Talon to reconsider the path they were on. Makayla was at war—drowning in glorious sensation while trying to contemplate how to get them to a more comfortable location.

Then she decided there was no reason that taking this to fruition against the wall of the mess hall wasn't a memory in the making, out here under the stars in the moonlight. She would worry about a bed next time. These thoughts raced through Makayla's mind and fed the pulsing through her veins, the throbbing at her core. They nurtured that growing emotion that resided in her chest, inflated her lungs, and beat its wings against the walls of her heart. And then the sound of approaching shoes on gravel imploded the entire erotic encounter.

Brock cleared his throat in an effort to offer Talon a warning. "I'm sorry, Talon. There's been another incident. Vandalism."

And that was all it took for the best evening of Makayla's life to come to an end. Well, she admitted to herself, the second best— it came in behind their night in the storm. Not that it hadn't been headed toward the best night of her life. *Fuck.*

CHAPTER ELEVEN

After she created some space between Makayla and herself, Talon tucked in her shirt. Then Talon turned to address Brock, back in full Commander de LaTerre persona.

"Tell me what happened." Talon's full attention was on him now.

"It was in the last few minutes since the dance let out. Inside the compound this time. A fire was set in the barn. Loose straw was placed in a pile and set on fire in the open space just inside the barn before you reach the corridor to the stalls. No way was it an accident." Brock rubbed his temple in obvious agitation. "Luckily, we had all our planned patrols on duty during the dance, so while not as many people were out and about, it was caught early. It could have spread and burned the barn down. Nobody on patrol claims to have seen anything suspicious before the smoke and flames alerted them."

Talon closed her eyes for a moment as she clearly struggled to control her rage. The fire-breather was defending her den. "I'll kill the bastard myself, once we have him." She snarled her initial reaction before she managed to regain command of her emotions. Makayla had no doubt that Talon recognized that there was a time for fury, but now wasn't the moment. "First, we have to catch him. Come with me to the barn, Brock, and let's have a look." It was evident Talon had started to shift her focus to thinking it through— to consideration of a more measured response and investigation.

She squeezed Makayla's shoulder. Then Talon signaled for Ash, who stood behind his father, to escort Makayla back to her room in the residence hall before she turned to leave with Brock.

"I'm going with you," Makayla told her.

"This is my job, Mak. I want Ash to take you to your room. You'll be out of harm's way there. Less to worry about." Talon's tone left no doubt that she was taking charge and didn't welcome resistance to her orders.

"But I need to know that my ravens are safe. They sleep in the barn, Tal. They would have been there." Makayla could hear the strain in her own voice as she worried for her not-so-unkindness.

"Brock and I will go to the barn. Too many people and too much chaos won't help the situation. The first thing I'll do is give orders to try to locate the birds." Talon's tone softened as she tried to reassure Makayla that she would make Ed, Al, and Poe a priority.

Makayla frowned, but Talon clearly didn't want to take the time to argue. "I promise," she said gently, speaking solely to Makayla. "I know you love them."

Makayla nodded. Talon might be difficult, might be temperamental, might even be an ass at times, but she trusted Talon to care for her birds. Talon knew how much she'd already lost. And she'd seen evidence that the ravens were important to Talon too. "How will I hear?"

Talon looked at Makayla as she obviously registered her distress. "Go collect Betty. He's in my bedroom. Ash can take you there." She took a key out of her pocket and handed it to Ash. "You take Betty back to your room, Mak, and make sure he's safe. I'll follow through on your birds. Either I, or someone I send, will come to update you. Okay?"

There was a gathering crowd of patrollers now watching them, both men and women because there was no gender division of duties when it came to the protection of the compound. Makayla didn't care who observed their interaction, but she thought that Talon might. She didn't want to compromise Talon's leadership authority or make her look soft. "Okay, Commander." Tears overwhelmed Makayla and streamed down her cheeks.

"Oh, bullocks." Talon swore under her breath as she leaned in and used her shirt cuff to wipe the tears away before she planted a kiss on Makayla's forehead. "Thanks for trusting me, fledgling." Then Talon turned and was gone into the night, the gathered patrollers following on her heels.

❖

Ash led Makayla through the compound to a small building on the perimeter of several other similar structures. "This is Talon's place." He used the key Talon had given him to open the door and told her to wait while he lit some candles. Once he'd accomplished that, Makayla could see that the place was solar-powered, but with limited salvaged storage batteries in the compound, everyone was in the habit of conserving energy when they could.

She peered around Ash into a small common area with a wood fireplace, some chairs, and a drop-down dining counter with two stools. A small kitchen area extended off the end of the room near the dining counter. A doorway that revealed the foot of a bed in Talon's sleeping room was located on the far side of one of the chairs. Talon's living quarters were compact but neat.

They moved into the common area, and Betty exited the bedroom and walked over to brush against Makayla's legs. The loud rumble of his welcoming purr filled the chamber. Betty rubbed the entire length of his body against her shins, then did a reversal and side-swiped his other side for a classic feline, full-body caress.

Makayla bent down and lifted the well-fleshed boy. "Good to see you too, Betty. Let's grab a couple of bowls for water and your food—you're going to be my roommate for the night." It dawned on Makayla as she talked to Betty that Talon's entire purpose in having her collect the cat was to offer her comfort and a distraction while she waited for word on her birds.

Ash carried the bowls and the cat food while Makayla hugged Betty close as they headed to her residence hall room. Makayla thanked Ash for his help, then he left to join the patrols. Makayla and the tomcat settled on her bed. She tried to doze but didn't have much success. Betty had no such issues.

It was over an hour later that there was a knock at Makayla's door.

"Who is it?" Makayla called.

"It's Calvin. I've news about the fire." The door muffled his voice.

Makayla opened the door a crack, just enough to converse with him. He put his hand in the crack and tested it with some pressure, but her foot held the door in place. She knew what Nina had indicated about her boss, and Makayla wasn't about to let him in.

"The entire barn has been searched and the birds aren't there. Talon's assumption is that they'd headed out to find an alternative sleeping spot when the fire was set," Calvin said. "You look worried. Maybe I should come in and keep you company."

Makayla didn't want Calvin's company. Maybe he was harmless, but she didn't trust him. He was too friendly. It felt like he wasn't interested in what he could do for her, but in what she could do for him—and there was nothing she could do for him.

"Thanks, I'm fine. I appreciate that you brought me the message." Makayla pushed her door shut, locked it, and stretched out on her bed. The news didn't prevent Makayla from worrying. She wouldn't rest well until she'd seen that the ravens were unharmed.

She didn't hear any more from Talon during the course of the night, but she hadn't expected that she would. Talon was occupied with the repercussions of the vandalism.

After tossing and turning until the first light of dawn, Makayla finally gave up. She left Betty asleep in her blankets and headed out to see if she could make contact with her ravens. As she walked from her quarters toward the barn, Ed flew in and landed on Makayla's arm. He offered her his special welcoming croak. Al and Poe were not far behind and landed on the ground near her feet. Makayla had a hard time containing her relief as the upset birds shared their disgust at the situation. She stood and let them vent until Talon appeared in the early morning light outside the barn.

"I was coming to tell you that it seems they moved to the orchards last night and are now back and full of opinions." Poe flew up and landed on Talon's outstretched arm. He let Talon stroke his head. "They're mad, but not as furious as I am." She looked more exhausted than enraged after the long night.

"Any idea who did it?"

"None, at this point." Talon's tone expressed just as much disgust as the ravens. "I bet your birds have the answer though. They don't miss much."

"It's a long shot, but there's a guy named Bull Puckett who's been upset with the Aurora leadership, and now the enclave alliance we're working on. He's in his mid-forties and a hothead. He wants more power. I'm not sure what he might do." Makayla imparted some of the information she'd learned at Aurora.

"Thanks, Mak. I'll see if I can't send someone to Aurora to check out his whereabouts. It's time to update the members of Aurora's contingent on our efforts at meeting with the other enclaves about the NATO progress, and how you're doing as well. We can write an update summary on our treaty efforts for both our consultation councils too, after our meetings this next week. Do you want to go to Aurora with whomever we send?"

Makayla shook her head. "I'll stay here and work with you. It's not like I still have any family there to visit."

"I'm glad your birds are all right." Talon made an effort at a smile—a tired smile. "I've been up all night, so I'm heading back to my place. Why don't you go get something to eat? I'm going to get some sleep, and then I'll be meeting with Brock and Willow today before the enclave leaders from Sylvan and Eden arrive. Can you keep Betty with you for now?"

"Sure," Makayla replied. "And, Talon?"

"What?" Exhaustion came through in the tone of Talon's question.

"Thanks for the last dance."

Talon now gave her a full smile. "Hell of a dance." Then she shook her head. "As I keep telling myself, you're dangerous."

Makayla became serious. "I'd never hurt you."

"Sometimes it's not on purpose. But me, I can't give you a long-term relationship. I can't give you what you need, and that will hurt you."

"Then like I asked before, just give me one day at a time." Makayla hoped she wasn't making a mistake, but she'd decided that she wanted to see if Talon would change her mind about their relationship. She was sure that Talon had feelings for her. Hatching, brooding feelings.

Talon closed her eyes in a prolonged blink, then opened them and looked at Makayla. "Thanks for watching Betty." She turned and headed toward her quarters, and Makayla watched her walk away until she was out of sight.

The ravens flew back into the barn to check it out. Makayla looked in after them before she headed to Sunday morning breakfast in the mess hall. The buzz was focused on the barn fire, and she was relieved that as she entered, no one paid any particular attention to her after it had become obvious at the dance that her relationship with Talon might be more than commander to commander.

Makayla collected some tea and fruit, waved into the kitchen where she could see Joe working, then headed toward a table where Nina, Ivy, and Derrick were eating breakfast. Nina signaled for her to sit as they stopped their conversation. Ivy smiled while the other two studied her. Joe came from the kitchen and joined them for a moment, but didn't take a seat.

"So, you and Talon, huh?" Ivy cut to the chase, a hint of awe in her voice.

"We've been working together on the defense alliance, and on Friday she told me she'd come to the dance and for me to save one for her." Makayla downplayed her interactions with Talon, but couldn't help the blush that she could feel infuse her face.

"It's rather obvious she has a soft spot for you," Nina said. Then she added, "Watch your heart, Mak. She's damaged goods."

Makayla wondered again exactly what had happened between Talon and Nina—Talon had indicated there'd been no long-term attachments. So was it more of a one-sided torch that Nina carried for her, and Nina's heart had been impacted? She certainly acted like she'd been burned.

"Talon's untouchable, or a one-and-done." Nina made her declaration and then focused back on her plate of eggs and fruit.

Well, it didn't appear to have been a romantic relationship. At least not on Talon's part. Makayla concluded that it must have been just that, a one-and-done, which was obviously not what Nina had wanted.

"So, I guess your rejection of us guys is more than just the fact that you're here temporarily and busy with your commander duties." While Derrick added his disgruntled assessment, Joe watched the exchange.

"Hey, guys, cut Makayla a break," Ivy said. "It's her business."

Makayla offered Ivy a smile. She felt a bit nervous, but it was time to make the fact that she was a lesbian clear to this group. "Thanks, Ivy. The truth is that besides the fact that I'm here on commander business, I also like women."

"Well, how convenient for Talon." Nina's sarcastic tone certainly indicated she wasn't pleased.

"Shush." Ivy kicked her under the table.

"It doesn't mean we can't be friends." Makayla ignored the interplay between Ivy and Nina and spoke to the entire group. "I'd like to get to know you all better."

They nodded, spent a few minutes eating in silence, and then the conversation turned to the barn fire and the worry about the safety of the entire compound.

"Do they have any idea who did it?" Derrick leaned back and waited for her answer.

"Not as far as I know," Makayla said. "I'm just glad my birds are all right."

"So am I," Ivy replied. "I hope the culprit's caught."

Everyone had finished their breakfast, so they cleared their table. As Makayla and Nina headed out together from the mess hall, Calvin came up to them and asked Nina about some furniture in her classroom, but the entire time that he was talking to Nina, Calvin was glancing at Makayla.

"Watch out for Calvin." Nina warned Makayla again about her boss as they moved past him and across the compound toward the residence halls. "He thinks he's a lady-killer, no matter your orientation, and he doesn't like taking no for an answer. I suspect he sees you as fresh meat."

"You work with him. Does he try to cross the line with you?" Makayla asked.

"Not anymore. Calvin's got an ego, but Talon intervened when I asked her to—she told him I wasn't interested in him, and he'd better get lost if he knew what was good for him." Nina's mouth quirked up at the memory. "He was pissed, but since then, he hasn't bothered me in the same way he had before."

"Good to know." Makayla considered that she was already wary of Calvin, but Nina's disclosure put her on even higher alert.

Makayla wished her a good day and headed back to her room to spend several hours buried in the book Nina had loaned her, in the company of Betty.

By midafternoon, she and Betty were restless, so Makayla grabbed the cat and headed out to get some exercise and fresh air. She stopped by the barn, but because the ravens were out somewhere else, she decided to head to the gardens on the perimeter of the compound. As she passed the woodshop, she ran into Derrick. He was just leaving from a project he'd been working on there.

"Hey, Derrick. Looks like you've been productive today." Makayla smiled at him.

Derrick looked at her, then Betty. "I've just moved some boards over from the warehouse where we store them—so we'll have them for use tomorrow. What are you doing out here?" He still seemed a little miffed after finding out that she wasn't a dating prospect.

"Betty and I are just out for a little fresh air. I thought we'd walk to the garden area." Makayla nodded out toward where the garden space was.

"You walk a lot?" Derrick asked.

"When I get a chance." As Makayla answered him, the not-so-unkindness flew in and circled. "Maybe I should see what they've been up to. Good to see you."

"Yeah, see you around." Derrick raised his hand as he turned and headed back toward the residence hall area.

The birds didn't seem to want to lead Makayla anywhere, so she led the way to the gardens with Betty and the flying threesome followed. After a tour of the plants, they wandered back toward the barn where the ravens left the excursion and entered the building for some rest. Makayla and Betty headed to her room. The next few days would undoubtedly be busy with the coming NATO meetings, and she wanted to be prepared.

CHAPTER TWELVE

As evening approached, Makayla went back to the mess hall and collected two plates of food. Her guess was that Talon hadn't taken time to eat a decent meal since yesterday. In the mess hall, she heard that the contingent from the Sylvan and Eden enclaves had recently arrived and been fed before being shown to their quarters, so it looked like tomorrow's Monday meeting would happen as planned.

Makayla took the two plates she'd dished up and headed to Talon's office in the leadership building. She couldn't imagine that Talon had remained in her living quarters after the other two enclave groups had arrived. As she reached the door to the building, Brock and Willow were just exiting.

"Hi, Mak. Are you looking for Talon?" Brock always seemed happy to see her.

"Yup. I've got some dinner for her. I suspect she hasn't eaten." Makayla tilted her head toward the two plates she carried.

"We're just on our way over to my place for dinner." Willow offered Makayla a smile. "I've been hoping to have you to dinner while you're here. We need to make a plan."

Makayla liked Willow. Ivy was lucky to have such a kind, warm mother. "I'd enjoy that." Then Makayla looked down at her full hands. "I brought dinner for Talon."

Willow nodded. "I don't think she eats on a regular basis. I'm glad someone is looking out for her."

Brock held the door for Makayla so she could enter without trying to juggle the two plates of dinner. "Good for you. She's in her office. That woman needs a keeper."

Makayla smiled. "*Keeper*. I suspect you mean a caretaker. But I'm thinking more along the lines of someone she doesn't want to dump—wants to keep."

Brock nodded at her forthrightness. "You're what she needs, trespasser. Don't let her run you off."

"Thanks, Brock. I'm pretty tenacious. There are times when it would be really nice if Talon was a pushover." Makayla considered that she probably wouldn't be nearly as attracted to a person who was a pushover, and Talon certainly wouldn't be Talon if she was one.

Brock laughed at the presence of "Talon" and "pushover" in the same sentence. "You've got my vote, kid. Go slay the dragon."

It was Makayla's turn to laugh. "That's the plan. Me—the dragon slayer."

Willow joined in the laugher. "Good night, Mak," Willow and Brock spoke in unison as they headed out.

Talon's office door was ajar, and Makayla kicked it with her foot because she didn't have a free hand to knock. It swung open, and Talon glanced up from her desk. Her hair was damp, and she looked like she'd had a bit of rest. Makayla hoped she wasn't in Commander de LaTerre mode. She'd loved the closeness she'd felt in their last few encounters, but Talon could pull back into herself at any time. She always seemed to do so just when Makayla was enjoying their connection.

"So, what did you bring me?" Talon asked. Talon's delivery was serious. Not a hint of flirtation.

"Some of your men were over at the ocean today and harvested a bunch of oysters. The mess hall was serving them for dinner tonight. Some veggies too."

"I haven't had oysters in forever. And James, the commander from Sylvan, got his hands on some chocolate and brought it as a gift. It's delicious." Talon pointed to a wooden bowl of chocolate chunks that were sitting on top of the lace-edged doily on the desk. She pulled the dinner plate closer.

Makayla raised her eyebrows. "Oysters. Chocolate. You know those are aphrodisiacs?" Makayla loved poking Talon a bit. She was just too serious sometimes. Makayla could leave Talon in control—Talon needed that, but she sensed that Talon also needed more. She'd shown that she wasn't immune to the banter, however much she tried to indicate that she was.

"Damn, Mak. You're a cheeky little flirt. You're going to be the death of me."

"That's the plan. Death by oysters and chocolate followed by..." Makayla couldn't keep the husk out of her voice as she gave Talon a very suggestive look, openly flirting. "But what a way to go."

"None of that tonight." Talon was obviously struggling to give her an admonishing look.

Makayla grinned. "Not tonight, huh? That means there's hope for another night."

Talon shook her head as she took a bite of an oyster. Makayla watched her as she lifted the morsel on her fork up to her mouth, passed it between those luscious lips, and then slowly chewed and swallowed.

Makayla suspected that Talon enjoyed the fact that she was one of the few people who didn't knock herself out to show reverence for Talon's status in this enclave, not that she didn't respect her leadership skills.

"I'm not asking for just one day at a time anymore," Makayla said.

Talon nodded. "Good. I'm getting through to you." She lifted another bite to her mouth.

Makayla held up her hand to stop Talon. "I'm changing my mantra. Just one *night* at a time." Makayla drew out the word *night* and looked Talon up and down as she said it.

Talon stopped chewing and gave her a warning look. Swallowed. When it seemed that she'd reproached Makayla enough with her gaze, she motioned for Makayla to sit down. "Let's talk about our meeting tomorrow for a bit."

"You're no fun." Makayla didn't want to change the subject.

"We've got commitments, Mak. A lot of people are depending on us." Talon took another bite.

"I know. And I take it seriously. We're ready for tomorrow—we've spent three weeks getting ready. I just function better when there's balance in my life."

This wasn't about lust. This was about that growing presence in her chest—that updraft of attachment that resided in her heart. It wasn't about the act of two individual people having sex simply for personal pleasure. It was about sex as another way for two people who cared for each other to communicate through shared pleasure—as its own language. She'd witnessed a Talon the Tenderhearted who'd been obscured by the Talon the Terrible lore. If only she could get Talon the Tenderhearted to converse with her in that language.

"Balance, huh? Because it seems maybe a dark and stormy night woke up the beast in you." Talon bit her lower lip in an obvious attempt to prevent a display of her amusement. Then she turned her attention back to what remained of her dinner before she pushed her plate to the side when she was finished. Makayla had only eaten a few bites of her food.

Makayla didn't want to joke about that night in the woods. "I remember that night. And I certainly wouldn't use the term *beast* for you. Your need was real, but you were so perfect. It's a night I'll never forget."

Talon frowned at Makayla, a mix of irritation and angst etched across her face. "Don't minimize my reputation, Mak. I keep telling you, I don't do romantic relationships. And ribbons—don't forget I'm ruthless. The only thing I'm committed to is Raptare. For the enclave—I can be relentless when I need to be. To get what Raptare needs."

Makayla thought maybe Talon was trying to convince herself. She decided to ignore Talon's declarations. "You can be an ass." Talon frowned some more at her, but Makayla held up her hand. "You are relentlessly dedicated to your enclave, not usually a bad thing. But also, relentlessly complex. Relentlessly intriguing. And relentlessly in need of some balance too." Makayla smiled at her. "And not to be left out...relentlessly gorgeous."

Talon sat and looked at Makayla across the desk. Her beautiful azure eyes darkened with feelings that she couldn't bluff her way through. "One night at a time, huh?" As she asked, Talon shook her head in a visual *no* while unconsciously licking her lower lip. Makayla knew Talon was conflicted and crossed her fingers. She needed to wait for Talon to come to her.

Makayla didn't care if it was a day at a time or a night at a time. She just didn't want Talon to walk away or push her away. Talon had feelings for her, and they were more than just physical. If only Talon would acknowledge their emotional connection. Makayla recognized that she needed to let Talon remain in control. She could do that.

Talon stood up. She walked around the desk and pushed Makayla's plate aside. Then she pulled Makayla up from her chair, shoved it out of the way, and lifted her so she sat on the desk before Talon stepped between Makayla's knees and faced her. She looked into Makayla's eyes.

"Not just hazel. Sienna and emerald—at least that's the color the hazel is projecting tonight." Talon stood and studied Makayla's face. "I'm probably only feeding that beast." Her hands grasped Makayla's top curls and held her steady as she leaned in and gently kissed Makayla's eyes closed. "This is about you—getting a little balance. Only so you're on your game tomorrow."

Makayla kissed her back. She tried to pour all her feelings for Talon into that kiss. She tangled her tongue with Talon's, explored the depths of Talon's mouth with a hunger she moderated into a languid seduction, and savored every moment of their encounter. "Got it. I'll be on my game tomorrow. For the enclaves." She pulled Talon close, just happy to be holding her.

Talon hesitated before she finally nodded, as if she'd made a decision. Then she reached between Makayla's thighs and danced her hand along the fabric. She touched her with those gifted hands until Makayla felt a hum, then a moderate roar at her center. Makayla rode that touch—the emotional, physical joining that dismantled the last fragment of control she'd been struggling to maintain. And when Talon added the sensation of alternately strumming and squeezing the peak of Makayla's breast through her shirt, it was all that Makayla needed for that roar to ascend to the heavens, to the summit of pleasure—it was the fulfillment her body had been craving for six long months—bestowed by Talon, the only woman in the world she wanted it from.

"Well, if I'd known you were going to be that easy, I'd have made it the appetizer instead of the dessert." The tease was evident in Talon's delivery.

Makayla thought it was time for her to lighten the tone too. She didn't want to scare Talon away by talking any more about how she cared for Talon. "Hey, I thought there was chocolate for dessert." Makayla pretended to look petulant.

Talon shook her head as she chuckled. "Never satisfied."

"Oh, I'm satisfied," Makayla replied. "Couldn't be more satisfied." She grinned. "But your turn."

"I'm having chocolate for dessert," Talon told her as she reached for the bowl of chocolate chunks still on the desk. "I really do have some things to talk to you about before tomorrow, Mak." Makayla frowned, not happy to be unable to reciprocate the pleasure that Talon had offered her. "Don't worry. You owe me, fledgling." Talon pointed her finger at Makayla. "And I *always* collect." Talon ate a piece of the imported chocolate, obviously not just to prove her point because she closed her eyes and emitted a soft moan as she indulged in the rare treat.

"Okay. Here's to the next *one night at a time*." Makayla gave Talon a prolonged kiss and savored the sweet sample of chocolate mixed with the taste of Talon. "But I hate owing you."

"Owing me. Just where I want you." Talon returned the kiss, slow and deep, until she determined they were done and gently pulled away, but with reluctance shadowing her expression.

And when the kissing was finished, while Talon still held her, they discussed the two enclaves they'd meet with tomorrow. Eden enclave was a religion-based enclave headed by a preacher named Elijah, and they agreed not to create issues unless it was in the best interest of their own enclaves—that definitely included not disclosing their lesbian status.

Talon then told Makayla that Sylvan, led by James, was an enclave formed by a group of families and friends similar to Raptare and Aurora. They reviewed their notes before they decided that Makayla would drop Betty off at Talon's office at about half past seven in the morning and then fetch breakfast for both of them before they were due in the conference room at nine o'clock. Brock and Willow would see that their guests had plenty to eat and drink before their meeting. And with that, Talon pulled Makayla off her desk, walked her to her residence hall, and hugged her.

"Good night." Talon swept Makayla's cheek with her knuckles.

"Good night, Talon the Tantalizing. I'm going to dream of you." Makayla kissed those knuckles before Talon turned to walk away. "And they'll be sweet, sweet dreams," Makayla promised her in a breathless whisper just loud enough for Talon.

The last sound Makayla heard before she entered the building to go to her room and the waiting Betty was rich, soft laughter as Talon headed out into the night. And that was balance, Makayla concluded.

❖

The next morning, Makayla deposited Betty in Talon's office. She was a bit disappointed that Talon wasn't there, but she suspected Talon was making preparations for the day. As planned, she went and collected breakfast for the two of them at the mess hall. She waved at Ash and Ivy, told Joe good morning as he stood refilling the buffet, then proceeded to collect the food. She ran into Willow as she finished filling the plates. Willow informed her that the visiting enclave leaders were in the conference room and Brock and Talon were making sure the breakfast set up for them was satisfactory. Willow suggested that once she'd finished her own breakfast, she could bring two mugs of tea over. Makayla agreed as she turned and headed back toward the leadership building with the breakfast fare.

"Good morning, Commander." Makayla greeted Talon with a smile when she found Talon in her office. She set the two plates on the desk and thought about what had happened on that surface last night. Her smile grew with the memory.

Talon noticed where she was looking and surmised what Makayla was thinking. "Don't make me sorry about how we finished our planning session." Talon was not as stoic as she wanted to appear with the impassive mask she tried to present—there was no hiding the twinkle in her eyes. "Commander Odin, we've got serious work to do. Focus."

Makayla fought for an impassive mask too, but knew she wasn't as successful as Talon. "Oh, the sacrifices of leadership. I think we need to do more *planning*." Makayla let that last word drag out.

"As they say, it's a hard job, but somebody's got to do it." The corners of Talon's lips twitched up.

"The *planning*, or the leadership?"

"The leadership, Mak. Our enclaves need us." Talon's tone became resolute.

Talon was right. It was time to eat and end her flirting before a long day of work began, so she concluded with a final quip. "No wonder they call you Talon the Terrible. I think you enjoy torturing me."

"Probably too much. But from your response, I don't think last night was torture. Now let's eat before we don't have time to."

The cat was settled on his chair and watched Makayla while she quickly ate her breakfast. "I brought some extra eggs, you old tomcat." She set her plate on the floor, and the feline leapt down and charged over to eat. "Betty was a good guest."

Talon finished her last bite and nodded. "Thanks, Mak."

Just then, Willow arrived with the two mugs of tea. "Brock is taking a tray of tea to the conference room for the two visiting enclave commanders and the seconds-in-command they brought."

Talon shifted her attention to Willow. "Thanks. If it's okay with Commander Odin, I think we'll take our mugs and head down to the conference room to join the others."

❖

As the Raptare and Aurora commanders entered the conference room, the contingents from Sylvan and Eden looked over at them from the table where they sat. They'd just finished their breakfasts and had been drinking tea while they waited for Talon and Makayla. The visiting commanders had met with Talon for a moment the day before, but Makayla introduced herself as the co-commander of Aurora and welcomed them. They offered their condolences for the family losses Makayla had suffered, and then the meeting moved to focus on the other enclave contingents.

The commander from Sylvan introduced his second-in-command. Then Eden's commander told them that he preferred to be referred to as the Prophet instead of as a commander and that he had brought his disciple, rather than a second-in-command. Talon showed no sign of being thrown off her game and asked if everyone was ready to begin discussions. The entire group affirmed that they were, and so Talon nodded to Makayla.

Makayla took charge and explained how the MidLand invasion had led Raptare and Aurora to negotiate a more formal agreement directed at working together toward a shared defense strategy. It would encompass a specific agreement that resulted in a cooperative call to arms if the situation warranted that action. She related how discussion between the two enclaves had led to the idea of reaching an alliance among all six neighboring enclaves.

When she explained the NATO title inspired by the 1949 alliance, the visitors chuckled their appreciation. Makayla didn't look at Talon when she made this reference to history. There was no point in poking the dragon during these meetings. The two visiting enclave contingents had come because they had been made aware of the topic. They'd all suffered from the MidLanders' attack, and the deployment of their populations to the MidLanders' fight.

It was afternoon by the time Talon and Makayla had completed their strategy of introducing the mission and goals their two enclaves had started with. They explained that the plan was to initially introduce these preliminaries, and then share the Raptare and Aurora specifics. There would be a total of six enclaves in this alliance to begin with, and these first meetings would each include two enclaves.

They moved on to the defense agreement that had already been negotiated between Raptare and Aurora and explained that the representatives could return home with those specifics to share and discuss possible adjustments with their own councils. They would meet again with all six enclave commanders present and work out a final alliance on a date they'd agreed to in a few weeks' time.

Makayla also explained that Raptare and Aurora had negotiated an additional trade agreement aside from their initial defense agreement, and some of the other enclaves might wish to do the same, depending on the focus of goods each enclave produced and needed. All this was received with enthusiasm. By the end of a long day of discussion and a shared dinner, everyone was ready to turn in.

The Sylvan and Eden groups would return to their homes in the morning with the information for their councils to consider. The commander from Eden offered them all a long final prayer that revealed a great deal about the religious tenets of his enclave, a prayer that included a focus on the sins of others, and Makayla realized how different some of the enclaves were. She was grateful for the work both her grandfather and Talon had done to make their own enclaves inclusive.

At the end of the day, Talon wished Makayla good night in full Commander de LaTerre persona after they'd already seen everyone else off to their quarters. She told Commander Odin to get some sleep before she turned to leave the conference room and collect Betty from her office. Makayla missed the banter but knew that when Talon was in leadership mode, even when it was just the two of them, there was no dissuading her. She hoped that Talon didn't regret their last personal encounter because she certainly had no regrets. It had been intimacy, connection, and hopefully, a step on the path to discovering what a balanced life meant. And that seemed to be what bothered Talon.

CHAPTER THIRTEEN

The next morning was Tuesday, and after learning from Willow that the Sylvan and Eden guests had departed at the crack of dawn, Makayla headed to collect breakfast for herself and Talon. She arrived at the office with scrambled eggs for breakfast and several apples for later day snacking. Talon wasn't there, but the lights were on and Betty was asleep in his chair. She deposited the food on the desk and turned to leave when Brock showed up in the doorway of Talon's office.

"Hey, trespasser. I was just coming to look for you," Brock said.

"I'm looking for Talon."

"She's over at the woodshop. She said to tell you to check on your birds at the barn and then come join her there."

"I've brought two plates of breakfast to her office because I assumed we'd debrief after yesterday. I guess I'll grab the apples I brought and take them with me, and maybe give Betty some scrambled eggs. But he can't eat all of these."

"Take the rest to the barn cats. They'll love you forever." Brock smiled.

As Brock turned to leave, Makayla offered her thanks and gave him a wave. Then she offered Betty some eggs after she'd transferred a large portion into a bowl to take to the barn. If she was going to the woodshop, Makayla decided she wanted her backpack, so she returned to her room to grab it. She hauled the bowl of eggs along, dumped the apples into the pack, and ducked back into the mess hall to collect a handful of jerky because Talon most likely hadn't stopped to eat.

After all the errand running, Makayla finally headed to the barn to leave the rest of the now cold eggs for the hungry barn cats and collect her ravens. The not-so-unkindness welcomed her with their usual enthusiastic croaks. They flew down from the barn rafters to join her as she whistled for them, and Ed even offered the hoarse "hi" that he'd mastered for greeting Makayla. She welcomed their company on her walk out to the woodshop.

The birds left to find a convenient spot to perch when Makayla entered the building to find Talon, who was talking to the enclave's senior craftsman in charge of the woodshop.

"Come on over, Commander Odin." Talon gestured for her to join them when she realized that Makayla was at the woodshop entrance. Talon was still in formal leader mode; there was no hint of anything but the compelling commander demeanor, which didn't invite banter from Makayla.

"I want to introduce you to Vince, who runs the woodshop. He's Ivy's father."

Vince seemed to want to clarify, so Makayla listened. "Willow was my girlfriend years ago. We had Ivy but aren't together anymore."

He was a dark-complexioned man who was about sixty years old and couldn't have been more welcoming as he grinned at her. His rich brown skin explained the beautiful light brown tone of Ivy's complexion. After she'd returned his friendly grin and shaken his hand, Makayla shifted her attention back to Talon.

"We have a few days' break until we speak to the last two enclave leaders on Friday, so I thought we could make some of that time beneficial to your education as co-commander of Aurora," Talon said.

Makayla realized that Talon wanted to reestablish the walls she loved to build whenever she felt threatened that they were coming down—that the personal connection between herself and Makayla was growing. Any acknowledgment of a relationship beyond a strictly professional one wasn't the mood Talon was in. At least not a mood she was willing to display to Makayla today. Makayla sighed as she worked to pay attention and respect Talon's feelings.

"Because our two enclaves trade so many goods, I thought you should have a tour of our woodshop. Especially since Raptare trades our furniture for the products from your enclave's reclamation shop, and our two enclaves have now formalized those trades in our recent talks. There also may be expansion to broader trade agreements with the other enclaves if our initial defense talks are fruitful." Talon finished her speech.

"If you two commanders would follow me, I'll give you the grand tour." Vince proceeded to show Makayla the workspace while Talon trailed behind. It was obvious he was proud of the goods the shop produced. Makayla realized that while the shop had different equipment and different products, it wasn't that different in concept from the reclamation shop at Aurora. She toured the work areas with several pieces of furniture in various stages of fabrication.

There were many tools visible: hand planes, saws, hammers, chisels. Two scavenged table saws that were powered by salvaged solar panels stood to one side. A few woodworkers were present and Makayla waved at Derrick when she recognized him. He nodded and watched them complete the tour. One area of the large shop contained finished pieces, and Makayla complimented the beautiful work. Talon stood back and let her appreciate the facility. After they'd finished and expressed their gratitude for the tour, they left the building.

"So, what did you think?"

"Very impressive." Makayla knew Talon well enough to discern that she was proud of the shop, even if she tried to hide that pride.

"It offers us something to trade with the other enclaves, and for goods to bring to Gull Town, as well. It's how we get many of the little pleasures in life we don't produce here." Talon couldn't completely suppress the satisfaction that infiltrated her tone.

Little pleasures in life made Makayla smile. And of course, Talon knew what she was thinking and gave her a disapproving look. "Come walk with me. We can go check out the garden. There's a wooden bench there."

As they silently made the short walk to the garden bench, the three ravens joined them. Ed and Al settled on the ground a short distance away, but Poe landed and walked right up to Talon's boot and dropped a wild daisy on it.

"Looks like you've got an admirer." Makayla smiled at Talon. "As if I need competition," she added with a manufactured groan.

The comment touched Talon's eyes. Made them dance for a moment, but then she gathered herself and inhaled deeply. "I need to talk to you, Commander Odin."

Talon's tone was formal, obviously intended to keep her distance from Makayla and maintain the invisible barriers designed to negate or diminish any emotional bond between them. Makayla wondered what Talon wanted to tell her. She suspected that Talon was again having regrets after the recent intimate encounter in Talon's office the other night. That emotional connection she'd felt, and she was certain Talon had felt it too. Makayla had certainly perceived an element of romance, and she knew that romance scared the hell out of Talon for some reason.

She didn't think she was ready for whatever declaration Talon was going to make this morning. Talon's somber mood didn't give her confidence that this was going to be a conversation she wanted to have. Makayla took a deep breath before she nodded, set down her backpack, and reached inside.

"Did you have breakfast this morning?"

"You're such a mother hen." Talon's stiff posture softened as Makayla handed her an apple and two sticks of jerky. All three birds moved to Talon's feet and waited expectantly. They knew she was a pushover when it came to sharing with them.

"Mother hen? I thought I was a songbird. And how do you know I didn't bring that food for my not-so-unkindness?" Makayla nodded at the waiting ravens. "Maybe I'm just trying to improve your standing with them—letting you disperse the goods. Just me doing my best to improve that Talon the Terrible image."

Talon leaned forward and offered each bird a small piece of the meat, then leaned back and began to eat the breakfast Makayla had brought her.

"Mother hen—you bringing nourishment for the three malevolent musketeers. That's what I meant." Talon obviously didn't want what she'd said to be taken as feelings of attraction between the two of them.

"Of course it was," Makayla noted as she fought to contain an eye roll. Talon was covered in so many layers of self-protection. Would she ever be able to allow that soft center to embrace Makayla fully?

Makayla had seen Talon's heart. A good heart, but wounded and shielded by years of assembling that armor. Like chainmail, a piece-by-piece mesh so carefully constructed that only those closest to her had even glimpsed what it protected.

She was a woman who would be worth loving, or so Makayla's own heart had decided—that autonomous organ refused advice from her brain. Her brain was beginning to doubt that she'd ever be able to dismantle enough of that protective barrier and become a part of the beat of Talon's heart—the way Talon had embedded as the upbeat of hers.

"I certainly didn't mean taking care of me. I don't need taking care of," Talon huffed.

"It's undoubtedly one of the great mysteries of the universe, but I want to take care of you." Makayla couldn't help but be the transparent individual she usually was. "I care for you," she whispered.

Talon focused on the ravens. She bit off and shared chunks of her apple before she cleared her throat and spoke again. "First, before I get down to the topic I need to discuss, I want to let you know that Brock sent a couple of the patrol men up to Aurora early this morning to ask them about this Bull Puckett you mentioned. To check on his whereabouts. They should be back by tonight or tomorrow." Talon gave Makayla a moment to assimilate that information, then shifted topics. "Now, let's address what I wanted to talk to you about."

Makayla nodded her understanding. Then she waited as Talon watched her. Talon appeared to be gathering her thoughts, and Makayla looked at the birds, then back at Talon.

"So, is this a Talon-to-Mak talk, or is this a Commander de LaTerre-to-Commander Odin talk?" Makayla asked.

Talon's bright sapphire eyes shifted to indigo as she contemplated Makayla. There was no misinterpreting the desire there.

"Commander-to-commander. I'm trying to help you, Commander Odin. You'll be going back to Aurora. To lead. And the more you know and understand, the better leader you'll be. That's why I wanted you to see our woodshop—because of the trade agreements between our two enclaves."

Those words nettled Makayla, wedged under her skin like thorns. She knew that her return to Aurora and commanding the enclave had always been everyone's plan for her, but she needed to sort out the uncertainty that she was feeling. What did she want for her future?

Makayla was aware that she enjoyed some form of a leadership role, but she was becoming convinced that she didn't want to go back to Aurora. There was no longer any family there. Aurora felt more and more like her past. And she didn't think her leadership strengths were in the broad array of issues that impacted an enclave—as a commander. She liked focus. What irritated Makayla was that it hadn't just been her family, even Talon had expectations for her. Now Talon was presuming her future.

"I've mentioned Gull Town before," Talon said. "Maybe you even went there when you were younger."

"I know it's a major commerce town for WestLand enclaves, but I haven't been there. I think Lilly, Aurora's director of inventory, acquisitions, and finance, worked with the reclamation center for most of that trading. I know Aurora trades for small items, and also for the larger ones that other enclaves produce and Aurora doesn't. My grandfather and father went on occasion. And maybe some individuals did some private bargaining there too."

Makayla didn't bring it up, but she'd heard rumors of an unofficial industry that catered to a sex-and-alcohol-seeking clientele, an industry that operated on a more personal exchange level in Gull Town. She suspected that individuals went there for mutual voluntary liaisons. An image of Talon finding women there for her one-night stands flashed through Makayla's mind. Fuck.

"It's a hub for trading. Where we can get some items that we can't get here," Talon said. "Like coffee."

"And chocolate." The memory of the taste of chocolate on Talon's tongue flooded Makayla's thoughts. There was no forgetting that connection to her on an evening when they hadn't just been fellow commanders—when they'd been Mak and Talon.

"And chocolate." Talon obviously wasn't immune to the memory either—she licked her lower lip before she took control of her reaction. "Gull Town. A place with a trading post where items are brought, credited, and exchanged. Run by a man named Ferril, and other people who live and work there in the commerce business. We bring furniture down to Ferril and he credits us. We get credits to use for acquisitions that we want, and he trades off our furniture. We do our own trading with local enclaves, but it's a trade hub for the entire Pacific Coast and some inland regions, and even down into areas in Central and South America. People arrive by land and by water. Gull Town is a port town with a harbor." Talon glanced at Makayla, clearly offering her an opportunity for any questions she might have.

"So, are you thinking of talking to this Ferril fellow in terms of joining our NATO alliance?"

Talon's eyes widened. "Sometimes you amaze me." She shook her head. "I hadn't thought of that. You were born for these negotiations. Of course we have a significant interest in keeping Gull Town intact and safe for ongoing trading. And Gull Town has a small community that could join in any defense strategies our alliance group finds necessary. Great idea, Mak."

Makayla smiled at Talon's praise. She felt even more elated when she registered that Talon had just called her "Mak." Not "Commander Odin."

"Wipe that grin off your face." Talon's tone was gentle, but she frowned. "I'm working to keep this on a commander-to-commander level. It's in your best interest, Commander Odin."

Makayla was losing patience. "Why is everyone but me deciding what's in my best interest?" she seethed. "And besides, I think that you think it's in your best interest for everything to be commander-to-commander. But maybe it's not. Can we talk about you?"

Poe moved over to stand at Makayla's feet as he recognized her agitation. Ed and Al had flown up and settled in to watch from a nearby tree branch. Then Poe walked back over and pecked on Talon's boot. He ignored the daisy that now lay on the ground. Talon reached down and picked up the flower as Poe looked up at her. He scolded her, then vocalized a corvid chuckle before strutting off.

Talon's eyes followed the bird, and she didn't look at Makayla as she responded. "We're not talking about me. We're talking about you." Talon's voice was full-bodied and low. As always, Makayla found it enticing and provocative. But it was also insistent and carried a hint of vulnerability. "I'm making a trip with Ivy and Ash down to Gull Town to deliver some furniture for credits. It's a six or seven hour journey each way with a wagonload of tables and chairs. I thought you might like to come and see the place, to enhance your commander experience."

"Overnight trip?" As she considered both of their current stances, Makayla tried to remain stoic about another night with Talon. It would probably be torture. Then she decided that any time with Talon was better than time without her. And she didn't actually know what would transpire.

Talon nodded. "*Separate* rooms, Mak. There are rooms that I exchange credits for when I go. Ash has a relative in Gull Town, and he and Ivy plan to stay in his quarters."

Makayla digested what Talon had just told her. Talon did not want to spend the night with her.

"We can make the trip down, stay the night, and come back the next day. You can certainly stay here if you don't want to come. I just thought if you hadn't been to Gull Town, it would expand your horizons."

Clearly, Talon wanted to keep this on a purely professional level. Makayla was trying to figure out the mixed signals she was positive she was receiving from Talon. To understand why their close connection always morphed into distance. To sort out the emotional from the physical. But nothing was straightforward. Makayla's head told her that she wanted nothing to do with a relationship based on unrequited feelings. It was wearing her out. But her rebellious beating heart wasn't listening.

Makayla inhaled deeply, an effort to force herself back into her professional role. She could at least succeed at that. "Can we meet with Ferril and explain our NATO plan? See if he's interested?" Makayla studied Talon. "It seems that at least broaching the topic while we're there would be a step toward assuring Gull Town is protected, and that's advantageous for both our enclaves."

"It would be, Commander Odin." Talon seemed pleased. "I know Ferril, and I suspect he'll meet with us." Talon considered their schedule further. "Today is Tuesday. Tomorrow, we need to go over the details of the last two enclaves. Their contingencies will arrive late on Thursday, and then we'll spend the day with them on Friday. So, I'm thinking of heading to Gull Town next week on Monday to avoid the weekend crowds there."

Makayla nodded. She was still hoping to at least be *Mak* for part of the trip with Talon. She would also be acting in her role as Aurora's co-commander in Gull Town, in talking to Ferril about the alliance. Now, if she could only come to terms with the personal versus this professional aspect of her life—and with Talon's stance on it all.

CHAPTER FOURTEEN

The next day Makayla met with Talon in her office during the limited time Talon had to spare, and they prepared for the Friday meeting with the leaders of the last two enclaves. Those enclaves were similar to Raptare and Aurora, composed mostly of families and friends with similar beliefs. One enclave was called Woodland and the other enclave was called Brighton. Their presentation shouldn't be significantly different from the one they'd had with the leaders of the Sylvan and Eden enclaves.

After they'd finished discussing the planned meeting, Talon changed the subject.

"I wanted to update you on Aurora. The patrol returned last evening. Quinn and Rosa send their greetings to you and want you to know that everything is fine there. The news on Bull Puckett is that they haven't seen him lately. He disappeared not long after you came here, so there's no telling if he's involved in the vandalism or not."

Makayla regretted there wasn't a definitive answer. She understood how upsetting the tree cutting and barn fire were for Talon. "I'm sorry they made the trip and didn't get an answer."

"Well, we'll keep him on the suspect list. It sounds like he's a renegade with self-importance issues from what you and Aurora's leadership have both indicated. Thanks for trying to help." Talon stood. "I have a meeting with Brock and Willow—making sure everything is in order here before the trip to Gull Town. I think we're ready for the Friday meeting, so why don't you take tomorrow off. The two contingencies won't be here until late." In typical Talon style, that last wasn't a question.

Makayla took it as the directive it was intended to be, and because she knew how much Talon had to do, she agreed. She wanted to review and organize her notes so she had everything at her fingertips on Friday, spend a little time outdoors with the birds, take Betty for a walk, and maybe read one of the other books she'd borrowed from Nina's library.

She'd finished the book she'd initially borrowed from Nina and decided that Talon certainly had some of the characteristics of the powerful main character, but those were necessary for a woman to be successful in many leadership roles, and both women were leaders. However, Talon had displayed a softer side than the fictional leader displayed, at least in her estimate. She didn't know all the dynamics of the tyrannical character's pain, although there was childhood poverty and divorce. And she didn't know all the dynamics of Talon's issues either. In fact, Talon was pretty much a closed book when it came to her history. All she'd revealed was that she had no grandfather, and there had been someone in her life who'd loved birds.

❖

On Friday, the introductions had been mostly a formality because Talon was very familiar with both the Woodland and Brighton leaders, who had expressed excitement at the proposal that Makayla had presented. Both of their enclaves had suffered losses at the hands of the MidLanders, and they thought their enclaves would benefit from the proposal and agreed to take the idea back to their consultation councils for further discussion. They also agreed to attend the meeting of all six enclave leaders scheduled in a few weeks to see if they could finalize a group alliance.

Because Talon needed to catch up with Brock regarding enclave issues, Makayla walked the Woodland and Brighton enclave leaders to the mess hall for breakfast before they left on Saturday morning.

After they'd all dished up, it was obvious the two visiting leaders wanted a chance to carry on a discussion between themselves, so Makayla left them to it and went to join Nina and Ivy, who were sitting at a table across the dining area.

Nina nodded at Makayla as she approached and Ivy said, "Haven't seen much of you in the last few days, Mak." Ivy greeted her with a wide grin. "Been busy being a commander?"

"I have," Makayla replied. "Most of this week."

"That's good." Ivy turned, frowning at Nina. "Right?" she asked.

"Uh. Yes. Sorry, I was just distracted," Nina said.

Ivy offered her a smile. Makayla thought that Ivy must have noticed that there were some feelings that Nina held for Talon, even if they weren't reciprocated. Makayla didn't want to hurt Nina any more than she seemed to be hurting after she'd found out Talon had wanted that last dance with Makayla.

"Hey, changing the subject…" Ivy glanced between Makayla and Nina, then shifted the conversation. "I hear we're both going to Gull Town on Monday. Delivering furniture for credits."

"We are." Makayla nodded. She didn't want to get into a list in front of Nina of who planned to go, but Ivy seemed to have no such qualms.

"Ash and I will drive the wagon with the furniture, and you and Talon will ride horses."

Nina sat up straighter when she heard Talon and Makayla were both going.

"You and Ash are staying with a cousin of Ash's, I hear. Talon and I each have separate rooms reserved." Makayla hated admitting that she wouldn't share a room with Talon, but she thought Nina might appreciate knowing the room setup. "We're hoping to meet with Ferril, who runs the trading post. He seems to be the one we'll discuss our NATO proposal with. Getting his agreement to join and defend Gull Town seems like a good idea for all of us."

Ivy agreed, and as they finished up their breakfasts and stood up, Joe came over and greeted them. They chatted for a bit longer. Joe was interested in their plans and wished them a good trip before he headed back to work. Then Ivy told Makayla she'd see her on Monday, took Nina's arm, and led her out of the mess hall.

Makayla headed to the barn to check on her threesome, and once she saw that they were just getting ready to head out to the orchards, she took the breakfast food she'd collected for Talon and Betty and headed to Talon's office. She fed the welcoming Betty some omelet and left the rest for Talon, who was again nowhere to be found. Makayla wondered if the timing of her absence was on purpose.

Talon remained in full commander mode when Makayla dropped by her office late on Saturday afternoon. The breakfast plate was absent, and Talon sat behind her desk studying a leatherbound notebook when Makayla knocked. With her head still tilted down as she perused the notes, Talon cleared her throat and commanded, "Enter."

Makayla was fairly certain that Talon wouldn't have invited an unknown person to enter, so she must have ascertained that it was Makayla. Makayla was tired of the unrelenting professional formalities.

Bloody hell, why was she supposed to be what everyone else dictated she was supposed to be? She wanted to be herself—at least part of the time. Professional when she needed to be, but open, and even teasing when circumstances allowed. And she needed to flirt because she knew that her flirting was part of her connection to Talon, whether Talon would admit it or not.

"How did you know it wasn't some marauding soldier at your door?" Makayla entered and leaned against the doorframe. "Or a sex-crazed maniac?"

"Oh, I knew it was a sex-crazed maniac, Commander Odin," Talon deadpanned, keeping her head down, but looking up at Makayla through hooded lids. As stoic as she managed to maintain her tone, she didn't manage to suppress the slight upward quirk of her mouth.

"Hey, I prefer to be recognized as a well-adjusted fan of life balance," Makayla said.

"Is that so?" Talon looked up and her gaze locked on Makayla's. She offered a full display of the amusement she was trying to suppress. "How can I help you, Commander Odin?"

Makayla suggestively wiggled her eyebrows. "Are you really asking me that? Because I'm happy to tell you how you can *help* me."

"Of course not. You must have misheard me." Talon's eyes crinkled at the edges as she tried to suppress her obvious enjoyment of their banter.

"Well, rats." Makayla let herself put on an air of sulking before getting serious. "I'm here to make sure I'm ready for the trip to Gull Town. To find out what time we're leaving and whether there's anything special I need to know. Also, to see if Betty would like to take a walk to the barn."

Talon sat back in her chair and relaxed. "If you're packed for an overnight trip, I suspect you're ready for Gull Town." Makayla was anxious to see the trade center town on the Pacific Coast of WestLand, south of Raptare. "We'll leave after a very early breakfast on Monday. It's about a six-hour ride on horseback down the coast. Maybe a bit slower because Ash will be hauling furniture in the wagon to deliver for credits. With an early start, we can arrive by midafternoon." Talon's brow knitted. "I've been a bit overwhelmed with our meetings and getting ready to leave, so I've neglected Betty. I'm sure he'd love a walk."

Before Makayla could even look at the cat, he'd jumped off his chair and was leading her toward the door.

"Would you be willing to keep him for the night?" Talon asked. "I won't have much time for him before we leave, and he seems to enjoy your room." Talon watched the tomcat as he rubbed against Makayla's legs. "And your company," Talon quietly acknowledged.

"I'm happy to have him," Makayla said. "Who's watching him while we're gone?"

"I've arranged for him to stay at Willow's place. She's watched him before, so he'll be fine there. She'll take good care of him."

Talon the Tenderhearted. Makayla remained silent, but she lifted an eyebrow at Talon while her heart gave the familiar flutter that occurred when she witnessed Talon being soft-hearted toward the animals around her—especially when Talon was caught doing it at the expense of her hard-ass reputation. She could tell it made Talon uncomfortable, but that was half the fun of indicating that she'd noticed.

Talon gave a little embarrassed cough, then sat up straight in a full-on commander pose. "Betty is an invaluable rodent catcher around here, Commander Odin. It's the duty of a commander to look out for the enclave assets. Bring him back late tomorrow afternoon, and I'll have Willow come collect him here, so we'll be all set for an uncomplicated departure early Monday morning."

Makayla smiled at Talon as Betty impatiently persisted in rubbing against her legs. "Do you have an agenda planned for our time there?"

"I assume you mean the agenda that includes delivery of the furniture to Ferril for credits, talking to him a bit about our cooperative defense treaty, and checking into our two rooms. Two rooms," Talon repeated before shuffling a few papers on her desk. "Probably in that order. I might show you a few of the attractions of Gull Town too, for your enlightenment, after we've checked in. Gull Town is an important trade center and information hub for our enclaves. Just to reiterate, this is a commander-oriented trip to accomplish some of my commander duties and educate you in your own leadership role, so you can go back and be the best commander you can be at Aurora."

Makayla let out a loud sigh. The more her future life was pushed on her, the more apprehensive she became. Makayla picked up Betty and nodded at Talon without saying anything else because she didn't know what else to say as Commander Odin. Out of the corner of her eye, as she headed out of the office with Betty, Makayla caught Talon leaning forward and touching the edge of the doily sitting under the chocolates on the desk.

❖

Sunday was a slow day, and Makayla and Betty slept in. Makayla took Betty to the barn with scrambled eggs for the felines. Once she'd confirmed that the birds had already headed out, she and the tomcat headed to the orchards too. Ed, Al, and Poe greeted them with enthusiasm as they reached the apple trees. It was a beautiful day. Makayla enjoyed an hour of sunshine and the chatter and melodies of the local foraging birds before she returned to her room to pack for the trip to Gull Town.

Before she packed, Makayla emptied her backpack. She discovered the ball of cotton string she'd used to fix a crutch for Talon out in the woods so many months ago. It had remained there since she'd cut off a few pieces for Betty to play with. There was also a remaining stick of the jerky she'd taken out to the woodshop for Talon to eat.

She didn't remember placing anything in the two small interior pockets, but decided to make sure they were empty too. She realized she hadn't done that since before her trek home from the battlegrounds because there in the bottom of one of the pockets was the petite, gold, heart-shaped pendant that she'd found in that warehouse where she'd spent the night. The night before she'd found Talon trapped under the tree.

Makayla studied the perfect little heart. Remembered when she'd found it in that box of abandoned trinkets with little utilitarian purpose in today's world. She'd saved it because it had reminded her there had been love in the world at a time when she needed to remember that. She'd hoped there still was—that she would find it for herself. Makayla caressed the heart and then opened the top drawer of the dresser and carefully placed it in the front right corner.

CHAPTER FIFTEEN

Monday morning, after a quick breakfast on the run, Makayla met Talon, Ash, and Ivy by the barn. Brock would remain behind to run the enclave, but he was there to see them off. Betty was staying with Willow.

Two horses were hitched to a wagon filled with a small dining table and four chairs, two dressers, and three end tables, all produced in the woodshop. Two additional horses waited for riders. One was Babe, and Makayla assumed Talon would ride her. Her not-so-unkindness was busy on a nearby fence; all three birds were keeping an eye on the humans and anxious to accompany Makayla, wherever her destination.

"Good morning, Mak, I'm so excited." Ivy gave her a bubbly greeting. "Give me your pack, and I'll put it in the wagon."

Ash waved at Makayla as he finished securing the furniture in the wagon bed with a rope.

Babe was bridled and saddled, and Makayla thought that Talon would ride her because she knew Talon was bonded to the horse, whether she admitted it or not. Talon was finishing preparations on another horse, that same black feisty stallion she'd ridden into Aurora. He was pawing the ground and snorting with energy.

"Ready for this, Commander Odin?" Talon gazed over at Makayla, then turned to check the bridle on the spirited animal. There was no saddle. Makayla gulped. She was a fairly decent horseback rider, but she wasn't sure she could handle this high-strung equine, especially bareback.

Without looking back over, Talon told her, "Don't worry, Commander Odin. You're on Babe for this trip. I'll ride Thunder."

Makayla nodded her appreciation as everyone finished what they were doing and prepared to mount up. Ash and Ivy climbed onto the wagon seat. Talon grabbed the mane and swung herself up onto the prancing, snorting horse before she took the reins and pulled them back to hold him in place.

"You're sure his name is Thunder? Not Pansy, or Lulu, or Gertie? Just thinking of Betty and all. Not that I don't think Thunder is an appropriate name from what I can see." Makayla didn't try to suppress the tease she knew her tone conveyed.

"He's a handful, and certainly likes to try to live up to his name—a challenge. But he does fine once he knows who's in charge."

"You like a challenge," Mak mumbled. "And you love to be in charge."

"That I do." Talon offered no hint of an argument. "Now hop on Babe and let's get this trip underway." And she proved with that stern command that she did love to be in charge.

Brock held Babe's harness while Makayla grabbed the saddle horn and mounted, then he handed Makayla the reins. "You all have a safe trip. We'll plan to see you tomorrow afternoon or evening." With that, the group rode out of the Raptare compound toward Gull Town, and the ravens flew along in accompaniment.

It was late spring and the weather was pleasant. There had been enough rain that the majority of trees looked healthy and the open spaces were blanketed in the colors of wildflowers and green grass. They made good time as they traveled a route that followed the coast—a roadway that Makayla knew had once been asphalt, but was now dirt and only maintained by the passage of travelers who kept the grass and weeds at bay. Where the coast had shifted inland with climate change, the route curved to accommodate that shoreline shift.

After a short stop to eat a packed lunch and rest the horses and ravens, they arrived at Gull Town in the midafternoon. The bird trio took off into the wooded area that was adjacent to the town. They would be much happier staying there than being too close to the strange buildings and people.

The settlement was a hub of activity with the compacted dirt main street extending through the middle of the town. There was a saloon, a handful of structures that served as sleeping quarters with available rooms, and a large storefront that Talon indicated was the trading post where they would leave the furniture for credits and collect supplies.

Additional smaller buildings lined each side of the main street, one a sheriff's office, and Makayla suspected there might be a brothel. All the structures were composed of wood or stone or reclaimed brick, and wooden plank sidewalks ran in front of them down each side of the street. At the far end of town, set back a distance from the other buildings, Makayla could make out a large barn and attached corrals.

It was a Monday, so the commerce center was probably not as busy as it was on weekends when local enclave visitors came to satisfy their cravings, but there were still several people wandering about. Off in the distance to the east, Makayla could see a cluster of what she suspected was housing for the locals who worked in and ran the town. Off to the west was a view of the harbor peppered with the silhouettes of several anchored sailboats, and the Pacific Ocean out beyond.

Ash drove the wagon back behind the trading post where there was a warehouse with open doors. A silver-haired man with a full beard came out to meet them. He had a merry, booming laugh that resonated from his broad chest as he welcomed Talon.

"Talon. How are you, my girl? I haven't seen you in a while." Makayla assumed this was Ferril. He walked over to where Talon had dismounted the still-energetic Thunder and pulled her into a big hug. She stood there with her arms at her sides and let him squeeze her. Makayla had the impression that he'd been squeezing people for years, including Talon. Makayla took it all in.

"Hi, Ferril." Talon returned the greeting with an amiable nod. "We've got a load of furniture to exchange for credits. We won't use them all up, but we do need two rooms, and Ivy has a list of supplies that we need at Raptare. I believe you know Ash and Ivy. And this is Commander Odin, from Aurora, Shep Odin's granddaughter. I suspect that you've heard that Shep, as well as Commander Odin's..." Talon offered Makayla a sympathetic gaze. "She also lost her father and brother—related to the MidLander invasion." Talon continued to look over at Makayla as if reassuring herself that Makayla could handle the spread of this news. "She and I want to catch you up on a few things too. If you've got time to talk for a bit."

"It's nice to meet you, Commander Odin. I heard about your family, and I'm so sorry. They were good men." Ferril scowled and his face turned red in agitation. "World's gone batshit crazy. We've got to protect ourselves better."

"It's nice to meet you too." Makayla reached out and shook his hand. Her grief was still present, but time was helping her come to terms with her losses. The pain was less acute.

"I've got a few lads here who can take your two mounts and get them set up down in the barn. While they're doing that, my people can assist in the unloading of your wagon—they'll take inventory as they do it. When the lads return, they can help Ash and Ivy get the wagon and those horses settled too. Two rooms for the four of you?" Ferril looked sideways at Talon and then took a harder look at Makayla. The trading post was a hub of news and gossip, so he probably knew that Ash and Ivy were together, and he seemed to have heard something that suggested a single room might work for Talon and Makayla. Or maybe he just knew Talon's reputation with women—as that thought crossed Makayla's mind, she felt a pang in her chest.

"You remind me of your grandfather and father. But much better looking." He smoothed his beard and waited, obviously trying to figure out the sleeping arrangements.

Talon seemed entertained as Ferril studied the group. Finally, she clarified the plan for accommodations. "Ash and Ivy are staying with Ash's cousin, who lives in the settlement." She indicated the housing cluster off to the east. "Commander Odin and I will each stay in one of the two rooms I need here in town."

"Rooms down the street at the Shoreline okay with you?" Ferril asked. Looking at Makayla, he added, "Separate rooms, common bathroom setup."

"Whatever you've got." Talon didn't give Makayla a chance to respond. "Two rooms at the Shoreline will work."

"Good. Then follow me inside while we finish the inventory and calculate the credits, collect the list of supplies you want, and catch up a bit."

Ash handed Makayla both her backpack and Talon's. Talon took her pack, and they followed Ferril inside the trading post and down a hallway.

When they reached Ferril's office, they left the packs in a corner. "Let me get you two ladies some coffee." Ferril pointed at two chairs for them to sit in that faced his desk.

"That would be great." Talon took a seat and indicated with a look that Makayla should take the one next to hers.

Ferril stepped out and returned with two steaming mugs filled with the aromatic brown brew. "Premium beans sailed in from a new place in South America," he proudly boasted as he handed them the mugs and waited for their response.

Makayla took a sip. "Delicious." She hummed her appreciation. It had been a long time since she'd had coffee and never any this good.

Talon chuckled and savored a taste. "Only a few pleasures in life as good as this," she purred with a side-eye glance at Makayla, leaving him to think it was the coffee when Makayla suspected the reference was just a bit of added torture aimed at her. Oh, the pleasures in life. Coffee and desktop planning sessions.

He nodded. "Speaking of pleasures in life, I hear that your friend Grace Wilde is in town."

Talon's posture shifted as she subtly straightened for a moment before relaxing again to continue drinking her coffee. "When did she get here?" Talon asked with a smile.

Makayla sat back and listened. Ferril's news had certainly garnered Talon's attention. She was interested in the fact that Talon had someone referred to as a "friend," and she wanted to know about her.

"Anchored this morning, so I'm sure she'll be in town tonight," Ferril replied. "Brought me some inventory from Central and South America, and she's restocking supplies on her vessel."

Talon filled her lungs with air and let out a long, slow exhale—she and this Grace Wilde must have a history. Probably part of Talon's past. Maybe that buried past. Then Talon changed the subject.

"Commander Odin and I have been meeting with the commanders from the neighboring Sylvan, Eden, Woodland, and Brighton enclaves. We're formulating a defense treaty in case of a future invasion like the one with the MidLand soldiers. Commander Odin is the lead, and she can explain it to you. We're thinking you might want to have Gull Town join in. You're not an enclave, but this trading post and the town are important to the enclaves. And you're at risk during an invasion." Talon nodded for Makayla to take over the discussion.

Leaning forward, Makayla engaged Ferril's gaze before she began. "Aurora and Raptare initially worked out a defense agreement between our two enclaves because we lost so many to the MidLand invasion."

Sympathy filled Ferril's eyes. "Again, I'm so sorry about your family, Commander Odin."

"Thank you. Call me Makayla. I'm a co-commander right now at Aurora. Quinn is my equal, and they're heading the enclave while I work with Talon on what we're calling a WestLand northern enclave NATO defense alliance. North Area Tactical Optimization—a twist on a touch of *history*."

Ferril shook his head and snorted in appreciation. Talon clenched her jaw at the way Makayla purposefully drew out the word "history," her piercing blue eyes locking on Makayla's.

"We've now met with those other four enclave leaders I just mentioned," Makayla explained, "and in a few weeks we'll hopefully finalize an alliance for a common defense in the northern region of WestLand, in the event of another invasion. Hopefully, strong enough to deter any invaders. Basically, a defense cooperative."

"I guess you personally know the repercussions of an invasion, Makayla," Ferril said.

"Not only did she lose family, Ferril, but she was taken from Aurora for two years," Talon told him.

Ferril looked at Makayla in confusion. "Oh my God. I hope you're okay."

"Her father helped her cut her hair off right after their capture. She was disguised as a young male. They never realized she was a woman," Talon said.

"Not exactly lucky." Ferril nodded as understanding dawned. "But luckier than being captured as a female. I've heard some stories." His expression darkened.

Makayla didn't want to dwell on her captivity. "Anyway, we thought Gull Town might want to consider joining the alliance. Strength in numbers and all. We brought you some information so you can look it over and discuss it with the rest of your town leadership."

Ferril was interested in the alliance, in the added security it might offer both the enclaves Gull Town served and the town itself. He accepted the papers Talon and Makayla had brought for him to consider, papers with a handwritten outline of the proposal.

He promised to make sure the requested trading post supplies would be ready for loading into their wagon before they departed the next day, and then after telling Makayla how pleased he was to have met her, he reminded Talon again that the *Hell's Belles* sailboat was in the Gull Town harbor. They thanked him and headed out to find their rooms.

CHAPTER SIXTEEN

Makayla's room was three doors down from Talon's. A relaxing tub soak at both Raptare and Aurora with added buckets of fire-heated water was a luxury Makayla had enjoyed on rare occasion, but there wasn't going to be a warm bath tonight in the common bathroom facilities shared by the Shoreline residents, so she washed her face in a bowl of cold water after the long day's ride. The plan was for Talon to collect her for a tour of the town and dinner, and it wasn't long before there was a knock at the door.

"Are you ready, Commander Odin?" Talon seemed determined to maintain her distance, even when she revealed hints of remembering their more personal interactions.

"I am, but can we walk over to the edge of town and check on the ravens before we go anywhere else?" This was an unfamiliar place with many strangers nearby, and Makayla's room was a few blocks from the woods. She was concerned because it wasn't like Aurora or Raptare, where the birds could spend the night in an enclave barn where they were known and welcome, and it wasn't like their nights in the trees when she'd been outside and sleeping close by.

"We can head over to the woods right now to make sure they're settled in for the night. Then we can go to the saloon to have a drink and order some dinner. I don't know if Ash and Ivy will be there, but I suspect they'll settle in at Ash's cousin's place." Talon turned to lead the way out of the building and onto the main street of the town.

"If not, we made arrangements to meet for breakfast at the saloon in the morning so we can organize and head back."

They walked along the wooden sidewalk in front of the shops until they were at the interface where the town ended and the woods began. Makayla moved past Talon and out into the trees. She whistled, then called the birds' names, and within a minute Ed and Al flew to her and landed at her feet. Talon came to stand next to her, and Poe flew over and dropped a small pinecone in front of them.

"You all set for the night?" Makayla asked. The birds answered her and flew up into the trees. "We'll see you in the morning then."

Makayla looked over at Talon. "Thanks."

"No problem. Let's go get some dinner at the saloon. I'm hungry." Talon turned back toward town. Makayla wished Talon wasn't maintaining such a personal distance, but she sang softly as they walked because her birds were fine and she wanted to fill the silence. Talon turned and smiled when she hit the first few notes, then seemed to catch herself and focused back on their route to the saloon.

It might have been a Monday night, but the saloon was crowded with people drinking and talking, both men and women. The women's attire was unevenly split between the majority who wore the shirt-and-pants attire of females taking a break from a day of accomplishing chores for their enclaves in Gull Town, and the minority who wore some form of skirt or dress in pursuit of catching someone's attention or just enjoying an evening removed from their normal roles of hard work and enclave duties.

As Talon stood and looked over the many women in the room, her expression didn't change. Makayla couldn't tell if she was searching for someone in particular, or if she was just surveying the scene. Talon's gaze did not linger on anyone but quickly came back to the host as he approached them.

Most of the tables were full. However, there was an empty table in the back, so they followed the host through the crowd. Heads turned as Talon moved across the space toward their destination.

Dressed in her signature sepia attire, tall and regal with inherently striking looks and a commanding demeanor, Talon drew notice. She paid no attention to the curious stares as she crossed the rowdy room while Makayla trailed behind.

Makayla had been in two enclaves, she'd been on southern battlefields, and she'd been in many locations on her trek to and from the south, but she'd never been in a place like Gull Town, or a saloon filled with such a diversity of people. She observed several attractive women dressed in clothing designed to reveal their physical assets, but her interest was only curiosity—none of those females captured her attention in the way that Talon did. It hit her again how devasting it would be when the time came for her to return to Aurora. She fought to shake off the sobering thoughts and enjoy this evening's new adventure in a new place with Talon.

Ten minutes later, Talon sipped tequila from a small metal shot glass, a drink that wasn't readily available at Raptare, and Makayla had a tankard filled with a bronze ale in front of her. The dragon embellishing the side of the shot glass amused Makayla. Drakaina.

"See something entertaining, Commander Odin?" Talon's tone didn't conceal that she had started to relax.

"Just enjoying my beer, Commander de LaTerre."

"Are you going to be able to drink that tankard and still behave yourself?" Talon arched a questioning eyebrow.

"I hope not." Makayla gave her a playful smile.

"Just take it easy. This isn't a good place to get drunk." Talon tilted her head toward the crowd and the constant roar of noise filling the room as all those strangers drank and talked and jostled and flirted and argued with each other.

"Thanks for the advice. Do you have plans besides babysitting a tipsy me tonight?"

"I never know what my evening plans are when I come to Gull Town." Talon didn't offer any additional information.

Makayla again considered this might be where a lot of Talon's one-night stands took place. That thought only made her want to drink more. She picked up the tankard and took another long swallow just as a server brought them their plates of food. Talon had questioned the server about a rabbit dish they were offering and then settled on fish. Makayla had the fish because she couldn't bring herself to eat a rabbit when there were other choices. They just seemed so innocent.

They were finishing their dinners and their drinks, and Makayla was feeling the buzz of the alcohol when Talon's clear blue eyes widened. Her fork hit her plate with a clang. Makayla followed her stare to the other side of the saloon, her gaze landing on one of the more interesting women she'd encountered in a long time.

This woman was very attractive with solid, well-proportioned features. Makayla thought she might describe her as captivating. Not compelling in the same way as Talon, but compelling in her own way. Her distinctive curls and a vitality mixed with an aura of self-assuredness were attention-grabbing. Her complexion was cast in golden undertones, and elation shone in her honey-hued amber eyes—eyes that had locked on Talon.

As Makayla watched, she wove her way around the talkers, the drinkers, and the tables in the saloon. Her convoluted path had an ultimate goal—she was working her way toward Talon and Makayla's table. When she drew near and was no longer partially blocked by the crowd, Makayla noted that she was probably about Talon's age—fortyish. The bottoms of her dark pants were tucked into her mid-calf boots, she wore a berry-dyed wool vest over her outer pale shirt, and she carried a distinctive brown leather tricorn hat in her right hand. But it was that mass of liberated chestnut-brown curls perched on her head like an autonomous untamed forest creature that was her most notable feature. Renegade curls that probably needed that tricorn cover to keep them from going completely mutinous on the open seas.

Talon stood and stepped away from her chair as the woman reached them and dropped her hat on the table. Then she grabbed Talon in a bear hug and rocked them both back and forth. Talon hugged the woman in return as she swayed with the embrace.

"Commander de LaTerre." The woman drew out the greeting in a deep, delighted drawl that indicated the use of Talon's official name was a joke between the two of them. Her dark dancing eyes locked on Makayla's as her chin rested on Talon's shoulder in the prolonged front-to-front clasp.

"Captain Wilde," Talon responded in a similar seductive drawl as she kissed the woman on the cheek. "Ferril told me that you anchored the *Hell's Belles* this morning in the harbor. I was hoping to see you."

Captain Wilde released Talon and stepped back to look her up and down. "You're as breathtaking as ever, darling. How have you been?"

A wave of jealousy shot through Makayla as she witnessed the intimacy of the encounter, and it displaced the mellow feelings that the beer had induced. She was suddenly sober again. Who was this woman?

As if she could read Makayla's mind, Captain Wilde stepped around Talon and extended her hand. "I'm Grace Wilde. Captain of the *Hell's Belles*—the largest sailing ship out there in the harbor." Grace tilted her head in the direction of the water. Then she turned toward a table across the room behind her, full of loud, laughing, drinking women. "That's most of my crew, there."

Makayla looked at the table of females and took in their boisterous mood. Then she stood and shook Grace's hand. So, this was the Grace Wilde that Ferril had mentioned to Talon back at the trading post. The dichotomy of her name gave Makayla pause—grace and wild. Was the captain as multifaceted as Talon de LaTerre?

While Makayla contemplated this, Talon introduced her. "Grace, this is Commander Odin, from the Aurora enclave. She's working with me on a defense alliance that we're hoping will initially include six enclaves and Gull Town. Maybe more later."

Grace glanced at Talon before she turned her sparkling amber eyes back to Makayla. "You're gorgeous, sweetie. I hope this old friend of mine hasn't corrupted you." Captain Wilde nodded toward Talon with a playful grin on her face.

Makayla heard the reference to "old friend" and wondered again about Talon's past. As the reference to corruption registered, she felt herself flush and knew her cheeks must be a distinct pink shade.

Grace scrutinized Makayla, and then Talon. She cocked an eyebrow as if trying to figure out their relationship.

"So, what are you doing in Gull Town?' Talon appeared to deliberately cut off Grace's assessment. "And how long will you be here?"

Grace cast a quick sideways smile at Makayla before addressing Talon again. "Long enough to catch up with a drink or two, darling. And maybe a bit more."

Makayla wondered if they were just old friends, or had they been something more to each other? Maybe they still were.

"Then sit down and join us, Grace," Talon replied. "It's been a while. We do need to catch up."

"You've convinced me." Captain Wilde laughed. Then glancing at Makayla, she winked. "Not that I'm easy or anything, but I'd love to upgrade my image by sipping a few with you two beautiful ladies." Grace looked around for an empty chair.

Makayla wasn't sure if she wanted to stay and see how things played out, or if she wanted to leave them to their drinks. As much as she would love to remain and listen in, Makayla decided that she would be more uncomfortable as a third wheel. Talon hadn't introduced her as Makayla. She'd made a point of making sure that she'd limited the introduction to their professional relationship.

"I'm exhausted from a very long day. I think that I'll leave you two to catch up while I head back to my room. It's nice to meet you, Captain Wilde."

"Just call me Grace—that's fine."

"And Makayla is fine for me," Makayla replied before adding, "Good night." Then she offered Grace her chair without looking at Talon, who she could feel watching her, and she left to return to her room.

CHAPTER SEVENTEEN

It was a long night and Makayla struggled to fall into a deep sleep. The soft glow of morning light was just beginning to filter through the curtains in her room when she awoke after a few final hours of much needed rest. Since Talon hadn't collected her for breakfast, Makayla dressed and headed out into the hallway. Talon's door was shut, and rather than risk waking her, Makayla decided to take the short walk to the woods to check on her birds.

The town was quiet and Makayla suspected many of the visitors were sleeping off a late night. Approaching the tree line from the edge of town, she could make out the morning activity of the local bird population. Flitting, chattering, chirping. Makayla whistled her customary greeting to her own birds. Ed and Al flew out from the foliage. In full panic, they vocalized their distress in shrill calls of alarm.

Makayla's heart rate escalated when she didn't see Poe, especially with the state of frenzy Ed and Al were conveying. "Where's Poe?" she asked in dismay.

She looked around and didn't see him. She headed a short distance into the woods, following the two distraught ravens, but saw no sign of her third bird. After considering for a few moments, she decided to return to their lodgings to see if Talon would join her. She didn't know what was in the woods, and she might not be found if she ran into trouble. That wouldn't help Poe. Nobody knew she'd left her room or where she was.

Makayla assured Ed and Al that she'd return as soon as possible, then took off running for the building that had housed them the previous night. She skidded to a halt in front of Talon's bedroom door and pounded. She was having difficulty catching her breath, between the exertion of racing back to the Shoreline and the anxiety that flooded her entire being.

The door swung open. Grace stood there in a long, button-down shirt. Her shapely bare legs protruded from beneath. "Good morning, sweetheart." She tilted her head as she took in the distraught Makayla. The shock of realizing that Grace and Talon had spent the night together hit Makayla with an additional blow to the chest, almost crippling her, but Makayla fought to ignore the added emotional pain. She had to focus on the crisis with her ravens.

"Is Talon here?" she wheezed as she fought hysteria.

Talon came up behind Grace, fully dressed. "What is it, fledgling?" The look of concern on Talon's face was obvious.

Grace's eyebrows lifted in interest at the term of endearment Talon had used to address Makayla.

"I went out to the trees to check on the ravens. Something's happened to Poe." Makayla choked on the words. She and the birds had been through so much together. They were the only family she had left. She couldn't let anything happen to one of them now.

Talon turned back into the room, grabbed her long knife, and joined Makayla. "Let's go. I'll lead since I've got a weapon. You follow." She looked back toward the doorway where Grace still stood and she addressed her. "I'll catch up with you later. If you have to sail before we get back, I'll see you at Raptare." Then Talon took off at a sprint and Makayla followed.

When they reached the edge of the woods, Ed and Al flew out. Ed landed on Talon's arm.

"We'll follow you," she said to the bird.

With Ed and Al leading, Talon and Makayla headed deeper into the trees. The undergrowth was thick, but there was a dirt path that the two ravens seemed to be shadowing, a path that made the passage through the thick foliage much faster for Makayla and Talon. After about fifteen minutes of rushed hiking, they approached a small clearing where the faint smell of wood smoke hung in the air. Talon put her finger up to her mouth to signal they should be quiet. Then with fluid stealth, she moved up on the camp, Makayla behind her.

There, next to the glowing embers in the fire pit was a scruffy man who needed both a haircut and a shave. He was thin and anxious, jerking his head in all directions before staring down toward the ground, probably having heard the approach of the two noisy birds through the trees, and maybe the two of them as well. He finally looked back up, his eyes partly occluded by long, dirty blond bangs.

At his feet where he'd been gazing, a wooden cage held a trapped Poe. Next to the cage was a bunched-string net, and next to that was a chunk of meat he had undoubtedly used as bait to capture the raven. He opened his mouth and told the vocal Poe to shut up, revealing that he had several gaps where teeth had once been.

Talon moved forward and did not slow down as she approached the man. She showed no hint of hesitation in moving ahead to challenge Poe's captor. He did not have much in the way of height on her, and she drew up only a few feet from him. "I think you have something that belongs to us," she announced.

He stared at her in surprise. "Doesn't seem like it's yours, considering it's here in my cage. Who are you, bitch?" Spittle sprayed from the man's mouth as he made his pronouncement.

Makayla had seen some off-putting men on her journeys. This man wasn't repulsive simply because of his appearance, but also because of his attitude.

"Nobody is taking this bird from me." He scowled before he added, "Over my dead body."

Talon placed her hand on the handle of her long knife, which was still in its sheath.

"Well, I'm the nobody who is going to take that bird from you," Talon calmly replied. "And *over your dead body* can be arranged. We can do this the easy way, or we can do it the hard way." Talon's voice shifted to almost a purr, as if inviting him to incite his demise. "Don't test me."

Her warning was a presentation of complete calm, but Makayla knew Talon and felt the rage boiling beneath the surface, ready to erupt with any further provocation. As Talon remained in full control of herself, it wasn't what Makayla saw, but what she felt—Talon would kill the man if that's what it took to save Poe. This was the Talon who inspired the lore. Makayla was shocked to realize that she would agree with Talon's actions. Poe was her family. The man had no right to him. But she hoped it wouldn't come to violence.

The scruffy fellow glared at Talon. He clumsily tried to grab Talon as he sneered his response. "Bitch." He repeated his offensive name-calling. "Fucking bitch."

Talon easily side-stepped him. Before the fool could react, her long knife was out of its sheath and at his throat. His eyes widened beneath the hair that fell across his face, and he gulped.

"I'm trying not to kill you," Talon said. Her knife nicked a thin line of crimson that ran down his neck. "For her sake." She tilted her head toward Makayla.

Makayla stepped forward as Talon held Poe's captor's life in her hands. She wanted to talk some sense into him. "That's my bird, Poe. I've raised him from a baby."

"I've got him now." The man was obviously fighting to remain defiant, but fear tinged his voice.

"And she's got you." Makayla tilted her head toward Talon and the weapon threatening his life. "Do you know the name of that woman you just called a bitch?"

"Don't know. Don't care." The imprudent man didn't let up with his attempted bravado.

"Talon the Terrible. Ever heard of her?" Makayla asked as Talon gave him a chilling artic blue stare.

The man's eyes widened and he choked. The knife moved a fraction of an inch deeper as his Adam's apple bobbed. "I was gonna sell him. To a taxidermist. Good money—ten credits. What are you going to give me?"

"I'm willing to offer you your life." Talon looked at Makayla again, as if offering the option of not killing the man on the spot was a concession to her. "What'll it be? The raven for your life, or a bit of slice-and-dice—and me with our bird anyway."

The man offered a high, nervous chuckle that bordered on hysterics. "Well, if you put it that way. Take the goddamn bird."

Talon nodded at Makayla to open the cage and free Poe, keeping the weapon at his neck. As soon as the cage door was unfastened, Poe pushed against it, hopped out, and flew off into the trees where he joined Ed and Al. They welcomed him with a commotion of avian relief. Talon lowered her knife and nodded at the still terrified man.

"I'll leave word in Gull Town with Ferril, at the trading post, to transfer a hundred credits to you. Enough to buy you several meals or drinks. That should more than cover what you would have gotten for Poe. Much more. But only on the condition you don't touch these birds while I get breakfast and arrange the credit transfer." Talon studied the man as he absorbed what she'd just told him. Then she raised the knife a bit. "You even think of touching them—I'll hunt you down and finish you."

The man raised his chin and nodded. "Glad we could come to an agreement."

Talon couldn't completely stifle a snort. Makayla just watched the exchange. The fellow didn't have a clue how lucky he was. What would Talon have done to him if she wasn't present and watching the entire encounter?

"What's your name?" Talon asked. "So I can tell Ferril and make the arrangements."

The man cleared his throat before he responded in a loud voice, making sure she heard his name so that he would receive the credits. "Weasel. Weasel McGee."

Talon held out her hand for a shake on the deal. "Just so it's clear that we understand each other." Then she held him in a long stare as she added, "Weasel" with a clear element of disdain in her voice.

Weasel shook her hand, then puffed out his chest in an effort to save his pride. "Nice doing business with you. One hundred credits. Any time." His tone indicated that he was proud of himself. Makayla thought he was a fool for pushing Talon.

Talon shook her head. Then she sheathed her weapon, very slowly, as if she really would rather have used it instead. "You're a lucky bastard, Weasel McGee. I hope your luck holds—for your sake." Then she turned and led Makayla and the birds on the hike through the trees to where the outskirts of Gull Town met the woods.

When they reached the juncture of trees and town, Talon spoke to the not-so-unkindness. "You birds stay here. Out of trouble. We'll take care of business and be back to collect you so we can head back to Raptare." Poe flew down and landed on her shoulder, then brushed his head against her cheek. "Crap." Talon blinked a few times. "I think I got some of that smoke in my eyes."

"Sure, you did," Makayla muttered before the enormity of the entire situation hit her.

Maybe Talon never allowed herself to cry, but Makayla did. She knew how close she'd just come to losing Poe—to a fucking taxidermist. Makayla wiped the tears streaming down her face before she bent over and began to dry heave into the weeds at her feet.

Talon waited patiently until she was done, then reached over to embrace her. "It's okay, fledging. It's okay."

Talon continued to hold her close as Makayla tried to calm down. Makayla inhaled deeply, secure in Talon's arms. When enough time had passed, Talon kissed her on the forehead, then took her hand and led them both back into town.

Talon walked Makayla to the saloon, her hand on Makayla's back to steady her. Ash and Ivy were already eating breakfast at a table, and so they joined them. Before another conversation began, Talon turned to Makayla.

"You need to eat before we head out. Something to drink and some food," she gently advised her.

"What's going on?' Ivy had obviously noticed how disheveled Makayla appeared. "We stopped at your room, Talon, to find out the plan for heading home. We saw Captain Wilde in the hallway. She said you two left in a rush, then she asked us to tell you that the *Hell's Belles* was sailing north this morning. That she planned to be at Raptare tonight."

Talon nodded, then gave Ivy and Ash an abbreviated version of what had transpired in the woods while coffee, and then eggs and toast were delivered. She downplayed her role in saving the raven.

When Talon finished, Ivy shook her head. "Oh my God. I can't believe what almost happened to Poe. Are you okay, Mak?"

Makayla had started to feel a bit better about the incident and the positive outcome. "You wouldn't believe Talon in action," she said to Ash and Ivy, who replied in unison, "Oh yes, we would."

Talon ignored the comments and concentrated on her breakfast. Makayla stopped to consider all the events of the morning. They'd saved Poe, but then there was Grace. She knew the place Talon occupied in her own heart, that her feelings were growing. However, Talon wanted no long-term emotional investment in her. Hell, Talon had just spent the night with Grace Wilde. And Grace was probably going to spend the night with Talon in Raptare again that very night.

"What's the matter, Mak?" Talon inspected Makayla's sad face with a piercing gaze. She leaned in and smiled at Makayla. "We saved Poe. He's fine."

Makayla shook her head, trying not to cry. She had no right to cry. "I know. Thank you, for what you did for Poe. You were amazing."

Talon's voice gentled. "So, are you going to tell me what's still troubling you?"

Makayla shook her head. She didn't want to tell Talon that her sleeping with Grace was breaking her heart. She looked over at Ash and Ivy. There was no way she could ever have this conversation in front of them.

Talon noted her glance at Ash and Ivy. She cleared her throat. "Eat up, Commander Odin. We have a long day ahead." Then she leaned over next to Makayla, her warm mouth up against Makayla's ear. "We need to talk—when we get back to Raptare, Mak."

After they'd finished eating, Ash and Ivy left to go hitch the horses to the wagon and have someone prepare Babe and Thunder for the trip home. Talon and Makayla walked back to their lodgings and collected their belongings from their rooms, then they headed over to the trading post where Talon had Ferril's bookkeeper transfer one hundred credits to an account they set up for Weasel McGee. The woman keeping the records gave Talon an inquisitive look, but Talon ignored her.

When that chore was completed, Ferril escorted two young men out of the warehouse loading bay with armfuls of the goods that had been on Talon's list of acquisitions needed at Raptare. Ash and Ivy pulled up in the wagon, and two stable boys walked behind them leading Babe and Thunder.

Ferril offered Talon his hand. She leaned in and gave him a hug. She must be feeling unusually sentimental, Makayla thought. "It's good to see you, Talon. Don't be a stranger." Then he turned to Makayla. "It's good to meet you, Commander Odin. Don't you be a stranger either." Makayla offered him a hug too. With all that had transpired on this visit to Gull Town, she was feeling rather emotional. Then Ferril waved at Ash and Ivy, who were still in the wagon.

With the new supplies loaded and the farewells complete, they headed to the edge of town where they collected the three ravens from the woods and made the return journey to Raptare.

CHAPTER EIGHTEEN

Upon their return to Raptare, Talon headed straight to the leadership building to check in with Brock. Makayla joined Ash and Ivy in the unloading of the wagon, the care of the horses, and the settling of the birds in the barn. Others came to help take the new supplies to a room where they could be stored until distributed.

After they'd finished the chores related to their return and deposited their backpacks in their rooms, Makayla met the other two in the mess hall for an early dinner. Nina and Derrick joined them. Their plates dished, they'd all just taken seats at an empty table when Joe joined them too.

"So, how was the trip?" Nina asked. "What did you think of Gull Town?" She turned to Makayla, probably more interested in what she would say about Talon than anything Ivy or Ash might disclose.

Before Makayla could answer, Ivy sputtered, "Oh, my God. A man in the woods outside of Gull Town captured Makayla's raven, Poe, to sell to a taxidermist."

"I'm so sorry." Nina's eyes had widened and she patted Makaya's arm. The news had Derrick's and Joe's attention too. The entire Raptare enclave knew of Makayla's attachment to the three ravens.

"It's okay. We got Poe back." Makayla smiled at the relief she still felt regarding Poe's rescue.

"From what Makayla indicated, Talon was fearless and saved the day," Ash told the group. "Talon the Terrible was a hero." Makayla knew that he didn't know everything because Talon had downplayed her role, but he knew enough from the abbreviated version at their breakfast discussion that morning to correctly surmise that Talon had saved Poe with her actions.

Nina, Derrick, and Joe stared at them, waiting for more information after hearing of Talon's role in the Gull Town rescue. Nina tightly clasped her fork, and although she tried to control it, there was the tiniest furrowing of her brow.

"So, just what did our fearless leader do to save the bird?" Derrick sat up straighter and crossed his arms as he waited for Makayla's firsthand accounting. His tone was hard to read. She wasn't sure that he thought Talon was fearless.

Makayla considered what appeared to be Nina's feelings for Talon. She felt sympathy for Nina—she'd acknowledged her own feelings for Talon, and she knew they weren't reciprocated in the manner she craved. Nina didn't need her feelings for Talon stirred up any more than they already were. Makayla didn't know if revealing Talon's aggressive actions would help Nina get over Talon, or if she'd find them enticing. Makayla had to admit that she found Talon's fierce loyalties attractive.

Makayla cleared her throat, a signal to Ivy and Ash that she'd like to be the one to tell this tale. She wasn't going to disclose how intimidating Talon had been. Talon had done what was needed to free Poe. She wouldn't share how she was in full support of Talon's hostile threats to save him from the fate of being stuffed as a trophy, or spiritual totem, or omen symbol—killed for whatever damn reason a person wanted a taxidermy raven.

"Talon let Poe's captor, Weasel, know that she had her long knife, so he didn't pull anything on us. She paid him a hundred credits to free Poe and leave my not-so-unkindness alone while we returned to Gull Town to prepare to leave. She was the right combination of intimidating, but fair. Talon solved things without anyone getting hurt." Except for that little nick in Weasel's neck, she silently added. Makayla waited to see how her answer landed.

Nina smiled and nodded. Downplaying the interaction between Talon and Weasel clearly hadn't dampened her feelings for Talon, but Makayla still couldn't judge if the truth would have escalated or diminished Nina's opinion of Talon. While Makayla didn't want to hurt Nina any more than she was already hurting, this probably wasn't her relationship to worry about. Makayla had her own issues with Talon to resolve.

Ash and Ivy simply nodded—they were already familiar with the story. Derrick seemed a bit skeptical with his pursed lips, and Joe just sat back and looked at her. As if she hadn't already realized it, Makayla sighed as she recognized that they all had their own perceptions of Talon. And the lore only added to those perceptions.

"Well, it sounds like you were lucky she was there and you got Poe back," Nina said.

"Did our fearless leader pull off a one-night stand while she was there?" Derrick asked. "You know she's famous for her womanizing." He said this as if he didn't have a hint that Makayla cared for Talon, even though he'd been a witness to their last dance in the mess hall.

A ghost of despondency played across Nina's face. The comment caught up with Makayla's confusion, hitting her square in the chest—a futile, flapping, fighting-a-headwind pain that made it difficult to breathe, but Makayla wasn't sharing any of that now. She chewed a bite of chili and washed it down with tea before she choked on it.

Ash jumped into the conversation. "We were at my cousin's house most of the time. I don't know what Makayla saw." Everyone looked expectantly at Makayla. She didn't say anything—couldn't think of anything to say. At least not anything she wanted to say.

Ivy spoke up, believing that she was redirecting the conversation after Makayla's silence and Nina's sad look. "The *Hell's Belles* was in the harbor and Captain Grace Wilde was there. She's a friend of Talon's, and we only saw her for a moment in the Shoreline lodging's hallway where she must have had a room. She's sailing here today and should be in Raptare tonight. I suspect her crew will stay on the ship or the beach, but I bet the captain will hike into the compound."

With the mention of womanizing followed by the reference to Grace Wilde, Makayla decided she was done with dinner. Also done with conversation for tonight. She knew she had no right to be upset. Talon had warned her that she didn't get attached. That she didn't do romantic. That she didn't ever spend the night after sex—that she'd been trapped into it out there in the woods because there was no other option.

Holy friggin' hope. It hit Makayla between the eyes—it had been morning when Grace Wilde answered the door to Talon's room at the Shoreline. So, maybe Talon hadn't slept with Wilde after all, if what she'd said was true about never spending the night together after sex.

Makayla felt a hint of relief. But then she considered that the captain wasn't wearing any pants when she'd opened Talon's door—her state of undress probably a clear indication they'd slept together. Makayla's heart sank. She was confused. Tormented. Was Talon busy in bed with another woman while Makayla was a few doors away—but refusing to share her bed with Makayla? Did Talon even care about her? Talon's words and actions were conflicting, confusing, and sometimes so damn depressing.

"I'm turning in." Makayla stood up and wiped the hint of moisture that had flooded her eyes. "It's time for me to head back to my room."

The others wished her a good night as she cleared her dishes and headed toward the exit. Just as she was ready to leave, the door to the mess hall opened and Brock walked in.

"Ash is over there." Makayla indicated the table she'd just left where Brock's son sat. She struggled to put on a normal, relaxed face for Brock. The man certainly didn't need to worry about her crybaby issues.

"Thanks, trespasser. I was looking for you." Brock took in her still damp eyes but didn't address his observations. "Talon told me about what happened to Poe. I'm so glad it worked out."

"Yeah. Me too. Thanks to Talon's heroics."

"The woman can be fierce when she needs to be." Brock clearly supported his commander's actions. "Hell, she can be terrifying.

But there's no better person to have on your side." Brock patted her on the shoulder before he added, "I've known her for a long time."

"I owe her." As that declaration came out of Makayla's mouth, the memory of also owing Talon for the desktop *planning session* where she'd been left extremely satisfied brought heat to Makayla's cheeks. Would she ever be allowed to pay her back? Not that it would feel like payment—more like bliss. And now she owed Talon a hundred credits for Poe. Her debt was mounting. "You said you were looking for me." Makayla forced herself back to the moment and Brock.

"Willow is having a dinner at her place, maybe on Friday," Brock said. "She wanted me to let you know if I saw you. The younger generation is coming—Ash, Ivy, Nina. You're invited too. Willow's a wonderful cook. Beats the heck out of this mess hall food."

"That sounds great. I'll get the details from you or her this week," Makayla replied. "Thanks."

"Sure thing." Brock smiled before he waved over toward the table where Makayla's dinner partners still sat, then turned and headed out the door with her. "I'm heading over to Talon's place, to meet up with Grace Wilde. I haven't seen the *Hell's Belles'* captain in quite a while. Have a good night, Mak."

Makayla was unsettled the entire night and never fell into a prolonged state of sleep. Talon and Grace together, intertwined, was the predominant image that kept her awake and infiltrated her slumber every time she managed to achieve a dream state.

Makayla had nothing against the captain; she was an engaging woman. However, Makayla had to admit to herself that she was jealous of Grace Wilde. That she was also upset. Upset with herself for her one-sided desire for a future that didn't seem attainable. Upset that everyone expected her to be a leader at Aurora when her heart was telling her the enclave was no longer her home without family there. But Talon didn't want her here either.

After she finally conceded that the night was over and it was time to get up, Makayla crawled out of bed. She went down to the common restroom, cleaned her teeth, and washed her face, then returned to her room with plans to dress. The insistent rapping on her door offered no one-knock prelude to see if she'd answer. Makayla opened it a crack to find Grace Wilde standing there, tricorn hat in hand and her chestnut-brown curls wild and unruly as they haloed her head and fell to her shoulders. The twinkle in her warm amber eyes seemed perpetual. Makayla hadn't yet seen her when she didn't seem a bit delighted.

Eyes widening, Makayla stepped back to let Grace in. What in the hell was she doing here? Makayla pulled her jacket on over her skimpy sleepwear, a loose shirt and short shorts.

"So, Captain, to what do I owe this honor?" Makayla patted her auburn top mop of messy uncombed ringlets. Then she looked toward her dresser and eyed the wooden comb her father had carved for her, but she quickly decided that she was going to have this conversation as is. She was almost too tired to care what Grace was going to say to her.

Grace strolled confidently into the room, then turned around to face Makayla. She took her time looking Makayla up and down. "Well, bite me—I can certainly see what Talon sees in you. You're gorgeous even first thing in the morning."

Makayla flushed and cocked an eyebrow. What was the purpose of this visit? Was Grace Wilde jealous of her? She didn't look jealous and actually sounded rather friendly. Or at least approving.

"No, I'm not jealous of you." Grace sauntered over to the edge of Makayla's unmade bed and sat down. She seemed to have no problem taking charge and making herself at home.

How did she know what Makayla was thinking?

"Talon and me. That's not going to happen. That ship has sailed." Grace's guffaw at her own nautical joke made Makayla smile.

"Feel free to sit," Makayla muttered to her, even though Grace had already taken over the edge of her bed.

"Don't mind if I do." Grace shifted a bit to make herself more comfortable. She patted a spot next to her on the bed in a show of extending an invitation to Makayla. "Please sit down so we can talk."

Makayla thought about the last time she'd sat on this same bed next to Nina when she'd borrowed a book. It had been completely innocent, but Talon had been so upset.

Grace looked closely at Makayla. "I won't bite."

"No, but Talon does," Makayla said under her breath.

"I hope you're speaking metaphorically and not literally." Grace's scrutiny did not let up, then she laughed again. "Nope, not speaking metaphorically," she exclaimed. "I'm gifted at a few things, and one of them is reading people. And, sweetheart—you're an open book."

Makayla was certain her embarrassment was showing. Then she decided to sit down so that she wouldn't be facing Grace head-on. So that she wouldn't be quite so readable. Grace was taller than she was, so Makayla would have to look up a bit. After she'd settled down next to Grace, her hands clasped in her lap, Makayla asked again, "So, to what do I owe this visit?"

Grace shifted to face her at an angle, then cleared her throat and revealed that she had a serious side. "I've known Talon and been her friend for decades. We even fought together as the world went completely to hell. We've both changed, but we've remained friends." Grace looked at Makayla while that sank in.

"I didn't know Talon had friends," Makayla replied before she decided that was rather rude. She didn't know what else Grace was to Talon, but she'd already concluded they were friends. She wondered what Talon was like as a kid. "Sorry. I meant at least not in the conventional sense."

Grace chuckled. "Not much conventional about Talon. At least not anymore. I won't go into her history—that's hers to reveal. So much has gone into making her who she is, Makayla. But I came to talk to you before I leave. For a few reasons."

Makayla waited while Grace seemed to consider what she wanted to say.

"First, I stayed the night with her as her friend in Gull Town. We drank until late. I didn't have a room and was a bit too tipsy to try to make it back to my ship out in the harbor." Grace stopped for a moment to make sure she had Makayla's full attention before continuing. "All that happened in that bedroom was sleeping, if you get my drift."

Makayla's eyes widened. "And you're telling me this because…?" She was thrilled with the information, but she wasn't clear about Grace's motivation.

"As I said, I'm good at reading people. You care about her. She cares about you. I don't want to be an excuse to mess that up—Talon means something to me. We're two women in tough leadership roles. We have a history and we can relate to each other. I value that." Grace's voice was earnest. "There are enough obstacles without false assumptions, so I'm clearing up the assumption I saw on your face Tuesday morning when I opened the door to Talon's room."

"I do care about her. Probably too much," Makayla said. "I don't see her caring about me in the same way. I know she wants me physically." Makayla couldn't believe how much blushing she was doing in front of Grace. "And I think there's an emotional piece there too, on Talon's part, but I keep getting mixed messages. She won't admit it. She runs every time she seems to feel anything. She says that she'll only hurt me because she doesn't do romance."

Grace sat a minute, considering. "You're right. She is running. If you tell her I said this next part, I'll be back to make you walk the plank," Grace said without a touch of jest in her tone. Only a twinkle in her eyes offered a hint that maybe she wasn't serious. Makayla could see how she could run an entire ship.

"Do you even have a plank?" Makayla asked. She thought that was for pirate ships. And who made someone walk the plank these days?

Grace gave her a stern stare. "You wouldn't want to find out. Maybe it's me speaking metaphorically, but you understand what I mean." Like Talon, she knew how to be intimidating when she wanted to be.

Makayla swallowed and nodded her understanding. She recognized that Grace was trying to help her, and Makayla would never threaten Grace's friendship with Talon.

"It's not just that she's afraid of hurting you. She's afraid of being hurt." Grace puffed out a deep breath of air. "She's years in the making. Layers and layers of protective shell, but there's a soft core still in there. And that's all I'm going to say. It's Talon's story to tell."

Makayla decided since Grace seemed to be on a mission of honesty, she would be too. "Well crap, Grace Wilde. I really appreciate that you were willing to come see me, even before I'm dressed. And that you've cleared some things up for me. But you've left me with a lot of questions. I'm still really confused."

Grace stood up. "Glad to be of help, sweetheart," she dryly stated. "Talon's my friend. And if you can navigate the gauntlet, you two would be good for each other. Talon told me—after several drinks—that she can't seem to intimidate you, which is gold in loving her. She admires that. In fact, she needs that in her life. And yeah. I can tell that you love her." Grace gave Makayla a knowing look.

Makayla's eyes widened again, as she stood up too. There didn't seem to be any secrets she could keep from her. Grace Wilde: a contrast of deep intuition, mirth, and even menace when it served her.

"I'm not going to label what she feels, but she sure doesn't call you *fledgling* without some pretty significant degree of attachment." Grace captured Makayla in a tight hug. "I'm setting sail this morning for the coastal trading center north of Vancouver Island, now part of the Pacific Territory of what was Canada. So glad we could do a little bonding before I go. Good luck, darling. Don't cut Talon any slack—and hang in there."

And with that last piece of advice, Captain Grace Wilde turned and left Makayla's room, quietly closing the door as she took her leave.

CHAPTER NINETEEN

For fuck's sake, Grace had nailed it. Loving Talon the Terrible. How could she have let that happen? Stretched out on her bed, Makayla contemplated the irony that she'd spent so much time fighting to get back home to Aurora, only to find herself now not wanting that at all. Because of a chance encounter in the woods. Because of an intriguing, fierce, complex woman that she had no business loving. Talon didn't love her back.

Makayla wasn't fond of epiphanies. She appreciated slow-reasoned thought over the sudden solidifying moments that knocked a person completely off course. This wasn't a complete ambush by her heart. Not wanting to spend her life leading Aurora through the daily challenges of enclave life would have undoubtedly surfaced, even without Talon coming along—the multi-faceted Talon, who was more comfortable with the threat of cutting people to ribbons than letting Makayla know she loved a rescued tomcat named Betty.

The doubts had been brewing for a while, as had growing feelings for Talon. But now it had hit her full force, this epiphany that she loved Talon, didn't want to become the legacy commander of Aurora, wanted purpose, but also needed balance in her life. She didn't have the capacity to be both a fiercely dedicated, outstanding commander and be happy. She needed to find a leadership role that fit her personality, her needs, or she would spend her life miserable. This implementation of the vision of NATO was a focus she enjoyed. She liked spending time outdoors with her birds. And Grace was right—she loved Talon. She should have known. Her heart soared when she thought of Talon. Makayla groaned—self-awareness was hell.

With that final thought, Makayla dragged her sorry ass back off the bed and got dressed. She wasn't ready for the mess hall and breakfast yet. She needed to think some more and spend some time with her ravens, so she headed to the barn.

As Makayla left the warmth of the morning sunshine for the cooler, darker interior of the building, the feral cats rushed over to greet her. She gave a low whistle to her ravens, but the trio decided to remain in the rafters and keep the assault under observation as the swarm of cats charged her.

Makayla couldn't help but think about Talon, who she'd just admitted to loving. She'd initially entertained the thought that maybe Talon loved the chase way more than the capture. That maybe Talon was ice all the way to her core.

But Makayla had seen the layers and connected with the vulnerability that lay beneath the dragon-scale armor. Talon had felt the emotional connection too, although she refused to admit those feelings. And that refusal was the source of Makayla's confusion. Talon's rejections seemed to occur after each encounter when Makayla felt they were drawing closer, after each encounter when Talon acted like she cared. Why? It was so exasperating.

That exasperation, that confusion, was the reason she was here in the barn. The animals would ground her—their adoration was simple and constant. Uncomplicated. An antidote to her anguish. She was here for the solace her not-so-unkindness would offer. And a few welcoming rat catchers.

"Well, I don't have food this morning yet, so you're wasting your time if that's why you like me. And I'm not naive enough to think that a little bribery doesn't help keep me in your good graces," Makayla told the feral felines. As she reached down to stroke a few of the cats, Betty came from out of the shadows. Surprised by the tomcat's appearance, Makayla looked around. "So, what are you doing out here, little man? Where's that sexy woman you've adopted?"

There was a low chuckle as Talon emerged from those same shadows and walked slowly toward her. "Sexy woman, huh? That doesn't sound very commander-to-commander appropriate," Talon chided Makayla, but her tone indicated she was way more amused than upset.

Makayla let out a prolonged sigh. She felt like she was spending her life in the constant state of Talon's emotional flux. But she'd say what she needed to say. "No, that was the balance I want in my life speaking out. The cheeky little charmer wanting to kiss Talon the Tantalizing."

Talon let out a deep breath of her own. Then she began to approach Makayla again, never taking her eyes off her as the distance between them narrowed. Makayla didn't move, didn't take her own gaze off Talon's hungry one. When her lips were within six inches of Makayla's, Talon finally halted.

Makayla inhaled deeply. She glanced at that warm, inviting mouth, then back up into Talon's ardent blue beacons of desire. Makayla was sure her heart would pound right out of her chest, and that she would forget how to breathe, but she held her ground. Heaven help her, she wanted Talon.

"And what if I said that I don't want to kiss you?" Talon said in a smooth, sultry voice that screamed the opposite.

"Then I'd have to call you a liar." Makayla closed the six inches down to four and didn't break eye contact with her antagonist. All she could see was the reflection of hunger from Talon's darkened indigo eyes. Talon wanted her, but Makayla couldn't win this game unless she played it. She leaned in another inch and cocked an eyebrow.

"Screw it," Talon growled in an obvious war with herself before she eliminated that narrow gap in nonnegotiable, lip-lock fashion. Her hand grabbed the back of Makayla's head as her mouth captured Makayla's in a blitz of lips and teeth and tongue.

It might have started as a battle bound to take no prisoners, but it quickly veered into a long, shared encounter of unbridled passion, and Makayla decided that they were both winners. Whatever this was between them frantically continued until it was momentarily sated enough to finally allow them to simply stand in each other's arms—heartbeat to heartbeat—and gently caress and kiss and feel their undeniable connection.

"As much as I'd love to just head to the hayloft with you, we need to talk." With a last soft touch of her lips to Makayla's cheek, Talon stepped back and created space between them, both physical and emotional.

Makayla couldn't keep up with their cycle of feast, then famine—she could feel Talon's qualms after this shared moment. She knew Talon was chastising herself, but she couldn't understand why.

"I think that would be a good idea. So, what's your schedule today? Are you caught up enough to meet with me?" Makayla asked.

"Well, after this little encounter, I suppose I'd better find time. Betty and I saw Grace off earlier, and we were just checking out the barn before we head back to my office. I'd be there right now if I hadn't bumped into a distraction." Talon gave her a look that conveyed both tenderness and trepidation.

"I need to eat. What if I go get two plates in the mess hall and meet you in your office?" Makayla suspected Talon hadn't eaten yet today and wanted to make sure she did. The collection of some food would give Makayla a bit of time to calm down and gather her thoughts.

Talon nodded. She let out a loud puff of air, scooped up the cat, and headed toward the barn door. "Betty and I will be there, Commander Odin."

After she spent a few more minutes with the ravens, who then took off for the orchards, Makayla headed to the mess hall. Lunch fare was available, so she filled their plates and headed to Talon's office where Betty was back to napping in his chair, and Talon was studying paperwork at her desk.

"Come in, Commander Odin." Talon barely looked up, even though Makayla knew she was paying attention to her. There was an almost imperceptible shift in Talon's breathing.

Makayla rolled her eyes as she set the plates on the desk. The bowl of chocolate was gone, but the doily remained.

"Your choice—goat cheese and vegetable casserole on one plate, slow cooked venison on toast on the other. Plus, some applesauce. And a bit of baked bass for Betty." Betty perked up when he heard Makayla mention his name.

"Shall we share the main courses?" Talon continued to pretend to be absorbed in the paperwork in front of her.

"If that's not too intimate, Commander de LaTerre. Seems rather appropriate to me after this morning's commander-to-commander encounter."

Talon's head came up, and she clenched her jaw. "Are you trying to provoke me, Commander Odin?"

"Is it working?" Makayla was unrepentant. "If you're going to be a drakaina, I just can't help doing a little poking."

Talon shook her head and held Makayla with an imperious look. "How do I keep you in the commander box? There are boundaries you just don't seem to understand."

"Maybe I've got a bigger box than you—wider boundaries that encompass a little life balance. And from what happened in the barn this morning, and a few other times, you seem to need that balance too."

Talon reached for the lunch. She divided and shared the main courses between the two plates. She placed the bass chunks in a bowl, and Makayla reached over and set it on the floor where Betty could easily reach it. They ate in silence until the food was gone. Then Talon pushed her plate away and studied Makayla.

"Raptare is my first priority, Mak. There's an entire enclave of people who count on me. And you have an enclave of people at Aurora counting on you too."

"I understand that Raptare comes first for you, Talon. But I'm not sure that being commander is the best fit for me at Aurora. The enclave has great people who can do the job, better than me. I'm thinking of a more focused role—one fitting my skills and personality. And as I've said, I need balance in my life—and I believe that you do too."

"I don't want the kind of balance you're talking about, fledgling." Talon worked her throat in an obvious swallow. "You need to go back home." Her expression shifted from one of contemplation to one of sadness.

"I am home. Home is where the heart is, and my heart isn't in Aurora. Do you even like me?" Makayla gulped and her eyes grew moist. When Talon didn't say anything, Makayla added, "I think that you owe me an answer because I'm falling in love with you. I'm not asking for a commitment of forever right now. But what happened to one night at a time?"

"I need to apologize to you, Makayla." Not fledgling. Not Mak. But Makayla. Talon didn't usually call her Makayla, so that put her on high alert. This was going to be a serious discussion. "There are several reasons I can't get involved with you. We have a job to do. Your home is in another enclave. You want more than I can give— you deserve more." She observed Talon clenching and unclenching her jaw.

Makayla didn't know how to respond. She'd just told Talon that she was falling in love with her. She couldn't get more exposed than that.

"I will only hurt you, fledgling." Talon motioned between the two of them. Then she gulped and admitted, "And I can't do this." Her hand stopped on her own chest.

Talon couldn't do this—that was a huge confession from the dragon woman. Talon seemed to project confidence in doing almost anything. Makayla waited. Talon kept taking her from heaven to hell. Makayla knew what she wanted, but it all seemed out of her control. If she pushed Talon, she would probably only be pushing her away. But it was time for some answers. Makayla needed those—and she didn't want to think of the consequences.

"So, I know that something happened in your past that hurt you. Really hurt you to where you've closed yourself off from anything but short encounters, one-night stands—no romance. But I think you care about me. And I know how much I care about you. So, can you at least tell me what happened for you to give up on me? To give up on any chance of *us*?" Makayla fought tears.

Talon stood and Makayla was afraid she was going to leave. Or tell Makayla to leave. But then she turned to the small cabinet to the side of her weapons' case and pulled out the two metal tankards and the jug of hard apple cider. She filled one tankard to the top and the other halfway, shoving the half-full one across the desk to Makayla. Talon picked up her own and took a long drink before sitting back down.

Nodding to the jug she'd left on the side of her desk, she said, "I might be needing refills. So might you, lightweight, if I'm going to tell you this. A few people from my past know. Brock. Grace. But not many."

"Okay. I've said it before, but let me just say it again—I would never hurt you, Talon." Makayla ignored her drink—she wanted to be sober for this. She had to believe that someone had hurt Talon very badly.

"Fortification." Talon held up a hand to stop Makayla and took another deep swallow from the tankard. She set the drink down and looked directly at Makayla with a somber expression, then took a deep breath. "I know you wouldn't hurt me on purpose. But sometimes it's not because somebody didn't love us enough. Sometimes it's because we loved them too much."

Makayla waited. Talon seemed willing to finally tell her, and she didn't want to give her a reason not to. After taking another gulp of the hard cider, Talon looked at the ceiling for a long moment, as if gathering her strength before they had this conversation.

"Shauna. In my twenties."

Makayla waited some more.

"My wife."

Makayla felt the shock of the disclosure slam into her. She took a deep breath and grounded herself.

"Oliver." Talon disclosed another name, distress in her tone.

Where the hell was Talon going with this?

"My son." Talon stopped for a moment as she struggled with the statement. She blinked a few times. "Ollie was two years old. They both died when I was twenty-eight. I'm forty now, so twelve years ago. March of 2061. It was the pandemic that swept the globe in the late 2050s and early 2060s."

Makayla looked at her in disbelief. Talon closed her eyes, as if defending what measured emotion she'd shown, then mumbled under her breath what sounded like a reminder to herself, "Fuck—I don't cry."

Makayla tried to digest the information Talon had just disclosed. She hadn't expected anything like this. Maybe a girlfriend and broken heart story, but not this. Makayla walked around the desk. She stood behind Talon and leaned over, slid her arms around Talon and hugged her from behind.

"I had no idea, Talon. I'm so sorry." She spoke softly into Talon's ear. Then just held her.

"Shauna was the one who loved birds." And with that, Talon seemed to be done talking about the people she'd loved a dozen years ago. The people who had changed the course of her life. The people who had made her who she was today.

Talon let Makayla hold her for a minute, but then cleared her throat and shifted, so Makayla freed her and sat back down.

"It was a long time ago. In my past. Afterward, I came here and devoted myself to helping make Raptare the enclave that it is." Talon seemed to want to talk about herself. She spoke softly, her voice hushed. "I was angry. Aggressive. I made a reputation for myself, but those were trying times…for the enclave…for me." Talon straightened in her chair and made an effort to shake off the emotion that Makayla had just witnessed. More emotion than Makayla had seen from her.

"That's how the lore came about?"

"You might not believe it, but I've mellowed." Talon rubbed the back of her neck. "But I won't go through that again. Love someone too much. It's easier that way, Mak. So don't love me, because I can't love you back."

Makayla felt her heart rise to her throat, then drop in a nosedive. The pummeling of wings inside her chest—a bird hopelessly caught in a hurricane. She didn't think that love was a choice, but she didn't know how to convince Talon of that. Makayla knew that it was too late to be a choice for her—she loved Talon. Heartbreak was the risk of love. And now Talon had said those five words—"I can't love you back." Makayla would have to live with the heartbreak.

After she'd opened up, Talon pulled on that protective chainmail and become stoic. She advised Makayla that she had a great deal to do regarding her commander duties. She declared that the preparation for the alliance talks was mostly complete, and they were just waiting for their scheduled meeting with all the other enclave leaders, and maybe Ferril, on the Friday of the next week. The words were just muffled background noise to Makayla's pain; they simply conveyed that Talon wanted time to herself.

"If you're busy with enclave issues, is it okay if I have an outdoor date with Betty?" Makayla watched Talon finish her second tankard of hard cider. Maybe Talon wasn't going to get much work done after all. She knew Talon was hurting. But with more grief than Makayla could have imagined, she was hurting too—you couldn't make someone love you.

Chapter Twenty

While Makayla sat and waited for a response from Talon regarding escorting the feline on an afternoon of outdoor activity, she picked up her half tankard of hard cider. She hadn't touched it before their discussion because she'd wanted all her mental faculties to be functioning at full capacity, and she was aware that drinking alcohol compromised her mental acuity. Talon was correct—she was a lightweight.

Makayla contemplated the container of orange-brown liquid painkiller. Maybe not being able to hold her liquor was a positive in the growing onslaught of negatives: Talon couldn't love her, didn't want to love her, wanted her to go back to Aurora to be commander there. Being in full possession of her wits hadn't done a damn bit of good. And it only hurt like hell now. Makayla hoisted the mug and downed its contents in a quick series of greedy gulps. She knew she'd be tipsy this afternoon, but she desperately needed the ache in her heart to diminish. She needed the reprieve of numbness the alcohol would likely offer.

"Are you okay? I didn't mean to get you drunk. I think Betty would probably love another outing today." Talon frowned and shook her head as she watched Makayla drain her mug. "I'm sorry. I know I'm an ass."

"No, Talon. This isn't you being an ass. I know when you're being an ass—firsthand. This is you being afraid."

"Not an ass. Just a coward." Talon kept her tone neutral, but the heat in her eyes told Makayla that she didn't appreciate being called a coward. Makayla had no desire to cause her any more unhappiness. Talon was a proud woman. And she didn't want Talon to close her out any more than she already had—dammit, she loved Talon—so she altered her response.

"Now I'm being an ass. Sorry. I know you're protecting your heart. And I know there's heartbreak that can kill a person." Makayla thought of all the loss she'd suffered these past few years—her grandfather, her father, her brother. It hadn't killed her, but she'd certainly known the torment of grief. However, her response had never been to shut everyone out—that wouldn't have helped her begin to heal. And she'd wanted to heal.

Talon leaned back in her chair and listened to Makayla, watched her, but she didn't say anything. Then Talon reached out and touched the doily. It seemed to ground her.

"Is spending the rest of your life living without love better than taking a risk because love hurt you in the past? Some things are worth a risk. I just wanted to be one of those things. Aren't I worth the risk?" Makayla could hear the dejection in her own voice, but she didn't want to plead.

Talon pinched the bridge of her nose before she looked up with a tormented gaze. All the years of trying to protect herself from the pain of the past surfaced and flashed across her beautiful face before she quickly buried it again. Makayla hadn't seen her like this. Was she simply sorrowful for what had occurred years ago—for the things she'd buried—or was she conflicted about her decision to spurn Makayla? Rejecting any pathway to love had become her strategy for preventing emotional attachment and the risk of pain. All that armor was worn to protect her heart.

And to mask all that internal maneuvering, Talon lived behind such an air of bravado. Such a show of womanizing. Such an effort at no emotional ties. The fact that she'd once loved a wife and a son was profound. But did she ever want that again? Did she want to change? Could she?

Makayla walked back around the desk, leaned over, and gently kissed Talon. "I would never leave you if I could help it—if you asked me to stay. But you'd have to want that. Now, I have a few errands to run, then I'll swing by and pick up Betty." And with that, Makayla turned and walked out the door, away from Talon. The squeeze of despair lodged in her chest and the buzz of alcohol settled in her head.

❖

Makayla didn't want to be alone. She headed to the mess hall to collect some carrots. Betty would enjoy a visit to the corrals, and she could offer Babe and the other horses the treats, then feed some to the goats as well. Joe was working this morning and loaded the orange root vegetables and a few apples into a cloth bag for her.

At a table across the room, Nina was eating with a petite woman Makayla hadn't met before. They were laughing and appeared to be in a good mood. Makayla was feeling the alcohol buzz, but decided to swing past their table to say hello anyway.

"Hi, Nina. How's it going? I'm on my way to offer treats to the horses and goats." She held up the bag she'd collected from Joe.

Nina looked away from the woman and addressed Makayla. "Oh hi, Mak. I'd like you to meet Lea Chang. She's been sailing on the *Hell's Belles* for the past few years but is ready for some land time. She's going to stay here at the enclave for a while. She's a net and rope maker, so she offers Raptare some useful skills."

"Welcome, Lea. Nice to meet you, and welcome to Raptare. I'm Mak. From Aurora." *From Aurora*—it was difficult to say when she knew that she was coming to consider Raptare home. But Talon had been clear. She expected Makayla to return to Aurora in her commander role.

"Mak's a co-commander from the adjacent northern enclave, Aurora," Nina said. "She's staying here and working with our commander, Talon, on a regional defense alliance."

For the first time that Makayla had observed, there was no hint of the undercurrent of dismay that Nina had displayed in the past at the mention of Talon's name.

"Well, it's nice to meet you, Mak. I hope to see more of you. I think I'm going to like my time at Raptare, and I know that I'm enjoying Nina's company." Lea turned and smiled at Nina, who grinned back—their mutual attraction was obvious. Good for Nina. Maybe someone was going to find happiness.

Makayla swung back to Talon's office to collect the tomcat. She appreciated the anesthetizing effects of the hard cider but knew the numbing would diminish. Talon was gone, but the tankards were still out on her desk and Betty was in his chair, so she called to him and he followed her outside.

They made their way to the corrals where the horses and goats approached the fence as soon as they recognized Makayla because she'd fed them before. After offering the treats to the animals, she headed to the garden boxes where Willow was pulling weeds.

"Could you use some help?" Makayla needed to take her mind off Talon. Off the news that she'd once had a wife and a son, news that drove Talon's rejection of her—a rejection that was killing Makayla.

"I sure could." Willow looked up and smiled, her hands in leather gloves and full of weeds she would add to a pile she'd started. "I hear you're coming to dinner on Friday. We'll probably have Ash and Ivy too. And maybe Nina, Ivy's friend. I asked Brock to invite Talon, but she's a hard one to corner."

"Don't I know," Makayla mumbled as she reached down and started yanking out weeds alongside Willow. Makayla hiccupped and wiped her eyes.

"Are you okay, honey?" Willow didn't push any harder. She seemed to just be willing to offer Makayla a friendly ear. Makayla appreciated Willow's kindness. A friendly ear would be welcome, not that Willow could begin to fix the repercussions of Talon's declaration.

"I'm okay. I just need a break and a little time to wallow." Makayla tried to conceal the unhappiness in her voice. Then wanting to talk about something else, Makayla changed the subject. "I just saw Nina at the mess hall. It looks like she might have a new friend from the *Hell's Belles* sailboat who's ready for some time on land."

"Well, I guess maybe I'll need to get a bigger table." Willow chuckled. "I do love a crowd though, so I'll invite her too. What's her friend's name?"

"Lea. She's been part of Captain Grace Wilde's crew—a rope and net maker," Makayla said before she shifted the topic. "I wondered what all your roles are here at Raptare, besides defense. You're a gardener too?"

"That I am. I enjoy the agriculture aspect of the enclave. I'm heading out to the orchards next, to check on the trees, and make sure the bees that have set up natural nests out there are looking healthy for pollinating. If you want to come, I'd love for you to join me."

Willow seemed to sense that Makayla was upset and wanted to keep busy. Maybe it was the fervor Makayla had put into pulling weeds—but more likely, Willow had picked up on the pain in her voice and the tears in her eyes.

Makayla worked to keep her focus on her encounter with Willow. "Quinn, who's currently sharing the co-commander position with me, is the beekeeper at Aurora. There are colonies with hives Quinn has set up. They love being a beekeeper. I used to go visit the hives a few years ago. Before the MidLand soldiers came."

"I don't have any hives set up. Maybe I could learn a few things from Quinn. But we have a few natural nests and I like to keep an eye on them." Willow stopped pulling weeds and gazed over at Makayla. "I'm so sorry for what happened to you. The battlefields. Your losses. I'm glad you're here now."

Willow's presence made Makayla miss the mother she'd never known. She'd died giving birth to her. Maybe she would have been like Willow. Kind, supportive, caring.

"Thanks. I've met some wonderful people here. And Betty and I would love to go to the orchards with you. We were going to head out there anyway, to check my ravens." Betty was busy exploring an adjacent garden box as Makayla and Willow worked.

When the day's weeding was complete, Makayla and Willow walked up and down several of the rows of trees in the orchards, and the cat and birds joined them. Then Willow invited her to help bring the dairy goats to the barn for milking.

Willow showed her how to milk them, and Makayla concentrated on enjoying her company and the antics of the goats. The silly animals played with each other, chased Betty, and one goat, Tilly, showed off how she could walk on her hind legs. Willow, half teasing, told Makayla that she was welcome to join her for chores anytime, and Makayla thought she would make an effort to do so. Just like at Aurora, she was happiest when she was busy and had a purpose.

When she was done helping Willow, Makayla escorted Betty back to Talon's office. The room was empty. The jug and tankards were now put away in the cabinet where they were stored. She checked to make sure Betty had plenty of food and water in his bowl. Talon had left some fish down for him, so he would be fine.

Since she hadn't eaten since sharing the meal earlier in Talon's office, Makayla went to the mess hall to collect some dinner. She planned to take it to her room and eat alone. As she stood in the buffet line, she saw Joe and waved at him. She was heading over to say a quick hello to Derrick when Calvin, Nina's nemesis and boss, came up next to her and closed in on her personal space. She remembered the night of the barn fire—how he'd tried to push past the crack she'd opened in her door to hear about the fate of her ravens. How he'd tried to come into her room.

Makayla moved sideways along the buffet to widen the space between them. She diligently studied the choices and selected what she wanted to eat, but Calvin closed the distance again. As he brushed his hip and shoulder against hers, the smirk on his face let her know that he was fully aware of what he was doing. He didn't let up until Willow, who had come in for dinner too, noticed and interceded by casually cutting in line between them and inviting Makayla to come join her at a table with Nina after she'd given Calvin a sharp look.

Once they were far enough away from him, Makayla thanked Willow. Then they walked over and greeted Nina, who was sitting with Lea. Nina smiled at Makayla and pointed to an empty chair at the table.

"I've been out working with Willow all day. I think I'll take the food and head up to my room. I really appreciate the offer." And with that, Makayla headed to the residence hall. When she arrived back at her room, she focused on the events of the day. She needed to figure out her course of action. Her future.

Worrying about that future brought her thoughts to Talon. Makayla hoped Talon had eaten some dinner—she certainly skipped enough meals. But then Makayla considered that maybe she'd already consumed her calories in hard cider, and hopefully, she was taking it easy.

The revelations of the day had surely impacted Talon too—revelations about losses that Talon had never been able to move beyond. The loss of her wife and her son explained the distance Talon tried to create every time there was an indication of an emotional connection, a distance that Makayla worried could never be closed. Miles of distance, even when there was no space between them.

❖

Wednesday and Thursday passed without any encounters with Talon. Every time Makayla dropped by the office to touch base with her, Talon's chair was empty. The mauve chair held Betty, so she collected him each day after lunch and left Talon a note to let her know that he was out getting some exercise.

The note was gone both days when Makayla returned with him to an empty office. Betty appreciated the taste of eggs and goat's milk that she treated him to, and she appreciated the tomcat—a straightforward being who let her know exactly where she stood. He seemed to sincerely enjoy what she could do for him, and it made her smile. He lived in the moment and seemed to expect the same of her. He never let his difficult past impact the connection they had. The simplicity of their relationship touched Makayla. It was uncomplicated and wasn't going to break her heart.

After joining the ravens in the orchards and helping Willow with more weeding, she returned Betty to his chair on Thursday afternoon. Makayla's days were devoid of Talon, and if this was what Talon wanted, she needed to honor that.

Makayla went to bed on Thursday night but had trouble sleeping. She would attend dinner at Willow's place the next night. After that, there were no plans for another full week, when the six enclave leaders would meet to finish discussing and finalize the NATO alliance.

Wide awake at three a.m., Makayla decided to get up and go for a walk. It was now early Friday morning. The moon was a pale semicircle in the clear night sky, its solar reflections offering a soft cast of silver visibility to the quiet compound landscape as Makayla strolled. Walking toward the barn, she passed the corrals.

Suddenly, several of the goats who recognized her from her time with Willow approached. Their bleating of a wary welcome as they moved toward her, free of their pen, put Makayla on alert. Something was wrong. They should have been tucked away in the shed that was in the corner of their enclosure, not out here wandering the compound outside their confinement. Alarmed, she advanced closer to the corrals and identified a human shape in the chicken coop. Not knowing what to do, she decided to make a ruckus. Surely someone on patrol would hear her.

"Who are you?" she shouted at the top of her lungs, still several feet from the silhouette, only visible because of the soft cast of lunar illumination. She couldn't tell if it was a man or a woman. "Stop what you're doing. Now!"

Makayla couldn't remember ever yelling so loudly. Not even on the battlefield when she was fighting for her life. Maybe because the animals were at risk.

The figure heard her and froze, then burst into action and charged out of the chicken coop before running in the direction of the compound living quarters. Makayla didn't know if the person was actually heading toward the housing or crossing the compound to scale the fence in an area where there was no guard. As she stood and watched, Talon and the night patrol appeared.

The patrol dispersed as they searched for the perpetrator, and Talon rushed over to Makayla.

"Are you okay, fledgling?" Talon's tone was hushed and strained with concern as she held Makayla in a prolonged protective hug. "Just what do you think that you're doing out here?" The voice speaking into Makayla's ear turned into a throaty admonishment.

"I'm fine, Talon. We need to gather the goats before they scatter and get lost or hurt."

Makayla registered Talon's worry and it touched her, but again, this felt like part of the emotional whirlwind she was caught in. She hadn't seen Talon in two days, most likely because Talon was avoiding her. She'd listened to Talon's story. Seen her pain. Heard her statement—"I can't love you back."

"We'll get to them. I want to know that you're not hurt first." Talon's distress at Makayla's encounter with the vandal persisted.

"I'm not hurt. I came out for a walk because I couldn't sleep." Makayla cajoled her. "Let's collect the goats."

The patrol members who had gone in pursuit of the vandal returned without a suspect. "Whoever it was got away. We don't even know if they went into one of our buildings, or past the fence on the far side of the compound."

Everyone had gathered around to hear what Talon and Makayla had to say when Brock came from the direction of his residence and joined them.

Talon looked at Makayla. "Did you see who it was? Is there any kind of description you can provide?"

"I'm sorry, Talon. All I saw was movement and a human shape over by the chickens. I decided to yell as loud as I could. Maybe it was the wrong move. Maybe I should have quietly gone for help, but the goats were loose and the person was going after the chickens."

"I'm just glad you're okay. It wasn't wrong to make a commotion to stop them and alert us." Talon was surprisingly calm, although she'd been that way initially with the pear tree vandalism, carefully examining the crime. Makayla was pretty sure her rage would surface soon. And it did.

"Bullspit, piss off, scum-of-the-earth vermin. They. Are. Dead." Talon bit out the last three words, one by one. This was the Talon that Makayla had been waiting for, in full fire-breathing fury protecting her den.

Brock stepped forward and looked at Talon. She nodded at him and allowed her overt wrath to subside while he organized the group. Talon turned and watched her.

"I was never in any real danger."

Talon gave her the slightest nod and quietly said, "That's good." She closed her eyes a moment, then straightened and surveyed the situation. Makayla knew Talon had every right to be upset—Raptare had been attacked again.

"You gather the goats and check the chickens. I'll join you." Brock pointed at Makayla and several of the patrol members. Then he indicated the rest of the gathered patrol members, including his son, Ash. "You go back out there and make sure we didn't miss anything. Check the fence to make sure there's not a rope or ladder for entry and exit. Also, make sure no fence wire has been cut." Then he looked at Talon, a worried expression on his face. "What do you want to do?"

"Kill the son of a bastard," Talon said without a touch of humor. Then she inhaled deeply and slowly let out the air. "I'm under control," she assured Brock. "Let me take Mak back to her quarters before I join you to finish with the livestock and check things out."

"I'm going to help round up the goats and get them back to their corral." Makayla tried not to sound like she was taking on Talon and her overprotectiveness, but bloody hell, she wasn't going to be sent to her room while there were animals who might be in danger. Talon had no right to have a say if there was to be no relationship. She had no right to a say in her life. No right to a say in her future—maybe not the future Makayla would have chosen, the one with Talon in it, but she still needed to decide what came next.

It had been three a.m. when she'd left her room, and by the time Makayla had spent time doing all she could to help gather and secure the goats, the features of the out-of-doors became more distinguishable as a precursor to dawn and the eventual start of another day. Talon insisted on escorting Makayla to the front door of her quarters and assuring that she would come to no harm.

"I could have made it here on my own, Talon." Normally, Makayla would have appreciated the gesture of caring, but not if Talon really couldn't care for the long haul.

"There's a criminal out there who doesn't know what you saw…if you can make an identification or not."

Talon justified her hovering with an added long look at Makayla. They stood silently at the residence hall door. Neither of them seemed to know what to say.

Makayla decided maybe it was time to keep words out of it, to let the silence speak. Everything had been said unless Talon had something else to offer. Makayla felt the delicate, invisible threads that tied them to each other, woven into a tapestry that she defined as love. But Talon wanted to deny those threads. Or if she felt them too, then cut them with the shards of Makayla's heart.

Makayla wiped a tear. She said nothing. Then Talon leaned in and ran her fingertips across Makayla's damp cheek. "Get some sleep, Mak." Makayla turned and went inside. Alone. Damn, love hurt.

CHAPTER TWENTY-ONE

Once in her room, Makayla decided she needed to sleep; she would be too fatigued to appreciate the dinner at Willow's if she didn't get some rest. She wasn't sure what she wanted to do after she'd met that obligation. Being this close to Talon, but rejected, would rip her apart. Shred her. Cut to ribbons by Talon the Terrible. Makayla would have laughed if she didn't feel so miserable. If she didn't want to cry so badly.

Makayla lay on her bed and tried to doze until it was early afternoon. When she couldn't rest anymore, she made preparations to create a warm bath in the tub down the hall. The bath did nothing to relieve the ache in her chest, but she did manage to soak herself clean.

She left a bit early for Willow's place, swinging into the barn and corrals to check her not-so-unkindness and look in on the goats. Finally, after burying her feelings and plastering on a smile, she went to dinner.

Brock answered Willow's door with a grin and led her into the common area, which was very similar to Talon's residence. Like Talon's place, this main living area had a wood fireplace for heat, and at the far end was a compact kitchen area, and a door led into the bedroom with a small attached bathroom. However, Willow had set up the living area differently than Talon had arranged hers—a large table took up the open space that Talon had maintained. She did have an arrangement of chairs located off to one side, so the common area appeared well-used.

As Makayla entered, she could hear talking and laughter. Willow was in the kitchen working, but still able to carry on a conversation with Ash, Ivy, Nina, and Lea, who were sitting at the large dining table in the living room with hard cider in front of them. Makayla looked around, greeted everyone, and then in a low voice she asked Brock, "No Talon tonight?"

"We invited her, but she indicated she had a lot to do. I know these vandal attacks are consuming her, not that there's a lot she can do about them. I think she's just stewing." Brock looked directly at Makayla. "Over a number of things." Then he cleared his throat. "We're going to have to get lucky to catch the instigator. And when we do, it's probably not going to be pretty."

Talon was avoiding her—Makayla's heart quivered in the ache of what she knew to be the truth. Another round of rebuff. Makayla knew she couldn't continue this way. Especially when Talon had made herself clear—Talon couldn't love her back.

Talon had changed her these past several weeks, these past several months if she was being honest. Talon had caused Makayla to examine what she wanted in life, and that included balance. She'd led Makayla to believe in the future and given her hope. Makayla didn't want to try to live with a hollow void in her heart where Talon had lived. But Talon was offering her no choice. To stay in Raptare when Talon had rejected her, rejected love, would only fully shatter her heart.

And right then, Makayla made a decision. She'd make it through this dinner, then it was time to move on. She saw no reason to stay. She'd go back to Aurora to live and figure out with the consultation council the best fit for her talents. She needed to tell Quinn and Rosa that she didn't want to command the enclave. She could remain at Aurora, or return temporarily to Raptare for a few days with Quinn in a week to finalize the NATO defense if others were agreeable. That was the type of focus she liked and was good at. But it was time to get on with her life. Time to leave Raptare.

After burying the conclusion that she'd just reached at the dinner party, Makayla tried to make the best of the evening and immerse herself in the caring and congeniality that these people of

Raptare were offering her. They had become the closest thing to family that she had.

Willow had cooked a wild turkey stew with garden potatoes and carrots, and she'd made biscuits and a side salad. The food was delicious and the conversation was lively. The topics jumped around. They included Lea's adventures on the *Hell's Belles* sailing ship and stories of Grace Wilde as its captain, Nina's adventures in the elementary school classroom, Ivy's observations with the enclave healer May Lin, a refrained mention of the NATO alliance, and a final mention of the vandalism occurring at the compound.

Makayla didn't feel like talking, so she mostly sat and considered how she would miss these people. Not like she would miss Talon—nothing close to the anguish she felt with Talon, but she cared for them. She cared for Ash, Ivy, and Nina as friends, and Brock and Willow in parental roles—Brock had helped take up the void that the death of her father had created, and Willow was the image of a mother she'd never known.

It was after ten p.m. when Makayla wished everyone a good night with prolonged hugs and returned to her room. She would get some sleep and then implement her heart-wrenching decision. Her life had been in turmoil for well over two years now, and she couldn't keep living this way. She had to try to move on.

Makayla climbed out of bed while it was still dark. She'd filled her backpack with her belongings after she'd returned from dinner last night, so it was ready to go. She'd brought the full backpack and an additional bag of clothes when she'd arrived from Aurora for a prolonged stay, so not everything fit into the pack and she couldn't carry it all. She'd decided to leave some clothing items in the dresser and retrieve them when she temporarily returned for the final alliance discussions for a few days, or if she stayed in Aurora, Quinn could collect them. She left Nina's books on the bed so they could be returned to her, as well as the bowls for Betty's food and water.

Lastly, she went to the top drawer of the dresser and opened it. She ran her fingers into the front right corner and lifted out the little gold heart she'd placed there. She picked it up and carefully deposited it into a pocket of her jacket.

Makayla had written a note and placed that into her other pocket before she'd gone to bed last night—she checked to make sure it was still there. Then she took a final survey of the familiar room before she hoisted the backpack onto her shoulders and secured the sheathed machete to her waist, then quietly closed the door behind her. As she exited her residence hall building, the moon cast enough light for her to navigate without issue. Her feet knew their way to Talon's office.

She'd planned the very early awakening with the hope that nobody would be around. The main leadership building entrance door was usually open, but the individual offices were locked. Talon had given Makayla a spare key to her office door, and either Talon or Brock usually locked it after hours when Talon wasn't there.

After removing her pack and setting it in the hallway against the wall, Makayla opened Talon's door and headed to the bookshelf where she lit the candle. The taper offered a soft glow that filled the room, a room where she'd spent hours with both the commander of Raptare and Talon the Tenderhearted—one and the same individual, but two distinct personas. Not that the woman she'd come to love wasn't always present under those layers of leadership she chose to wear, layers she wore as protection against assaults on a heart that had once been completely broken. Seemingly, damaged beyond repair.

Makayla reached into her jacket pocket and took out the pendant. She set the little gold heart in the center of the doily where Talon would see it. It had been with her since the day she'd first encountered Talon. She touched the heart, then wiped her eyes. Under the doily, with a corner sticking out beyond the lace edge, she shoved the folded note. It was a simple note:

This is home…because home is where the heart is. And you own mine.

Love was never a choice for me—the fledgling fell in love with the dragon woman.

Your songbird always,

Makayla Melospiza melodia

After taking a last look at Betty's empty mauve chair, Makayla went over and blew out the candle. She started to set the key to Talon's office on the desk, but then decided to keep it because it was a tangible piece of her time with Talon. She placed it in her pocket after relocking Talon's door. She lifted the backpack onto her shoulders, then turned and took her leave down the hallway with a heart that was lodged in her throat.

Makayla slipped out of the leadership building, vigilant in her silent closure of the door, careful to tread softly on her walk to the barn. The black veil of darkness had barely begun to lift, even though the sun hadn't yet broken the juncture where the sky met land. A mist of fog ghosted the compound structures and revealed them as large looming boxes of various sizes.

As she headed to the barn, Makayla remained as quiet as possible so she wouldn't draw attention in case anyone was close. She listened for the patrols that guarded the compound but heard only silence. Her biggest worry was encountering Talon, but she hoped that Talon would still be asleep in her quarters with Betty at this early hour.

In her practiced greeting to her trio of ravens, Makayla expelled the softest whistle she could manage on entering the barn. While she waited for her not-so-unkindness to realize she was there, the feral rat catchers wandered out from their beds to see what was going on. They purred and meowed their welcome.

"I'm sorry. I don't have any eggs for you—it's too early. I'm going to miss you all."

Makayla fought down her feelings of loss. She'd made up her mind that she needed to leave Raptare, and becoming sentimental about the barn cats wouldn't make heading back to Aurora any easier.

When they realized she had no food to share, the cats headed deeper into the barn, probably looking to catch breakfast before returning to their sleeping quarters later in the day for a nap. After all, she knew that cats were naturally crepuscular—most active during the twilight hours of sunrise and sunset.

In the safety of the feline absence, the birds swooped down to the barn floor to greet Makayla with their friendly chatter. They noticed her backpack, which they seemed to know likely intimated more than a simple walk through the orchards. Poe strutted closer and offered her a questioning look.

"Yup. We're going for a hike. Back to Aurora. Are you three up for it? I need your company today."

Poe clicked his agreement, and Ed and Al croaked along. With the certainty that they would follow, she headed out the barn door into the early blush of dawn.

She had to exit through the gate because she didn't want to try to scale the fence with her belongings. Luckily, the young man on guard duty only half-heartedly lifted a hand to note her exit as she left the compound.

It would be a full day of travel back to Aurora, but Makayla was no stranger to long days of walking. She set a good pace because she had twelve miles to cover before nightfall. She'd placed several pieces of venison jerky and a few apples in her pack so that she could stop for a few breaks on the trek and refuel, as well as fill her bottles with additional water so she wouldn't dehydrate. Taking turns leading, circling, and trailing, the ravens resumed their established custom of escorting Makayla's progress through the woods.

As Makayla traversed that first mile of countryside on the trip north to Aurora, she mentally traveled her decision to leave Raptare and return to Aurora. Returning to Aurora felt nothing like the same trek she'd made six months ago. She was no longer heading home. Aurora did not offer the things she considered as defining *home*.

She believed in love—in loving and being loved. The beauty, the joy, the passion, the contentment. Makayla wanted those things with Talon, and it made her cry as she trudged away from the enclave. Considering her not-so-unkindness, Makayla noted how the ravens had each other. Sparrows grouped in a host. Hawks in a kettle. Eagles a convocation. Robins a round. Damn, even mythical dragons grouped in a thunder. But she, Makayla Odin, felt so alone.

Makayla and the trio were another mile into their journey, and the lower sky was glazed in a golden glow as the morning mist slowly evaporated in measure to the slow ascension of the sun. She moved forward, taking in her surroundings. The woodlands were lush and green, an ecosystem of plants and animals. Out here in the bushes and trees she could hear the morning activity of birds singing to their mates and seeking food.

The ravens flew above the canopy of limbs and leaves, descending on occasion to land on a branch near Makayla, stopping to chat and rest. They were not far inland as they headed north up the coast, and the foliage filtered the daylight and cast shadows on the path she walked.

Ed led the way, with Al and Poe taking turns trailing and circling Makayla. They had settled into a tag-like rhythm when Al let out a shrill call from behind, followed by the other two circling back to check out his warning. Makayla shifted to high alert while the birds remained above the arboreal blanket and at a distance, so they couldn't be easily injured.

The ravens' actions led Makayla to believe that she was being tracked, although she could not yet see or hear anything. They were reliable harbingers of danger—they'd proven so many times since she'd adopted them. Trepidation brought Makayla's mind and emotions back into the moment and increased her speed. There was no safety in reversing course and heading back into the hands of whoever was behind her.

The trio's alerts didn't let up as she picked up her pace and covered another mile, but Makayla had the feeling from the birds' increased anxiety that whoever or whatever was out there was gaining on her. The sun had fully crested the horizon and was slowly ascending upward as the morning progressed. Continuing to move north as rapidly as she could manage, she hoped it was fast enough.

Not having consumed any food or drink since the dinner the evening before, Makayla was feeling hungry and thirsty as she completed her fourth mile, but she didn't dare slow down. She readjusted her pack and pressed forward as rapidly as she could manage. At about mile five, with the birds still apprising her of danger, Makayla tripped on a branch that had fallen across the pathway. She went down hard, her backpack landing on top of her. As she started to get back up, ready to unsheathe her machete, arms grabbed her from behind. Turning over, she stared directly into the face of someone she never expected to see out here in the woods, and not many feet away was Babe. Her pursuer had taken the time to steal the horse before trailing her north.

"What the hell, Derrick?" Makayla couldn't help but express her anger and confusion.

Derrick looked nervous, his mouth pinched and his pupils dilated. As Makayla struggled to free herself, he held on tighter. Poe flew down to intervene, knowing that Makayla was in trouble. He landed a safe distance from Derrick, projecting a full threat display with facial feathers extended—throat hackles and ear tufts fluffed out to increase his size and villainize his appearance. Derrick reached behind his back and pulled an old handgun from his waistband.

"Cooperate, or I'll shoot your wretched ravens." He waved the gun around wildly with one hand as he clung to Makayla's arm with his other.

Makayla froze. She wasn't going to risk injury or death to any of her birds. She gave Poe an upward head tilt toward the sky. He flew into a nearby tree.

"That's better," Derrick said. "Now, throw your machete over there." Derrick pointed toward a tree a few feet to her right.

Makayla complied. "Where did you get the gun? I didn't know anyone at the enclave had their own gun. I thought they were in the enclave arsenal, except for maybe the few patrol and leadership weapons."

Makayla wondered who Derrick actually was. She'd thought he was just a guy in his mid-twenties who worked in the woodshop and the orchards at Raptare, but she'd definitely missed something.

"My cousin gave it to me. Part of my great-uncle Ezra's collection—he died a decade ago and was from an enclave you'd know, Aurora." Derrick sounded smug as he imparted information Makayla didn't know.

"From Aurora." Makayla considered this. She went through her memory, but the name Ezra didn't register. "I don't remember him, but he's been gone a while then."

His relaxed demeanor was nowhere in evidence as she continued to study Derrick. He seemed agitated and tense.

Makayla fought her panic. She didn't want to show her consternation in the hope that if she portrayed calm, maybe Derrick wouldn't do anything irrational. At least any more irrational than he'd already done. "So, how did you happen to be way out here this morning?"

"I was out in the dark. Going to destroy some of those orchard beehives at Raptare. But then I saw you leave and followed you." Derrick seemed pleased with his actions.

The more she heard, the more alarmed Makayla became, although she fought to show no signs of her state of distress. Derrick was involved in the vandalism at Raptare if he was out to destroy the beehives. The ones she and Willow had checked. The bees would have been inside them during the night. He would have done real damage if he'd killed a large number of bees because they were essential to the agriculture at any enclave.

"Followed me? Is there something I can help you with?" Makayla tried to keep the conversation on a friendly level.

Derrick scratched his head. It seemed his actions in following and capturing her had been rather spontaneous, a result of opportunity. That was probably better than a well-conceived and coordinated plan, but she knew that spontaneity could result in very bad outcomes too. And his admissions and actions suggested he was unbalanced.

"I'm taking you to a cabin. Secluded in the deep woods of Sylvan."

Sylvan was the enclave mostly east and slightly south of Aurora. So, that indicated the cabin was probably several miles from where they were now.

"What do you plan to do with me?" Makayla grew more nervous as she realized that she would be isolated and in the hands of a disturbed Derrick. Derrick had no soft spot for her. She'd rejected his advances. And he seemed to have a grudge against Raptare if he was the vandal.

Then, as Makayla was considering all this, Derrick took the handgun by the barrel, raised it, and hit her over the head hard enough that the world went black.

CHAPTER TWENTY-TWO

Makayla floated between awareness and sleep, the balance weighing increasingly on the side of awareness as she was gently rocked through her state of disorientation. Physically transported in a fore-and-aft motion. Was she in the rocking chair on her grandfather's lap? No, she was an adult and he was gone.

She slowly sobered to the fact that it hadn't been sleep. She had a severe headache and the side of her face stung, as if it had been scraped. Her throat was dry. She was sitting astride something, slumped forward, her hands tied at the wrists. Astride something that was shifting beneath her as it progressed forward. Slowly, she became more cognizant. She straightened a bit and rotated her gaze back and forth in a one-hundred-eighty-degree arc, realizing she'd been slumped forward with her wrists tightly tied to the saddle horn of Babe so she wouldn't fall off.

They moved through the trees with Derrick rapidly walking ahead and leading the horse, extended woodlands on either side of their path. She had no idea where they were, even as the events of the morning began to play back through her memory and adrenaline blasted through her body. Her heart pounded wildly in her chest. Do. Not. Panic.

The sky was a clear, beautiful cerulean, and the sun was overhead and slightly to the west with warm rays filtering in through the mix of oaks and firs. Makayla didn't think she'd been unconscious for too long, so it was undoubtedly still Saturday, and early afternoon. They were moving northeast based on the position of the glowing orb in the sky.

As she sat up even straighter and looked around, Makayla first saw Poe flying parallel to them, and in turning her head to look back, she took in Al and Ed trailing behind. All three birds were shadowing them, but keeping a safe distance.

They maintained that mode of travel all afternoon with a short rest stop, and then as twilight approached, they came to a green meadow with a stream. The water flowed rapidly past and broke in white caps around small boulders that barely exposed their smooth gray tops above the waterline. A mist began to creep in, chilling and dampening what little was left of the day.

Derrick decided it was time to stop. He helped Makayla dismount after he momentarily untied her wrists from the saddle horn, then retied them before he allowed her to relieve herself in the woods. There was no hesitation in his threat to shoot Babe or her birds if she tried to run, the same warning he'd made when they'd stopped for the afternoon break.

Once she was seated near the fire he'd built, he tied her ankles too. Derrick had obviously been in such a hurry when he left Raptare that he had no belongings and neither of them had bedding, although they both wore jackets.

"I have a little water and some food in my backpack."

Derrick grabbed her pack and rummaged through it until he found what he was looking for—her water bottles and some jerky and apples. Makayla managed to hold the drink and then the food between her tied hands. She gulped down the supplies, her mouth dry and her stomach empty and churning from hunger.

After leading Babe to the stream, Derrick let Babe drink while he refilled the bottles. Then he tethered the horse so she could graze without wandering off during the night. Makayla watched her not-so-unkindness move out a distance from the campsite to find night accommodations of their own.

Would Talon come looking for her? Makayla prayed she would, but it was more likely that she'd assume that Makayla had gone to Aurora after reading the note and learning her backpack was gone. Talon would have no idea where she was as Derrick took her northeast toward some cabin in the woods in the Sylvan enclave.

Although she was cold, Makayla managed to doze as she leaned against her backpack near the fire. Exhaustion simply overtook her, and she was grateful for the brief escape from her stress. In the morning, Derrick was up early so they could head out when the sun came up. The birds were awake too and remained off in the trees while they observed and waited to follow wherever Makayla went.

"It's Sunday? What's the plan today?" Makayla hoped she might be able to gather some useful information that would help her escape this dangerous situation.

"Yes, Sunday. We should be there by midafternoon. Walking is a lot slower than riding, but I don't think Babe would make it with two of us on her. She's getting old."

Makayla thought about Babe. How she was a victim of this abduction too. Well, at least maybe he cared about the horse. Or maybe it was just about making sure they reached the destination— he had threatened to shoot Babe.

"Why the vandalism against Raptare?" Makayla asked him.

"My sister, Rhea. She got tangled with Talon a few years ago. Totally taken with the bitch. Talon didn't return her feelings, and my sister finally left Raptare and had a fatal accident on her way to Gull Town. I blame Talon. I wanted to rile her. Shake the enclave's trust in her leadership. Payback." Derrick scowled as he fumed about what had happened to his sister.

Makayla didn't say anything. She knew Talon's history. Her story. Her reasons. And of course, she knew personally that you couldn't make someone love you, if that's what Derrick's sister had been looking for. She knew for a fact that Talon didn't lead women on—she crushed the first hint of attachment with her little speech about not doing romance.

"I'm sorry about your sister." That was all Makayla could think to say without running the risk of upsetting Derrick further.

With Makayla remounted on Babe, and Derrick trekking ahead with reins in hand, they moved into another long day of putting distance between Makayla and either enclave she knew. With her wrists tied to the saddle horn and her ravens never coming too close, they moved forward. Besides the fear and uncertainty, the realization that someone had again stolen control of her life infuriated Makayla.

❖

It was late afternoon, and sunlight tilted long shadows in the increasingly dim forest landscape. Their path broke from the trees onto an open clearing. Sitting to the far edge of the expanse was a cabin. Not a newer structure, but one composed of grayish-brown, weathered wood. The roof was in disrepair, and there was a pile of junk off to one side of the building. A tall, stocky man stood silhouetted in the open doorway. Who was that?

The distance between them and the man in the doorway diminished as they drew closer. Makayla could see that the porch and its handrail were missing boards, and the open-air windows were defined by interior cloth coverings that blocked the opportunity for an inside view. Makayla kept her attention on the man as they drew closer. At the moment, she could finally make out the features of his face, her breathing stopped. It was Bull Puckett.

Her expression likely mirrored his—absolute shock. But Makayla had to believe it wasn't for the same reasons—hers was instigated by feelings of loathing disbelief, his likely by jubilant disbelief. Then his expression morphed into an ugly, calculating grin.

"What have we here, cousin?" Bull slurred. He sounded like he'd spent the day imbibing. "I didn't expect to see you coming by for at least another week. I didn't think you could get away from Raptare."

"I saw an opportunity and took it," Derrick replied. "Makayla Odin." He nodded toward her.

"Co-commander of the enclave Aurora," Bull finished for him. Makayla knew that Bull had wanted the power to make decisions in Aurora. That he hated her family. That he, by extension, hated her. And that she was in deep trouble. She'd had no clue that Derrick was Bull's cousin.

"Well, bring her in," Bull said. "Show some manners." Then Bull sauntered back inside and only a black vacant hole in the doorway remained where he had just stood. A hole into the abode of the damned.

Derrick untied her wrists and watched as she slid off Babe. Then he took the horse to an ancient corral off to the side of the cabin where posts and boards barely maintained an enclosure, a corral that Makayla hadn't noticed as she'd scouted the man on the porch on their approach.

Her hands were momentarily liberated from the constraints of the rope, Derrick was occupied with Babe, and Bull was back inside the cabin, so Makayla reached into her pocket and tossed Talon's office key out as far as she could into the meadow. She watched Poe swoop in and retrieve it, then fly away in the direction of Raptare. Straight toward Talon de LaTerre. As the raven flies, she thought. And Makayla prayed that he would reach Talon.

Throughout Sunday evening, Bull continued to imbibe from a jug that appeared to be filled with a golden-brown hard cider. While Makayla sat trussed up in a corner, tied at the wrists and the ankles, she leaned with her back against the wall of the cabin's only room and watched as Derrick fretted. She listened as he and Bull discussed the possibilities. They sat in chairs at an old wooden table in the center of the room, the only furniture besides a couple of sleeping pads with blankets against the far wall.

"Aurora will want her back. They'll pay in goods like weapons and supplies." Bull studied her as he talked to Derrick. "And horses," he added, as the thought came to him.

"The commander at Raptare, Talon, has taken a liking to her. A personal liking." Derrick twisted his face in disdain as he mentioned Talon's name. "But Talon's a bitch. The one who got Rhea killed because she doesn't care about anyone. So, I don't know if we can get something from Raptare as well as Aurora."

Makayla heard Derrick's assessment. Maybe Talon refused to love her, but she hoped that Talon at least cared enough to come looking for her. Especially if Poe showed up, hopefully with Makayla's key to Talon's office as a hint that Makayla had sent him.

"We'll need to think about the logistics of this. What we want. How to collect without getting caught, and making sure if anyone is going to die, it's not us." Bull drank more while he talked. Derrick let Bull carry the conversation, although no useful decisions were made before Bull finally passed out and Derrick fell asleep.

Makayla was terrified and uncomfortable. Her head still pounded and the side of her face stung where she'd abraded it when she'd passed out from the gun blow to her head. She dozed from exhaustion but certainly didn't feel rested when daybreak finally arrived. She remained silent as Bull's and Derrick's snoring persisted while the morning progressed. The more prolonged their sleep, the more chance she had of being rescued before Bull and Derrick took any action that would lead to confrontation and her harm. At least she hoped that was the case.

Finally, the amount of light entering the cabin interior through the tattered cloth tacked over the window space reached a level consistent with the luminosity of late morning. It was Monday. Derrick woke up, but Bull slumbered on. Makayla wouldn't be surprised if he had a hangover when he finally surfaced.

Derrick headed over to a metal box in the corner of the cabin and opened it. He rummaged through the contents and extracted some flat pieces of dried venison, saved from foraging woodland creatures by their placement in the container. There was no food left in Makayla's backpack. Derrick placed one piece of meat into her tied hands, ate one himself, and put one on the table for Bull.

After untying her wrists and ankles, Derrick escorted Makayla outside to an outhouse behind the cabin after he'd brandished his pistol at the corral where Babe waited patiently, a warning that Makayla had better not cause trouble. She noticed there was a wooden bucket in the corral with water for the horse. Tall clumps of green grass sprouting from the corral floor indicated the absence of any recent animal presence in the pen. Makayla was hopeful that

Babe had enough to eat. When she saw Ed and Al in the trees, her anxiety was eased. The fact that Poe was absent offered her a sliver of hope that there was a chance she might be rescued.

Bull was awake when Makayla and Derrick reentered the cabin. His hair was uncombed and spiked out in various directions, and he needed a shave. He looked unkempt but alert. Makayla returned to her corner, her wrists and ankles resecured by Derrick. Then Bull and Derrick sat at the table, a quill pen, walnut ink, and paper in front of Bull.

Bull and Derrick drank all day. They talked and planned and argued about a course of action. It seemed that neither of them had come well-stocked with food, but Bull had remembered his hard cider. Sparse offerings of dried venison were the only food available. Finally, after the sun set again, her captors passed out.

Makayla had another painful, fitful night as she tried to get some rest, bound up on the hard floor. She was grateful when Derrick woke up on Tuesday morning and took her outside for some relief. Then, Bull and Derrick spent another day trying to decide on a plan.

Bull was sober enough that he wrote as he and Derrick talked. He made a list of items they would demand as ransom from Aurora for the return of Makayla. She heard Bull tell Derrick that his plan was to ambush the ransom delivery person in a remote site; the person would be instructed to appear alone. They would surprise the individual, steal the supplies and horses and weapons they'd placed on the list, and then return to the cabin. Their scheming called for them to repeat the plan with Raptare. After that, they'd ride and lead the horses out of the area with the goods they'd acquired.

Makayla saw a lot of things that could go wrong with the plan, and a great deal of opportunity for someone to get hurt, including herself. Especially because they hadn't made it clear what her planned fate would be. Bull was no criminal mastermind, and Derrick was simply a sidekick. A sidekick who would leave for Aurora the next day, Wednesday, to deliver the note.

That evening was another several hours of heavy imbibing by Bull. There was little food left, and because Bull was drinking his dinner, Derrick divided the last piece of dried meat in the metal box with Makayla. As it grew darker, she tried to relax. Tired, stiff, and extremely hungry, she prayed for rescue. Her face hurt, and she still had a headache. She'd experienced some extremely dangerous times with the MidLanders that she'd survived, and she only hoped that she'd survive this ordeal too.

❖

Makayla's eyes flew open as the ambiance of Wednesday's morning light filtered into the cabin through the window cloth, and defined the shapes that filled the room. The hours were dragging. Last Saturday, the day she'd left Raptare, felt like weeks ago. If she was lucky enough to share a retelling, maybe it would seem that time flew, but in the moment, she felt every tick of time.

Makayla realized that the sun had been up for a while by the degree of clarity. Bull and Derrick were recumbent on the bed pads spread out on the floor, their snoring and heavy breathing the only sounds she could hear. Two cups and an empty jug of hard cider sat on the wooden table, abandoned from last night. Then, from outside, she heard what she thought was Poe's croak. She was afraid it was just wishful thinking—she wanted so badly for this nightmare to end.

After carefully inching herself up to a sitting posture from her painful, slumped position on the floor, Makayla listened intently. She tried to shut out the cacophony of respiratory noise that filled the room—an atrocious serenade of sniffling, snorting, and wheezing racket that would have kept her up all night if she hadn't been so physically and mentally drained.

Above this auditory pandemonium produced by her two snoozing captors, Makayla heard again what she thought was Poe's call. She silently pushed herself up even straighter. She was sitting there quietly and putting all her energy into trying to decipher any noise coming from outside the cabin when she heard a rush of movement and the front door flew open.

After that, the cascade of events became a series of actions that unfolded in slow motion: Talon and Brock bursting into the cabin—Brock raising his gun and Talon raising her long knife—Bull sitting up and wildly firing his weapon at Makayla—Talon throwing her long knife at Bull before Brock could fire off an initial shot—Talon saving Makayla before Bull could fire off a second shot—other people, including Ash and the Sylvan commander, James, entering behind Talon and Brock—Derrick raising his hands in surrender—Talon rushing to throw herself over Makayla to shield her—the roar of chaos filling the room—the soft sound of Talon whispering into Makayla's ear. Five whispered words.

In the past, Talon had spoken five words that now lived in Makayla's broken heart. *I can't love you back.* She'd told Makayla that she didn't do romance. Makayla's charted future had been inadequate before the events of recent days, always charted by others. And always plans that didn't consider who she was and didn't take into account the things she really desired from life.

Makayla wanted plans that included a leadership role with a focus, but not a commandership, even if Talon refused to be in her life. And now she'd woken this morning in even deeper despair—once again a captive of monstrous men holding her as a tool for their goals of influence, dominance, and power.

But now, suddenly, spectacularly, Makayla was immersed in hope. Talon's admission, with those five words just now whispered into her ear altered who she might finally become to Talon. Maybe Talon didn't simply see her as the commander of Aurora, but maybe she saw Makayla in a more fitting leadership role.

Not only had Talon rescued her from her captors, but with those five words, Talon had given her back hope. Hope that her life could be balanced with the things she valued. And it wasn't because Talon had simply repeated the three words Makayla had spoken to Talon, "I love you," but because Talon de LaTerre had admitted, "Oh God, I love you."

❖

Makayla couldn't believe that Talon had finally declared her love, said the words she wanted to hear. Words she needed to hear.

And, as if the prior admission had broken a dam and she couldn't help herself, Talon spoke again, so loud that everyone could hear, "I love you, fledgling."

Makayla was hopeful that meant Talon was willing to consider a future with her in it, that Talon had decided she was worth the risk that came with loving someone, and that Talon wouldn't create emotional distance every time they grew close.

Makayla wasn't exactly sure what the future held, but now she had hope that all decisions wouldn't be made for her. She would be able to live a life more aligned with both her personal and professional desires. Makayla wanted to do good things, but she didn't want to do them with a huge void in her heart—the place that Talon occupied. And with those thoughts, Makayla breathed easier for the first time in a very long time. She wanted to go home. To Raptare. Where her heart was.

Talon untied Makayla, but had her remain in the corner while the chaos in the cabin started to subside. James and his patrol told Talon and Brock that they were happy to have been able to assist them, and then they mounted up and headed back to Sylvan. They'd encountered the three Raptare riders tracking Poe's flight yesterday and joined them in the search for Makayla. They'd camped with them in the dark, then accompanied them as they'd followed Poe to the remote cabin this morning to assist in whatever way they could.

Brock and Ash took charge of burying Bull, who hadn't survived the knife to his chest. Derrick sat tied to one of the cabin chairs as he awaited his return to Raptare, guilty of vandalism and kidnapping—and stupidity. Makayla almost felt sorry for him, but his fate would be up to the consultation council at Raptare, and he had caused a great deal of mayhem. Makayla had faced death these past two years, and she accepted that Talon had taken the only action she could against Bull if she hadn't wanted to end up dead. Hell, Makayla was extremely lucky his shot had missed her.

Talon confirmed that everything was under control before leading Makayla outside where she could be with her birds and enjoy some fresh air. Talon didn't let her out of her sight. After Makayla had a chance to calm herself a bit more, Talon ran the back of her hand gently down Makayla's cheek, the one that hadn't been hurt. The touch was light and caring. It suggested Talon wanted physical contact just to confirm that Makayla was truly there with her.

"How did this happen?" Talon nodded to the injuries on the other side of Makayla's face. The tone of her voice left no doubt she had no qualms about the demise of Bull Puckett, that there was no measure of forgiveness for what had happened to Makayla.

"Derrick knocked me out—it happened when I fell to the ground."

The rage in Talon's eyes was evident. "Did they harm you in any other way?"

Makayla assured her that the two men hadn't personally touched her, a declaration that probably prevented an immediate death sentence for Derrick.

Talon nodded. Then she pulled Makayla in for a long, slow kiss. She gently explored Makayla's mouth with her tongue, held Makayla's lower lip between her own lips, and then surrendered Makayla's name in a low sensual moan. Talon refused to let her go until their departure was imminent.

"If you're going to give me a hot, fuck-me kiss, you'd better mean it," Makayla advised her.

"Oh, I mean it, Mak," Talon advised her right back. Then she led Makayla over to the group of people organizing to depart the cabin. Each of the Raptare members had a horse. When clean-up was complete, Brock put on Makayla's backpack and mounted his horse, then escorted the wrist-tied Derrick to Babe and helped him mount.

Ash climbed astride his horse and headed out first, in the direction of Aurora.

"We'd ridden north all the way to Aurora before Poe found us. Ash needs to let them know that we found you," Brock told Makayla. "Aurora has people searching closer to their enclave."

Talon indicated that she would help Makayla onto the saddleless Thunder. Makayla's eyes widened. The stallion, Thunder. Bareback.

"It's okay, Mak. I'm going to be sitting right behind you. I won't let anything happen to you."

Before they mounted the horse, Talon came up to Makayla and faced her. Makayla took in the signature golden swathe streaking Talon's dark tresses. She took in those brilliant blue eyes, then she studied the moist, delectable lips that she'd just kissed. Makayla had been so afraid that she'd never see Talon again.

A piece of cotton string, the twine Makayla had shared with Betty in Talon's office, hung as a necklace, encircling Talon's neck. Makayla let her gaze drop to the top curves of Talon's smooth breasts, exposed by the three-button opening at the throat of Talon's sepia shirt. Nestled in Talon's cleavage, suspended at the bottom of that cotton string, was the little gold heart that Makayla had left behind on the doily for Talon on the morning she'd left the note. The heart that was a reminder that there was still love in this world.

Brock rode his horse and led Babe with Derrick tied to her saddle. Talon, regal as a raptor, perched atop Thunder with Makayla encased against the front of her warm body, arms almost hugging Makayla's torso as they extended forward and held the reins. The stallion seemed to sense how fragile Makayla was and offered none of his normal attitude.

The hero of the day was Poe, who escorted them with all the attitude that Thunder had suppressed. He landed in branches along the way, puffing out his chest, and vocalizing his pleasure regarding the entire outcome of his actions. Al and Ed followed from behind as the group rode through the woodlands, southwest toward Raptare in the pleasant afternoon weather.

Talon exhaled warm air onto the back of Makayla's neck and actually touched her mouth to the primed area on occasion as the horse jostled her forward and Makayla backward. Neither of them tried to prevent the intimacy.

Talon leaned forward to speak into Makayla's ear, not missing the opportunity to press her front even more tightly against Makayla's back. "We're going to have to camp for the night when the sun goes down. We departed in a rush, soon after I found the note you left. I was busy and didn't see it until late on Saturday, so we only made a little progress before the sun set that evening." Talon kissed the area behind Makayla's ear. "And we were headed due north to Aurora, but we were searching with no luck. Poe showed up with the key on our third day out, yesterday, after we'd gone from Raptare to Aurora and then left Aurora without encountering you. We wouldn't have found you without him. He must have flown to Raptare to find me, then up to Aurora, and now here." Talon tortured her a little more, letting her lips capture Makayla's ear lobe. "So only a few blankets to share strapped to Brock's saddle. I guess we'll just have to keep each other warm." Talon didn't sound too distressed about the sleeping situation.

"Almost like old times. Except for these chaperones."

"Chaperones. Lucky for you." Talon nuzzled Makayla's neck again. Then she growled. "You scared the hell out of me, Mak. You've got some penance to do."

Makayla was drained, but Talon was rejuvenating her. This was the Talon she knew and loved. "Penance, huh? Now the dragon woman is scaring me." Makayla chuckled.

"You should be scared. I'm not happy with you. We're going to have a serious talk when we get back to Raptare." Talon's tone was much lighter than her declaration of "a serious talk" indicated.

"Is this talk going to be before or after the penance? Because I think I'd like to do *the penance* first. Soften you up for the talk." Makayla hoped Talon could hear the humor in her voice. "Maybe the kind of penance that doesn't require a lot of attire."

Talon chuckled. "That doesn't sound like penance to me."

Makayla wished she wasn't facing forward, away from Talon. She wanted to look at her. Kiss her. "You know that I love you. It's the only reason I left. So that you wouldn't break me."

"I know you love me, Mak. And now you know that I love you. All we have to do is figure out the rest."

"We've done the hard part. And we both know Raptare is home. So all we have to figure out is if you're finally going to let me into your bed," Makayla replied.

Talon leaned way forward and kissed the side of Makayla's throat before moving back and speaking into her ear. "No. All we have to figure out is if I'm going to let you *out* of *our* bed."

❖

They spent the night in the woods, Makayla wrapped around Talon, but she behaved herself with Brock and Derrick sleeping only feet away. Or at least mostly behaved herself. She wasn't going to release Talon. She'd thought that she'd lost her forever, and she'd felt hollow without her. Empty. But tonight, Talon's love made her whole. The only one in the world who could complete her. And she thought she was finally the same for Talon.

They woke early the next morning and finished the trip to Raptare by late afternoon. Makayla was still exhausted by the time they arrived, and Talon kept her upright on Thunder. Brock took the horses and headed to the barn with Derrick still tied to Babe.

"I'll make sure your birds are settled in, trespasser," Brock said. "I'll see that they have food and water. They're heroes in my book. I'll get one of the patrol members to take Derrick over to the building with the local Raptare law enforcement. He's lucky we're not leaving him to the mercy of Talon because I don't think she'd show him much."

Makayla was more exhausted than she'd been in a long time. Talon took Makayla to her home, where Willow had left Betty. Betty was pleased to see them and jumped down from Talon's bed as they entered.

Makayla gave Talon her best exhausted, but suggestive look. "So, is this going to be our first night together in a real bed? I owe you, and you once told me that you'd collect."

Talon's indigo eyes blazed with desire, but she took on a stern demeanor. "You're taking a bath, and I'm going out to greet the commanders who have started arriving. Tomorrow is Friday, and it's the day of our big multi-enclave NATO meeting, in case you haven't kept up with your calendar."

Makayla looked at Talon in surprise, but as she considered, she realized almost a week had passed since her dinner at Willow's place with Brock, Ash, Ivy, Nina, and Lea—the night she'd made her decision to leave Raptare for Aurora.

"What can I do to help?" Makayla asked.

"You can get clean so you don't ruin my sheets, then crawl into bed and get some sleep. I'll go do the commander greetings, catch up on the alliance work I need to do for tomorrow because I've been gone as well, and then come back to check on you. If you're not snoring, it's the wrath of Talon the Terrible." Talon gave her that menacing Commander de LaTerre glare before she pushed Makayla toward the bathroom. "I'm not staying, or I won't leave."

"So bossy." Makayla fought a yawn and lost. "But at least a good night kiss. And some food."

Talon grabbed her, pulled her close, and offered her a long, scorching kiss. "That's all you're getting for now. I'll have Ivy bring over some hot water for your bath before she fetches some food so you can eat after you soak. Then you sleep." Talon turned Makayla around and pushed her toward the small bath.

Makayla looked over her shoulder and frowned.

"You'd better take advantage of the opportunity to sleep. Tomorrow is going to be a long day." The corners of Talon's mouth twitched. "And tomorrow night is going to be a very, very long night." Then Talon turned and left through the front door.

CHAPTER TWENTY-THREE

A few minutes after Talon left, Makayla had her clothing off and was eyeing the tub. She didn't want a cold bath. Luckily, she heard a knock and Ivy came through the front door with a bucket of steaming water. She pushed the bathroom door open and shifted Makayla, bare as the day she was born, out into the bedroom while she filled the tub and added the hot water. In typical Ivy fashion, she spared Makayla having to think up half the conversation.

"So, it's a bucket of hot water for you and a warm bath. Luckily, there was this bucket of water warming over the fire in the laundry room. You get in, and I'll go and bring you a meal from the mess hall," Ivy told her. As Makayla sank into heaven, Ivy stuck her head back into the bathroom. "I'm grabbing your clothes for washing, and leaving you a towel and shirt." Then, with her arms full of dirty clothes and the bucket, Ivy stopped to study the naked Makayla in the tub with no chance of modesty on Makayla's part. As she took in Makayla, Ivy spoke again. "So here you are in Talon's tub. Without a stitch of clothes. Rescued by Talon, herself. So, fess up. Have you finally tamed the commander?"

Makayla laughed at her. "I don't think anyone tames Talon. Although I think we have an understanding. Now how about a bit of privacy, and maybe some food from the mess hall? I'd like to eat and crawl into bed if that's okay. I'm at my limit."

Ivy didn't let her load of dirty clothes and the empty bucket slow her down as she tossed back over her shoulder, "Yeah, that's the plan. I'll get the food."

"Thanks." Makayla yawned again, then submerged her head to wash almost a week's worth of misery from her entire body. She was ready to leave the dirt and forest from her kidnapping behind. She was ready to get a good night's sleep and then face tomorrow.

❖

Makayla had no recollection of anything that had occurred after she'd slipped between the sheets of Talon's bed. She'd never heard Talon come in. She'd never felt Betty snuggle up against her. But when she woke, there was the tomcat stretched out beside her and the bedding was mussed on the opposite side of the bed. From the light and the sounds floating in from outside, Makayla judged it to be close to eight o'clock on Friday morning. That meant she'd slept for almost fourteen hours.

She rolled out of bed, stretched, and then dressed for the day. When there was still no return of Talon to her quarters, she grabbed Betty and swung into the barn to find that her birds were already up and gone before going on to Talon's office. Makayla made sure that the tomcat had food and water and was comfortable in his mauve chair, then headed down to the conference room.

Talon saw her through the doorway and brought her out a mug of tea and a plate piled high with toast and eggs. Makayla hadn't stayed awake to finish her dinner last night, so she was famished. Then before joining Makayla so they could go down the hallway and eat at Talon's desk, Talon went back into the conference room and grabbed her own tea.

"I was wondering if you were going to make it," Talon said. "All the enclave leaders are eating and chatting. The plan is to start in about forty-five minutes, and I can run the meeting if you don't want to, but I'd rather you do it if you feel okay. Let's go into my office. I can bring you up to speed while you eat."

"That sounds good to me. I feel so much better this morning. I'd be happy to run things." Makayla knew this was the job she desired.

When they reached Talon's workspace, Makayla placed her food and drink on the desk and started to sit. Talon set down her mug and gathered Makayla into her arms—simply held Makayla against her own body in the privacy of the office before finally stepping back to gently touch her cheek, still red and healing.

"Son-of-a-bastard." Talon didn't hide her fury at Derrick as she looked at the raw area. "I still want to do him harm. Take him apart piece by piece, so it's a good thing it's out of my hands."

Makayla gave Talon a teasing smile. "That's the drakaina I love. Still a warrior woman. My warrior woman. I'm okay, Talon. Thanks to you." Makayla kissed Talon lightly on the lips. "Let me say it again—I love you."

"I know, Mak. You're good at so many things, but if there's one thing you're not good at, it's hiding your feelings."

Makayla offered her an exaggerated huff. "Now I'm offended. Maybe I'll just go about hiding my feelings later on tonight. That'll show you."

Talon laughed. "You can try. But by the time I'm done showing you *my* feelings, I don't think there's going to be any doubt about how you feel about me."

"Well, aren't you smug?" Makayla knew she wasn't hiding anything, that her eyes were dancing with the mental images of what the night would bring, and those images didn't help her focus on the upcoming meeting.

"Smug?" Talon said the word with disdain. "Confident, Mak. Confident. Remember paragraph number one of our strategic plan? I've been studying it. You know, fuc—" Talon stopped, her tone shifting to very much amused. "You're blushing."

Makayla sat down and concentrated on a piece of toast and the tea. "You're going to completely throw me off my game if you keep this up. Could you please sit down and talk to me about NATO? Maybe how it's in a class all its own." Makayla could see a flash of confusion cross Talon's face. "You know, N-A-T-O. *Nothing*

Approaching Tonight's Orgas—" Now it was Makayla's turn to stop and laugh. "Why, Commander de LaTerre. I do believe that you're the one blushing."

"Now I won't be able to think of the alliance with a straight face." Talon shook her head. "Someone's in for it tonight. I'm going to have you singing like the songbird you are." Talon's voice dripped with anticipation as she dropped a kiss onto Makayla's neck before clearing her throat. "Now get your mind on this morning's agenda and let me bring you up to speed."

At nine o'clock, Makayla called the meeting to order. She was seated at one end of the table with Talon at the other end. In the chairs on either side sat the enclave leaders from the Sylvan, Eden, Woodland, and Brighton enclaves. Ferril, from Gull Town, had also made it.

"As you all know, I'm Makayla Odin, and I've been heading these alliance talks. Talon and I have met with all of you over the past weeks, so I think we're all up to speed on the proposal for a shared defense plan to prevent a repeat of what happened to us with the MidLander's invasion. Hopefully, you've all had the opportunity to discuss the information with your consultation councils, and now we can get down to the business of entertaining questions, concerns, or additional ideas." Makayla looked around the table to assure herself that each member of the group was absorbing her comments. "Our hope is that by the end of the day, we have a final defense alliance that you can either sign or take back for final approval by your councils. Talon and I would like to think that if today is successful, we can expand our regional talks to other topics including trade, information and technology exchange, or any other ideas you might have."

And with that, animated discussion began. By the end of the day, all the enclave leaders had agreed to a defense treaty that would create a cooperative alliance of the six enclaves and Gull Town with the goal of safeguarding the security and freedom of the region through both cooperative political and armed means.

When those talks were finalized, James, the commander of the Sylvan enclave, loudly cleared his throat to garner everyone's attention. When he had it, he asked for the floor and Makayla gave it to him.

"I'd like to propose that we create a lead position for our NATO group. Someone to steer the process on through future decision-making and coordinate the implementation of those decisions, as well as help us communicate with each other and respond to any threats. We may even want to expand the alliance and add additional enclaves, once we're up and running. And even expand the scope of our mutual cooperation." With the other members around the table murmuring in agreement, James continued. "I believe that Makayla Odin has done an outstanding job, as co-commander of Aurora, of getting us to this point. I don't know if she'd be interested in the position, but I'd at least like for us to consider her." When he'd finished his proposal, he locked his gaze on Makayla and offered her a nod of his head.

The other enclave leaders and Ferril took turns enthusiastically expressing their support for the idea, and Makayla let everyone know that she'd been wanting just such a position because she'd already reached the conclusion that a commander role wasn't the best fit for her.

With James now taking over the meeting, and Talon sitting back and watching, it was decided that Makayla would step down from her co-commander role at Aurora and take up the position of Secretary of NATO. Quinn let the group know that while Aurora would miss Makayla Odin's leadership skills as a commander, every one of them would benefit from her skills in guiding the defense alliance to its full potential and hopefully, facilitating further alliances.

After James's proposal was affirmed, Willow and Ivy brought food for dinner and the gathering ended with cheerful conversation and comradery before the room finally cleared out as the visiting commanders were shown to their rooms for the night. It was getting late, and the schedule had been planned so that they could depart in the morning.

Makayla was amused with Brock's timely arrival. He promised Talon that he and Willow would see the enclave leaders off in the morning, a hint that he'd surmised Talon might not be up for an early send-off. He stepped closer to Makayla and lowered his voice. "Good job, trespasser. And I'm not just talking about the NATO job."

Finally, the conference room was empty of everyone except for Talon and her. Talon left her end of the conference table and came around to Makayla's end. She stood up to face Talon.

"So, *Secretary* Odin, it looks like life is going your way." Talon spoke in her Commander de LaTerre voice.

"I think so. I got the job. I got the girl. And if I'm lucky, I'm going home with her tonight."

"Nobody has called me a girl in decades," Talon harrumphed. "They wouldn't dare."

Makayla stepped back and looked Talon up and down. She studied her gorgeous face, stalled on her ample bustline, lingered at the curve of her hips before her inspection proceeded down past her boots and then back up again.

"Oh, I'd dare. But I have to concur that you're not a girl. You're an enchanting woman. The woman I love—just in case you didn't know that." The ability to tell Talon that she loved her, and knowing Talon wanted that love, made Makayla's heart soar. She knew that she'd never grow tired of telling her.

Before she grew serious, Talon's sultry gaze raked over Makayla in return. "I know that. I've known it for a while. And loved you back. It probably started from the time I regained consciousness out there in the woods and you presented as the cheeky little charmer that you are." Mirth captured Talon's expression, played across her lips, and put a sparkle in her eyes. "Must have been brain damage from the tree accident."

"Hey, you thought I was a male. *Boy. Cheeky little bastard.* That's what you called me." Makayla put on her best air of indignation.

"Yes, my attraction to you was perplexing," Talon replied in a low, gravelly voice. "I'll have to admit that I'm rather pleased that you're a girl."

"Now who's calling who a girl?" Makayla didn't even try to hide the amusement in her voice.

Talon leaned in and whispered in Makayla's ear. "Grown-ass woman. And it's a good thing considering the agenda for tonight. Penance...remember." Then Talon kissed her with enough passion to let Makayla know that she was indeed a grown-ass woman.

Makayla finally came up for air. "I think this meeting is adjourned, Commander de LaTerre."

Talon pinned her with a darkening sapphire response before asking, "Is that a hint you're ready for the next meeting on tonight's calendar?"

Makayla nodded, so Talon took her hand and led her out into the cool spring evening.

The upper rounded edge of the sun's sinking sphere barely floated above the distant treetops, the upper sky was streaked in shades of cobalt blue and violet, while that final end-of-the-day kiss of rose-gold glow cast out low across the compound. Passing gulls high overhead were the only witnesses to the slow stroll home, the first of what Makayla hoped would be thousands of evenings of such strolls. Tail in the air, Betty escorted the silent walk. The link of Makayla's fingers with Talon's was communication enough.

Betty led them toward the barn, and Makayla was grateful. Her birds, especially Poe, had experienced an ordeal at least as stressful as her own.

As they trailed the tomcat, Talon broke the silence. "Well, I think Betty has decided where our priorities should be. He knows we need to check your not-so-unkindness before we're distracted by other things."

"*Other* things?" The word "other" came out throaty and suggestive as Makayla communicated exactly what she had in mind.

Talon offered her a side glance. "Priorities, fledging. Brock has been checking on them, but let's make sure for ourselves that they're doing fine." Then Talon added in a tone of conviction, "After all, I owe them." She turned and looked at Makayla, and Talon left her with no doubt that it was love in her eyes.

Makayla snorted at Talon's adamant declaration of indebtedness to the birds.

"You're the one who owes the ravens?" Makayla decided to poke Talon a bit, not able to help herself. She loved to watch Talon react. "Okay, I guess maybe *your* calendar might be a bit different tonight without me."

Talon's eyes gave away her merriment, but she maintained an unrepentant tone. "Don't be ridiculous. It's about my commander role. They're assets to the enclave. We wouldn't want to lose our tracking birds. Rescue ravens."

Makayla laughed and gave Talon a gentle shoulder bump. "Certainly not, Commander de LaTerre. Every enclave knows rescue ravens are an asset. Right up there with tomcats named Betty."

The birds were up in the rafters of the barn and greeted them from their lofty perch. The threesome seemed to be healthy and alert, so Makayla didn't bother to whistle them down from their evening roost.

"Have a restful night," Makayla called to them. Then she looked directly at Talon and suggestively ran her tongue across her lower lip. "At least someone might have a restful night."

"Is that a hint that you have other things besides resting in mind, Mak?"

"Not at all. I was thinking that I'd go for a long walk to wear myself out, crawl between those sheets, and not stir until morning." Makayla struggled to sound perfectly serious.

"And I think that if you need to wear yourself out, I know a much better way than a long walk. Guaranteed to make you sleep like a baby." The words rolled from Talon's mouth in a seductive drawl.

"I thought babies kept you up all night."

"Exactly." Talon took Makayla's hand and led her out of the barn, Betty following.

❖

As they navigated through the last of the evening's visibility, Talon wanted to talk.

"I'm keeping your room at the residence hall for you."

Makayla stopped mid-step and looked at Talon, not sure if that meant Talon didn't want what she wanted. "Why?" She did her best to gulp down her concern.

Talon had stopped too. She faced Makayla. "Because there's a rumor that a person of reputable judgment thinks that I can be an ass on occasion. Even overbearing and difficult." The edges of Talon's mouth twitched up, not a full smile, but she was obviously entertained with the discussion. "I want you with me. The house will be *our* house. The bed will be *our* bed. We'll find you an office space. But I want you to have the option of some personal space to yourself if you need it." Talon stopped to look at Makayla, then firmly added, "Not at night. I want to sleep with you. But in case you need space to read or something. Because I love you." Talon's contained smile broke through. "And I can be an ass. I even enjoy being an ass sometimes."

Makayla worked to restrain her head nod to a minimum, trying not to come across as too enthusiastic in her support of Talon's self-assessment, but she couldn't suppress her grin.

"You don't have to be so agreeable," Talon admonished her, but her expression wasn't admonishing.

Makayla grew serious. "Okay. I want this to work. But I don't think I'll need that residence hall room. Anything else?"

Talon gently lifted Makayla's chin so her eyes were locked into Talon's darkening blue ones. Talon swallowed, then cleared her throat. "I've known terrible heartache because I loved someone. It almost killed me. I've fought this love, but damn if it hasn't reached a point that walking away will leave me more broken than taking the risk. You asked me if you weren't worth the risk, fledgling. I didn't want to say that you are, but I know the answer is yes."

In an effort to lighten the mood, Makayla held up three fingers and pledged in a teasing tone, "Thank you, Talon. I solemnly swear that I'll do everything in my power not to meet an untimely demise."

"And that brings us to the other topic on my list." Talon had taken on her professional persona again. Serious and in charge. "Promise me you'll never pull another stunt like you did this past week—you'll not take off on your own. We'll solve our issues by talking." Then Talon didn't hesitate to add some bark to the last part. "And that's an order from Commander de LaTerre."

"Well, I'd hate to cross Commander de LaTerre." Makayla saluted with a cheeky smile before becoming earnest. "I promise."

And with those words, Talon kissed her on the forehead, took her hand again, and turned toward the house. "Now, for the *penance*." She maintained her commander demeanor, but there was no doubt in Makayla's mind from the rasp in Talon's voice that they were both going to enjoy Makayla's atonement.

Betty squeezed through the initial crack in Talon's front door, followed by Makayla. Into the dark, warm den with Talon, who had done things to earn herself the reputation of being fire-breathing. But while Betty made it to the bedroom, Makayla found herself constrained against the inside of the smooth wooden barrier that closed the rest of the enclave away from what she knew would be a night she'd never forget, willful quarry to Talon's ravenous desire. Caught and smothered by lips so devouring that Makayla hoped there would be an opportunity left for her to show her love for Talon before she was completely dismantled.

After the initial capture of Makayla's mouth, her eyes, her neck, her clavicles, Talon took control of her unleashed passion. Makayla heard herself whimper with the more measured possession—with Talon's momentary restraint. This was the language of love, and their conversation had barely begun. There was so much more to say. Tonight, and so many nights ahead.

"I want this night to last. I want to do this in bed. *Our* bed." And with that, Talon guided Makayla into the bedroom, where a smart tomcat decided three was a crowd.

Talon gently pushed Makayla back onto the mattress, unbuttoned Makayla's shirt, slipped her out of her shoes and pants. Then Talon stood and pinned Makayla's nude body to the sheets with her focused approving appraisal, never looking away as she quickly removed her own attire. Makayla caught a glimpse of the skin art, the dragon, on Talon's back that helped define her very own drakaina. Her very own dragon woman. And the only item that negated Talon's state of nakedness was the small gold heart she wore around her neck.

Makayla couldn't separate the rising tide of arousal from the engulfing wave of love that she harbored for Talon. She'd waited so long for this time to come into the realm of reality—for the time when her physical and emotional connection to Talon could not be separated. For the moment when she felt fulfilled because she was secure in the knowledge that there was no imbalance between the two of them. Talon needed her as much as she needed Talon.

Talon first feasted on her breasts. Devoured her with caresses and kisses. She ascended the soft slopes to the peak of each rise until she changed course and descended down the tender skin of Makayla's abdomen to the arched bones of her hips, then traveled on to her inner thighs. She skipped the center of Makayla's need until finally, lastly, Talon went to that place that held intimate passage to Makayla's deep physical craving for her. With the touch of her lips and the faultless dance of her fingers and tongue between the delicate folds that concealed the sweet soft core of Makayla's desire, she took Makayla apart.

Talon stroked and caressed, sucked and licked. She was relentless, those gorgeous hungry eyes open and observant as she wreaked havoc on her. And finally, when Makayla could no longer restrain the escalating irrepressible moans of pleasure that filled the room, when she knew that she could endure no more, when the climax finally, fully claimed her, Talon held her close as the swell of her release consumed her. And as sensation roared outward from her core, Makayla thought her heart would burst with the volume of love she felt for the commander of Raptare. A love that had been worth all that had brought them to this moment. To a time when Talon de LaTerre loved her back.

When Makayla felt her completion, she didn't pause for recovery. She kissed Talon with all the passion she possessed, then rolled Talon onto her back, reversing their roles. Now the time to possess and bestow was hers—emancipator of Talon's self-imposed solitariness.

Makayla went back to that dream she'd had so long ago in the warehouse. She made love to that beautiful woman with the flawless skin and alluring shape. Melded seductive curves into her own gentle contours. Used hungry lips to capture that mouth, hold it hostage. Then, ultimately, she offered touches that sculpted exquisite ecstasy—not from heartache, because heartache had been left behind in her life, left behind in Talon's life—from a shared love that was worth the risk.

However, that wasn't the end of the night of lovemaking. It was only the beginning, as Makayla and Talon traveled together to places they had never been before and embraced the miracle of knowing they would do this again and again and again.

Makayla's heart soared to new heights as the first light of sunrise trickled through the wooden slats of drawn shades, and golden hints of the dawn's glow filtered into the room. Their bedroom. Talon cradled her as Makayla reveled in the morning symphony of feathered vocalists announcing this new day. And as she drifted among memories of last night's lovemaking in the comfortable caress of Talon's arms, Makayla barely registered the thump of the cat bounding onto the bed.

Talon groaned, then left with the feline following. It was time to feed the starving rat catcher. Makayla felt the absence of Talon, missed her while she was barely gone, knew that only Talon could make her whole.

And then Talon swooped back into their bed. She constrained the willing russet-topped sparrow under her lean long body, immobilizing Makayla against the sheets beneath. Talon feasted again on her bared chest, tasted her exposed throat, consumed her completely until there was nothing left but the sated body of *Makayla Melospiza melodia*.

Makayla crooned into Talon's ear, a melodious solo sonata with an avian accompaniment floating in from outside. *Love is this song sparrow trilling at dawn.*

When the sound of sniffling joined the bird chorus, Makayla opened her eyes and saw a trail of tears leaking from the beautiful blue blend of deep river currents and expansive cerulean sky. "Is something wrong?" she asked the woman who never cried.

"No, fledgling, everything is so right." And when the cat jumped up to join the love nest, Makayla knew it was perfect. The way it was supposed to be. Talon and the songbird. And of course, a tomcat named Betty.

About the Author

Julia Underwood (http://www.juliaunderwood.net) grew up loving animals and pursued a degree in veterinary medicine. She's been blessed to have wonderful family members, friends, and a parade of pets to enrich her life. She's an avid writer and reader. The joy of discovering the journey to novel writing cannot be overstated. She hopes her admiration for the love, dedication, and competence women bring to the multitude of roles they fill in this complicated world comes through in her writing.

Books Available from Bold Strokes Books

Beautiful Things by Emma L McGeown. A warmhearted romance of missed chances, undeniable chemistry, and a stubborn love that maybe, just maybe, can find its way back. (978-1-63679-934-6)

Love Takes a Village by Karis Walsh. As Lena Preiss struggles to manage a busy restaurant in the Bavarian Christmas village of Leavenworth, Washington, chocolatier Devin Meyer brings an unexpected richness into her life, along with her delicious desserts. (978-1-63679-902-5)

Secrets of the Heart by Jenny Frame. When a beautiful stranger starts asking questions about Nikki Sharkey, head of an infamous crime syndicate, Nikki will stop at nothing to protect her daughter Isla. (978-1-63679-653-6)

Talon and the Songbird by Julia Underwood. In a world where survival depends on strategic alliances, Makayla and Talon must navigate not only complex politics but also the dangerous territory of their hearts. (978-1-63679-970-4)

The Great Popcorn Romance by Georgia Beers. Opposites attract, and Riley Shaw stands no chance of resisting Hannah Kramer's magnetic pull. But opposites know just how to drive each other crazy… (978-1-63679-910-0)

Three Blissful Days by Dena Blake. Kendall Jackson attempts to make her ex regret dumping her by announcing she's dating beautiful park ranger Ivy Patterson. But there's nothing fake about how attracted Ivy is to Kendall. (978-1-63679-707-6)

Chasing Her Scent by MJ Williamz. When Sheridan Rousseau walks into Lisette Mouton's charming little bookstore in Quebec City, she unknowingly holds the key to a mysterious box hidden in a secret room. (978-1-63679-900-1)

Heart's Run by D. Jackson Leigh. Hoping to recover an escaped racing mare, stock transporter Tobie Mason locks horns with local wild horse advocate Maggie Wilkes. (978-1-63679-825-7)

Scandalous by Kris Bryant. When a Hollywood actress trades places with her twin sister, everyone's in an uproar about getting duped, but Lindsay's more concerned about finding out which twin she made out with. (978-1-63679-874-5)

The Art of Love by Ali Vali. When Mimi and Bianca both set their sights on Jolly, sparks fly, loyalties are tested, and hearts collide as they navigate the unpredictable nature of their hearts (978-1-63679-719-9)

The Other Side of Forever by Kel McCord. Will Kenzie and Rachel be able to make love work when Rachel's cozy suburban dream feels like Kenzie's worst nightmare? (978-1-63679-812-7)

The Secrets of Rhydian Hill by Ronica Black. A doctor in need of a new start. A woman running from a killer. A love story that could end in tragedy. (978-1-63679-880-6)

Feeling Lucky by Krystina Rivers. What happens when, despite suddenly having enough money to buy almost anything, Lucy and Tanner start to discover that maybe all they need is each other? (978-1-63679-876-9)

Iceberg by Gun Brooke. When Lady Arabella hires Zandra, she never expects to find love, especially not as a disaster looms on the horizon. (978-1-63679-908-7)

It Happened One Semester by Aurora Rey. After a Pride night hookup, can eager new Assistant Professor Hudson Greene and Dean of Advising Callie Shaw overcome the odds and ace falling in love? (978-1-63679-814-1)

It's Kind of a Bad Idea by Sarah G. Levine. What happens when an emotionally unavailable serial dater meets the one woman she can't help but fall for—who happens to be the one woman who told her not to? (978-1-63679-920-9)

Thankful for You by Tagan Shepard. Everyone deserves to find their person, maybe Karen has finally found hers? (978-1-63679-884-4)

What Happens on Location by Nan Campbell. How can Helen produce a successful movie when its director is the woman responsible for the demise of her marriage? (978-1-63679-904-9)

When Love Comes Around by Radclyffe and Ronica Black. Can Maya Sanchez and Nolan Wright trust each other enough to build something real, or will the past tear them apart? (978-1-63679-930-8)

Anywhere with You by Margo Glynn. On a road trip through the Great American Southwest, two friends discover nature, hope, and each other. (978-1-63679-907-0)

Burning Bridges by Lesley Davis. Can Clancy and Jude crack the case of eight missing women—and the secrets of their own hearts? (978-1-63679-872-1)

Dreams Entangled by Sophia Kell Hagin. Amid self-doubt, secrets, a pandemic, fear of attack and attempted murder, Pirin and Gracie's attraction turns to love and their lives will never be the same. (978-1-63679-892-9)

Echoes of Love by Catherine Lane. As Hazel's and Jo's paths intertwine, they're swept up in a whirlwind of long-buried secrets, sizzling chemistry, and memories that won't be denied. (978-1-63679-835-6)

Moonlight Obsession by Sheri Lewis Wohl. All it takes to stop a clever killer is moonlight, love, and a silver bullet. (978-1-63679-831-8)

My Boyfriend's Wife by Joy Argento. Amid betrayal and heartbreak, can two women discover a love that could heal their pasts and rewrite their futures? (978-1-63679-866-0)

Tapout by Nicole Disney. A struggling MMA fighter finds her edge in an underground ring, but as she falls for the magnetic and ambitious promoter behind the matches, their dangerous world threatens to destroy everything they've fought to rebuild. (978-1-63679-924-7)

The Fame Game by Ronica Black. Wild child Hollywood actress Luna Kirkman begins dating Hollywood's leading man, only to fall for his straitlaced sister instead. (978-1-63679-858-5)